Books by Wendi Zwaduk

Heart Attack

Over My Head

Haunted By You

Miss Me Baby

Immortal Love

Until the Night

Wanton Witches

Candlelit Magic

Jolly Rogered

Ruined by the Pirate

Clandestine Classics

The Phantom of the Opera

Lust Bites

Must Be Doing Something Right
Love Remembers

Sexy Snax

Firelit Magic
Sunshine of Your Love

Anthologies

Treble
Bound to the Billionaire
Wild After Dark
Over the Knee
Boots, Chaps and Cowboy Hats

Single Titles

Learning How to Bend
My Immortal
You'll Think of Me
Tangled Up
Careless Whisper
Please Remember Me
What Might Have Been
Ever Fallen In Love
Savin' Me
Someone Like You
When You're With Me
Still The One
Play to Him
Whip It Up
Honey and Decadence
Lasso Lovin'
Tying One On
Taken In
Silk and Decadence
Her Man
Between Us
My Favorite Mistake

My Favorite Mistake

ISBN # 978-1-78686-107-8

©Copyright Wendi Zwaduk 2017

Cover Art by Posh Gosh ©Copyright 2017

Interior text design by Claire Siemaszkiewicz

Totally Bound Publishing

Published in 2017 by Totally Bound Publishing, Newland House, The Point, Weaver Road, Lincoln, LN6 3QN, United Kingdom.

MY FAVORITE MISTAKE

WENDI ZWADUK

Dedication

SM — I'm glad I get to work with you again. Yay!
CD — thanks for listening to me when I worked through
the kinks in this. You rock.
JPZ — you're not a mistake, but you're mine.

Chapter One

"What are you talking about?" Molly Neff asked. "Say it again."

"Please tell me you've got a good idea that doesn't involve showing my ass." Austin leaned back in his chair and propped his feet on the edge of his desk. "The clothing company wants something that's simple and chic — that's your strong point, but I still don't see why you think I could be good for this."

Molly sighed and drummed her pen on her notepad. She'd worked with Austin for the last five years and still he managed to surprise her. The ad campaign they were working on didn't have to involve him showing his ass, as he'd put it. He didn't have to show up in the campaign at all. But what if she went with her initial idea and used him in the advertisements?

She stared at him. Austin Dean personified sex. From his perfectly cut dark-blond hair to his muscles and the way his clothes always fit just right, he could model. When he smiled, she melted — and so did just about every other female within a hundred-mile radius.

Molly picked up the shirt box and flipped up the lid. The T-shirt wasn't anything that special, but on the right body and showcased to its softest advantage it would sell well. Pair it with the boxer briefs and put the model in a casual situation…yeah, she could see the clothes selling well. Hell, she could see the posters now with Austin as the model.

"What are you thinking?" He moved his feet from the desk and leaned forward. "The wheels are turning. I see them."

She shook the shirt out and smoothed it across her notebook. If she wanted him to model, she'd have to tell him sooner rather than later. "Okay, so here's what I'm thinking. Aura Sportswear wants the clothes to look easy to live in. They're going for casual and fun. What if we did a series of photos of models in those clothes?"

"Isn't that the plan anyway?" He frowned, but his blue eyes twinkled. "Go on. What's your vision?"

The tips of her ears burned. He loved to tease her about her methods for coming up with the ideas for the different advertising campaigns, but the visions, as he called them, almost always worked. "I'm seeing black-and-white images. Casual. Like, the male model stretched out on the bed, wearing glasses maybe, and dressed in the shirt and boxers. He's reading the paper. Another one is the same kind of guy, but on a balcony. Maybe it's sunset and he's got coffee. Bare feet, backside shot. Hot, but not overly grossly sexual."

She met his gaze and hoped the heat on her cheeks wasn't evident. When he laughed, she knew he saw everything.

Austin didn't answer right away but kept laughing. "Backside shot. Who says that?"

"I do," she muttered. She saw him as the guy on the bed, engrossed in the paper and debating what to do with his stock portfolio. He'd be damn sexy. She could probably make a mint off the posters alone. "The clothing is made for lounging. It's supposed to look soft and inviting, but sporty. Like this."

Molly placed the tablet in front of him. She pointed to the image she'd cobbled together on her photo manipulation software.

He stopped laughing and sobered. He laced his fingers together. "You used my face."

"It's the back of your head." She shrugged. She should've regretted her decision to photograph him, but it was too late now.

"Where is this?"

"I took it a couple hours ago while you were staring out the window. Your pose was perfect and the lighting was even better. I cut your body out and put the clothes in. Your body is the plastic mannequin body." She gripped the pen again, needing something to do with her hands. She'd crushed on Austin for almost ten years, but every time she'd tried to make a move, he hadn't been available. They'd only made love a couple of times because he'd wanted it. Her mild obsession with taking his picture was going to get her into trouble.

"I thought I was a little tighter in the back and ass section." He swiped the screen to another image and paused. "Did you take this?" He snorted. "What am I saying? Duh, you took this. It's your tablet." He turned it around. "Is this me, too?"

She shrugged again. Yep, her tendency to photograph him was definitely going to get her into hot water. "It was the lighting and your expression." He'd looked so damn cute and puzzled. "Sorry."

"For what? I want a copy so I can use it for my business cards or something." He leaned back in his seat again and crossed his arms. "Molls, I don't know why you got into the advertising game. Your photography is too good not to be shared."

"Nah." She picked at the tip of the pen. She'd considered working professionally as a photographer, but she liked creating advertising spreads. Truth be told, she craved the time she spent with Austin. They'd probably never get together as anything other than collaborators, but that didn't mean she couldn't dream about a romantic relationship with him.

Austin scratched his forehead then pushed away from the desk and stood. "What if — ? What if we did this? The ad campaign. We pitch the idea of the black-and-whites and see what Aura says? I'll do it, but *only* if you take the pictures. Yes?"

"You mean manipulate them together? Sure." She

nodded. "I've got a couple of shots of you I can put with the clothing and cut and paste into a good composition."

Austin rounded the desk and sat on the edge of hers. "No, I meant we actually shoot me in those clothes. Well, you do the photography and I'll pose. We can get a hotel room or something. I've got points we can use for it, or we could expense it once we get the account." He swung his foot and bobbed his head. "We could make a night of it. Room service. Order a movie... I'm in. What about you?"

She stared at him, unable to process what he'd just said. A hotel room? Seriously? Making a night of it? Uh, yeah, she wanted to, but probably not in the same way he meant.

"Molls?" He tipped his head to the side and his eyes widened. "What do you think?"

She wanted to strip him naked, ride him into the sunset and forget about the ad campaign—that's what she thought. "Are you sure?"

Where in the hell had *that* come from?

"Why wouldn't I be sure?" he asked. He stopped swinging his foot. "I don't trust anyone else to take my picture."

"Oh, yeah. That." Definitely not thinking the same as she was... "If you want real pictures, then sure. I'll take them."

"Get that overnight bag you keep in your car and meet me at the Madison House Inn. They've got the exact room we want for this."

"Sure." She paused. "I'm thinking more candid shots for these. Like the girlfriend taking the picture. Thoughts?" She shouldn't be hoping for more, but she did. Was she wrong to want to be the woman in his life and not just be his collaborator?

Austin nodded. "That's smart." He grinned and kissed her on the cheek. "This is why I only work with you."

She warmed from her head to her toes. She balled her hands to keep from reaching for him. Wanting him was so foolish, because he'd never see her as anything other than his friend, but still. A vision of him in bed with her, him kissing her and making love to her, came to mind.

She pressed her knees together and bit back a sigh. Naked, clothed, she'd didn't care — she wanted him.

"I'll meet you in the lobby in ten." Austin smiled and trailed his fingers over the back of her hand. The flirt. He packed his tablet and leather-bound notebook into his messenger bag then strolled out of the office he shared with her.

Once alone, she sighed and rested her head on her folded arms. Photographs, a room together, him in form-fitting clothes — she was *so* screwed, and not in the way she wanted. She should've used another head for the mock-ups, but she hadn't been able to resist. The thought of Austin modeling those shirts and shorts was too tempting.

She stuffed her own tablet and notebooks into her shoulder bag then tucked the box of shirts and underwear beneath her arm. She was going to spend the night with the man of her dreams, taking pictures of him. She could do this.

Ten minutes and three trips back to her desk later, Molly finally stepped into the elevator. She leaned against the back wall and sighed. What was she thinking? She should have turned him down. He *had* to know how she felt about him. Good God, they'd been friends for so long and she'd admitted she liked him at least twice after she'd had too much to drink when they'd slept together before.

The elevator car stopped and the doors opened. Austin stood in the lobby, but he wasn't alone. Her heart sank, along with her spirits. She'd talked herself into turning him down, but she hadn't expected him to turn her down first.

Austin widened his stance and smiled at the petite blonde woman. He laughed at whatever she'd said and seemed entranced by her.

Molly pressed the button to close the elevator door. She'd seen this too many times and knew exactly where he'd take the evening. He and the blonde would end up spending the night together. He'd come into work the next day and tell her all about whatever it was they'd done. A movie, dancing, hanging out at a basketball game, going to an art gallery opening—whatever. She'd play the role of the trusty friend, listening and being supportive.

Screw support. She was tired of being the best friend.

Just before the doors shut, Austin rushed up to the car. "Where are you going?"

"Back upstairs. I forgot my purse." She'd lied, but she hoped he couldn't see the gigantic bag dangling from her arm.

"Molls." He stuck his arm between the doors. "You've got everything. Might take you a dozen trips, but you never come downstairs without it all."

"Guess so." She averted her gaze. "Look, Austin, this won't work."

"What?" He stepped into the car and pressed the button for the top floor. He leaned against the wall beside her. "Talk to me."

"Nothing to say." She couldn't meet his gaze. "When—when are you and the woman out there leaving?"

"Huh?" Austin tapped the emergency stop button and crossed the car to where she stood. "You mean Iris? I'm not spending time with her tonight. That's what I was trying to tell her down there. She's convinced we'd be a good team. Probably, but I already promised you we'd get the job done."

"Iris?" As in Iris Sommerville, the owner of Aura? The woman who wanted her and Austin specifically to do the ad campaign? *Shit.* She probably wanted special treatment and Austin in her bed. Molly closed her eyes. She'd just played right into Iris' hands and was about to deliver photos of Austin in Iris' brand of clothes.

"Hey." Austin curled his fingers under her chin. "We've got a job to do and we'll get it done. We'll have a good time doing it. Promise."

She didn't doubt they'd have fun, but she did doubt he wanted to spend the night with her. Work or not, he wasn't known as a playboy for nothing.

"You're finally tired of me, aren't you?"

"No." She wriggled away from him and pressed the button to start the elevator up again. "We need to get this done. Let me do some magic on the computer. I'll have the stuff ready for Monday's presentation."

"I don't think so."

The car stopped a second time, but when she looked up at the display she noticed they were on the ground floor. She shrugged past him and into the cooler air of the foyer. God, she was screwing this up all on her own.

"Hey." Austin caught up to her. "I don't know what's gotten into you, but we've got a job to do. We'll do it."

"Yeah," she said and choked back tears. She'd built up the evening in her mind and ruined things before they'd even begun. She blew out a ragged breath. "Let's go."

A muscle in Austin's jaw tightened. He didn't say anything as he escorted her to the parking garage. He didn't have to talk. She knew the play. Meet at the Madison House Inn.

"I'll see you in a few." She unlocked her car and dumped her things onto the back seat. "Meet in the lobby?" He didn't answer, so she glanced around the garage. "Austin?"

"In here." He opened the driver's side door for her. "You're driving."

"Oh." She shut the rear door and settled onto the front seat. Sure enough, Austin was in her car. He'd ridden with her plenty of times and hung out with her plenty more, but there was something different between them.

"We might as well take one car. We're coming back here in the morning anyway." He rested his arm across the seat back. "Josh and his working Saturdays rule. The guy is nuts."

"He knows what he wants out of his workforce." She switched on the engine and managed to back out of the spot without hitting anything. She didn't know how she'd accomplished the feat, seeing as her hands wouldn't stop trembling.

She peeked over at Austin a couple of times as she made

the short drive across the city to the lakefront. Working in Avondale, Ohio, had its plusses — traffic, but not awful and a great view of the lake. Stores were within a decent distance and the cost of living was reasonable. Besides, Avondale had the Madison House Inn. Every room faced the lake and resembled a homey bedroom rather than a stuffy hotel room.

She turned onto the freeway and merged. Austin hadn't said anything since the garage. She drummed her thumbs on the steering wheel.

"There's a couple of T-shirts, three pairs of boxer briefs, a button-down shirt and a tie. Not sure why Aura didn't send over pants," she said.

"Aura makes jogging pants and base layers." Austin toyed with her ponytail, tugging her hair lightly. "Or the selection is their way of throwing us a curveball." He laughed. "They'll love the way we're going to lob that ball right over the left field wall."

She bit back a chuckle. Austin and his baseball analogies — what would she do without him?

"This is the exit." Austin sat up straighter and moved his arm. "I haven't been to the Madison in forever."

"I've only been there once." She stopped from elaborating on *that* visit. She doubted Austin would remember her being at the company Christmas party two years back. He'd come in long enough to say hi then left with his date.

"The party two years ago, right? I wished I could've stayed longer. Gigi wanted to leave. She hated large crowds." Austin tugged his wallet from his coat pocket. "Let me off at the door and I'll get the room."

"Sure." When she stopped, he jumped out of the car. She did as she'd been told and sat in the silent vehicle. She should have been happy as hell. A room with Austin. This should've been her dream come true.

Molly scrubbed both hands over her face and sighed. If she kept thinking the worst then she'd never get him out of her system. Tonight would be a fun night. Room service, she'd take pictures of him, and God only knew what movie he'd want to watch. Maybe more? She couldn't be sure. If she wanted a good time, she'd have to make it happen.

She gathered up her purse and her shoulder bag then climbed out of the car.

"Where's the box?" Austin asked. He jogged up to the vehicle. "You've got your hands full. What can I carry?"

"My other bag and the box, I suppose." She paused. "If I've got an overnight bag, what are you going to use tonight?"

"Thought I might bum something off you." He winked. "But seriously, I've got a few things in my messenger bag. I'll be all right." He gathered up the bag and box. "The room's ready. You're never going to believe it. The place is booked up so we hit the jackpot."

She locked the car and followed him into the hotel. She didn't say anything as she entered the elevator with him and held her breath until the elevator car stopped. Top floor.

"Bridal suite," Austin said as the doors opened. "Free upgrade."

"Are you kidding?" She crept out of the elevator and up to the third door in the foyer. "Really?"

"No kidding." He slid the card through the reader and twisted the handle. "It's going to be perfect."

"Sure." She hesitated to put her bag or purse down. She'd never been in such a lush room. The suite featured three rooms, not including the bathroom. French doors led to a balcony. Her mind worked overtime. She could see him on the balcony in the waning sun. Him stretched out on the bed, reading the paper. Cooking in the kitchen in nothing but his boxer briefs. She closed her eyes and bit back a sigh. Her body warmed again and her nipples tightened.

"What are you thinking?" Austin rubbed her shoulders. He pressed his chest into her back. "Got ideas?"

She swayed into him and swallowed past the lump in her throat. She couldn't speak. Not when she wanted to turn around and kiss him.

His breath tickled her ear. "Bet I'm thinking the same thing you are."

Bet he isn't.

Austin let go of her and left her things on the couch. He flopped onto the bed. "I'm thinking we need food, drinks and a movie — then the photos."

"Right." She rubbed her forehead with the back of her hand. "What did you want to eat?" Molly focused on unpacking the box and her bag. She needed to sort out what they had and what she wanted to do with the ad campaign. She set her laptop up on the desk and plugged in the cord. "Is there a menu anywhere?"

"I'll get us something." Austin disappeared onto the balcony. He chattered on his phone and waved his hand as he spoke.

Molly ignored him and finished getting her things out. She unfolded the clothes and arranged the items on the table. The colors needed to contrast just right. Austin strolled back into the suite and she rested her hands on her hips.

"I know they want bright color to sell the clothes, but what about black-and-white art shots mixed in? Like posters within the catalog?" She looked at Austin. "What do you think?"

"Like modeling stuff?" He sat on the arm of the sofa. "You're really getting into this one."

"I know what I want out of it. I've got a pretty clear vision." She twined her fingers together. "What did you order?"

He stared at her for a moment. "Molly, are you trying to sell me?"

"Kind of." Not really, but maybe, yeah, she was. She sighed. "I can see you in the photos, and they're going to be great."

"I believe you." He smiled and scooted onto the couch beside her. "I ordered pizza, beers and sodas. Figured we could watch an action flick or a dirty movie. Whatever you're in the mood for." He wriggled his brows. "I'm all for the porn flick."

"Austin." She'd watched more than a couple of dirty movies with him—usually when they'd needed inspiration and had been stuck in the midst of procrastinating. After a particularly hot movie, she and Austin had ended up in bed together. She relished the memories of making love with him. After those two times, he'd shied away from her for a week. Did she want to go through that again? The silent treatment? Not really.

"Okay, so no porn—yet." He tossed his keys and wallet onto the table then rummaged through his messenger bag. "I'm ditching my contacts. If the food arrives, let him in. I put it on the room."

"Sure." She twiddled with the settings on her phone and her digital camera. She'd probably get better shots with the phone but clearer images with the dedicated camera. She sat at the table and pulled out her notebook. Time to sketch out exactly what she wanted.

Molly barely noticed Austin moving around the room. She did hear the knock at the door and peeked over her shoulder. Austin wheeled a silver cart and whistled.

"This is great." He laughed and scooted the pizza box and drinks onto the table. "They think we're on our honeymoon." He plunked a vase with two roses onto her notepad. "Happy marriage?"

The cut-crystal vase sparkled and the fragrance of the roses wafted around her. She closed her eyes and breathed in the light scent. Roses were her favorite, but she hadn't had a boyfriend in forever, or a reason to buy herself flowers. When she opened her eyes, Austin had sat opposite her at the table.

"The roses are nice." She laced her fingers together. "Thanks for buying dinner."

"Molls, I couldn't invite you to a hotel room and not, at least, get food." He twisted the top off a bottle of beer.

"Want?"

"I'll have a soda for now, but save the bottle. It'll work as a prop." She finished her sketch then moved the tablet and vase aside. "So, how was your date with Serena?" She hated talking to him about his various girlfriends but she wanted conversation.

"Serena? She dumped me after two dates. Said I wasn't able to commit." Austin shrugged. "I'm not sure what she expected. It was only two dates, but yes, the last one was pretty bad."

"Oh." She slid a piece of pizza onto her plate. "I'm sorry to hear that."

"No you're not." He winked. "I know you. As far as you're concerned, I need to stop trying to find a date and focus on work."

"True." She willed her hands to stop trembling. For a moment, she thought he'd say she wanted him to stop dating and realize she wanted him.

"Iris asked me out." Austin downed another swig of beer. "Said we'd get the account if I went with her on a date. I turned her down."

"Wow." She picked at the pepperoni on her slice of pizza. "Guess you've got women falling at your feet now."

"Except the one I want." Austin munched on the pizza and stared at her. "One of these days I'll get my head out of my ass."

"But not today." She ripped the pepperoni away from the cheese. Any other woman would probably want to be in her position—with a handsome man in a hotel room and with the ability to make him strip. But he wasn't interested in her in a romantic way.

"You never know." Austin polished off a second slice of pizza then sat back in his seat. "So. I saw the notes. What's the plan, boss? I'm dying to see what you're going to make me do."

Make him do? She could make him explain his cryptic statement, or maybe tell her exactly how he felt about her.

But why make things easy? She met his gaze and part of the ice around her heart melted. The old-school black frames brought out the blue in his eyes.

"Well, first I want you to keep the glasses." She turned the notebook around. *Focus.* "How about you put the shirt and boxer briefs on and I'll mess up the bed. I thought I saw a newspaper around here somewhere. We can spread that out and make it look like you're reading it."

"Hunt out the sports page and I *will* read it." He tossed his wadded-up napkin onto the plate. "And don't finish the beer. Got it." He left the table and grabbed the clothing. "Be right back. Don't miss me too much."

She rolled her eyes and slumped in her seat. The man would wear her out. She waited for him to close the bathroom door before she hopped up from the table. They were comfortable with each other and he surprised her by not stripping right in front of her — while keeping up a conversation.

Her thoughts turned to Iris Sommerville. The woman knew good-looking men and if she did date Austin, she'd help him improve his social standing. She'd probably get him jobs in the modeling and film industries, too. Did Molly blame Austin for being interested? No.

She yanked the comforter from the bed and messed up the sheets. She wanted the lived-in style.

"Nice." Austin eased up beside her. He held the paper. "Almost looks like my room."

"I don't doubt it." She picked up her phone and camera. "I'll do some quick shots on the phone first to get the lighting right, then I'll use the SLR."

Austin plopped on the sheets. He crawled toward the headboard and stretched out.

Molly jumped back and whipped the camera from the bag. The man was a natural. She snapped half a dozen shots before he'd even settled.

"You're not giving me the chance to pose." Austin crossed his ankles and rested on his elbow. He smoothed the paper out in front of him then grabbed a pillow and tucked it to his chest. "Better?"

"Yes." Not really. The pillow impeded the view of the shirt, but she didn't have to use that particular shot—not for the campaign anyway.

He rolled onto his back and laced his fingers together on his belly. He bent his left leg and kept his right leg straight then glanced out of the window. The shirt stretched tightly across his chest and accentuated the taut planes of his body. When he breathed, his abs became more defined.

Molly wobbled as she clicked away, taking more photographs. He oozed sex. God. She was crazy. She could be taking the pictures for her own use, not to entice everyone else.

"Good?" He grinned. "I'm not sure I want to get up." He sighed and stretched then sat up. "I bet you want to use that light." He nodded toward the balcony. "It's that right time of the night. Creamy light or something like that."

"The sunset will make your skin look perfect—not that it's not already." She blew out a long breath. "Just go out there."

"Yes, ma'am." He scooted past her and onto the balcony again. The way he padded out onto the concrete and leaned against the railing was so casual and as if he spent many an afternoon out there.

Molly snapped a few shots with her phone then switched back to the single lens reflex camera. "Hold on." She grabbed the beer bottle then offered it to him. "That's better." She knelt a few yards from him and focused. "Be yourself." She wasn't sure what he'd do but she trusted him to know what she wanted.

Austin rested his forearms on the railing and crossed his legs. He swirled the beer in the bottle and nodded once.

Everything he did was exactly what she needed in the photos.

"That's great. I can work on other shots on the computer." She strolled back into the hotel room and placed her camera in the bag. If she spent too much more time out on the balcony with him, she'd admit she still hadn't gotten Austin out of her system.

"I don't know," Austin called. "I think we need a couple of selfie ones."

She froze. 'Selfie ones'. Yeah, a personal shot would be good. She handed her phone to him without looking back. "Go for it."

"Thank you."

She didn't bother to watch. She'd seen him photograph himself plenty of times. He always managed to take the best shots and never had his hair out of place or his eyes funny. She hated selfies or any other pictures of her.

"I did a couple." Austin eased up beside her and draped his arm around her shoulders. "Smile."

When she looked up, he snapped a photo.

"Why did you do that?" she asked and reached for the phone.

"Because you're adorable." He kissed her temple and took another picture. "And I love to irritate you." He kept her phone and strolled away from her. "Aura is going to love what you're doing. They're lucky we're doing this."

"Correction. They asked specifically for *you*. I got to do this because they had to take me." She tucked the notebook back into her bag and slid the memory card from her camera. "Want me to take off? You've probably got a girlfriend dying to spend the night with you."

Austin groaned and took the memory card from her hand. He led her across the room to the bed and tugged her down beside him. "You make me sound like I can't keep my dick in my pants."

She shrugged, not wanting to argue with him. Austin liked to date and loved to tell her about the women he'd seen. "You like all the girls you're with, then you sleep with them and the relationship falls apart. I don't know if the shine is gone or your attention span is that small, but you can't commit."

"You sound like Serena."

"I've been witness to almost all of your relationships since college." She stood, but he tugged her back onto the bed. "Austin, stop playing with my head, okay?"

"No." He grabbed the remote and switched on the television. "How can I stop playing with your head? I invited you to stay the night with me in a hotel room. I never said we had to fuck or that I expected something from you. The idea of the photos was your idea—a great one at that—but I'm just going along. Relax and let me give you a great night."

She scrubbed both hands over her face again and sighed. Being alone with him wasn't an awful idea. She'd fallen hard for Austin so many times. At least this time she had photos for later. After he moved on and found the woman of his dreams, she'd have a reminder of the man who owned her heart.

"Well?" He met her gaze and grinned. "What do you think?"

"Sure." What else did she have to lose?

Chapter Two

Austin stretched out and tucked both hands behind his head. Molly would be the death of him—even if she was his best friend and the only woman who hadn't given up on him. He'd tried to get her to open up so many times, but she kept a few secrets close to her chest. Why? They were partners. She should be able to trust him.

"Once you're done putting your stuff away, come over here." He patted the bed. "One of your favorite romancy movies is on the television." He bit back a wince. She hated how he used that word—'romancy'. "I meant one of those… movies you like." He'd eat his foot all the way to his knee if he didn't shut up.

"'Romancy'. Nice." She tucked the loose strands of hair escaping from her ponytail behind her ears. "Austin, we work together and the one shot we took at a relationship didn't work. We're good as working friends and friends-friends, but nothing else."

He scrambled off the bed and strode to the table in the living room area. Things were messed up and she had a point—having a relationship at work and in the bedroom again probably wasn't smart, but he wanted both, nonetheless. She'd taken his picture and the thrill of being desired had overwhelmed him. She made him feel important, but that was the thing about Molly. She wasn't like other women. She didn't beg for his attention. She made him take notice, and not just when they worked together.

He hated to admit it, but she was right—the one time they'd fucked, he'd screwed it up. Instead of running to her and confessing he'd had the best night of his life, he'd avoided her. He still wasn't sure how to deal with the way he felt about Molly.

Molly zipped her bag shut and rested her hands on her hips. He'd once been told she wasn't classically beautiful. What was classical? Because she wasn't nearly six feet tall and a hundred pounds soaking wet? Because she didn't have blonde hair or huge tits? Maybe that wasn't what he wanted in a woman.

Molly stood barely five feet three inches tall compared to his six-foot-three-inch frame, but she stood toe to toe with him often. He liked the way her hourglass figure fit against him. Her blue eyes sparkled and her laugh lit up a room. Her gravelly voice sent shivers down his spine and he longed to run his fingers through her hair. He loved her hugs. He needed her.

Damn it. She couldn't leave. Not yet.

"Will you stick around?" He gripped her shoulders, massaging the tight muscles. "We did some kick-ass work tonight and this past month. You deserve to have a good time for a change. When was the last time you had a night out?"

"College." She sagged in his arms. "Even Linc wasn't wild about going out."

Austin bit back his frustrations. He hated how she still talked about Linc, her damn ex-husband. He shouldn't dislike the guy, but Linc had never deserved Molly. He hadn't known how to love a wonderful woman like Molly and hadn't been able to treasure her. Like Austin had? "Then stay with me tonight." Austin kissed her temple. "Enjoy a night out and watch this movie with me. I'll buy ice cream or popcorn, or whatever you want."

"You don't have to buy me off." She grabbed her laptop. "I'll stay, but you need to help me edit the photos."

"Deal." He followed her back to the bedroom and settled onto the bed. His spirit soared as she cuddled up to him. He turned the sound on the movie down and wrapped his arm around her. So they worked together. So they shouldn't be involved. Did that matter? She understood him. He was on the same wavelength as her concerning her ideas on the different advertising campaigns. He needed to get over himself and admit his feelings.

"I bet the pictures are awesome." She swiped through the images. "Except this one."

He chuckled at the blurry image. "You got excited." He could've been in the shot, but then a lot of stuff could've been happening within the blurry matrixing.

"I did." She tapped the photo. "Delete."

"Don't get rid of all of them." He pointed to one of the images of him on the balcony. "In that one, you'd think I'm a model." He scooted closer and bit back a gasp. He barely recognized himself. Between the great lighting, the pose, and her ability to photograph him, he looked awesome. "No one will believe that's me."

"The Aura Sportswear Group will love these," Molly said. "Correction, Iris will love them. You'll get that date after all."

Iris. He'd be lying if he said he wasn't interested in her. She resembled a model, with her long blonde hair and slender frame. She dressed to impress and her business sense with Aura was sharp, but he didn't have much in common with her. Not like with Molly.

"Let's worry about her later." Austin pointed to another image, then trailed his fingers over the edge of the laptop screen. "I like this one the best." He liked the way he looked with Molly. Wasn't that how things were supposed to go? Her beside him and making him better? Then why did he feel the need to keep things platonic? Because he feared if they mixed work and play again, he'd ruin the best relationship of his life.

"That's got me in it." Molly moved the photo file to a separate folder. "I guarantee they won't want that in the campaign." She selected one of the pictures of him on the bed and adjusted the sharpness. She added a blurry frame around it then drew on the image. "Thinking of you."

"Nice. Like a postcard." He rested his head on hers. "Molls, this is why we work so well together. You know what to do and know how to tell me what to do." Why wouldn't she just tell him to get his head out of his rectum and admit he liked her? He had no idea.

"I had you pose. It wasn't that hard." She clicked the save button and switched to a photo of him on the balcony. "Make it black and white, add a haze to the edge," she said, explaining her process as she went. "I want this one, the last one and another to round out the presentation. Which one?"

"Undecided." He stared at the thumbnail images. Christ. Molly could use any of them, really. She'd captured the essence of the company—free-spirited comfort and accessibility—and enhanced his appeal. If she'd gone into professional photography, she could've made a mint with her artsy pictures.

"Yeah, I'm not sure, either." Molly drummed her fingers on the laptop keys. "How about the one where you're glancing over your shoulder at me?" She lined up the images. "Yes?"

He hadn't noticed that particular shot before, but yeah, she'd made him look hot—again. "Go with that one."

"Cool." Her fingers flew over the keys as she added type to the image. "And send."

"Send?" He frowned. "Sent what?"

"The proposal. Iris should have it in her hot little hands as soon as the email arrives." Molly closed the laptop. "I need to plug this in." She left the bed. "I kill more batteries working on photos, but it's fun."

He pieced through what had just happened. She'd already submitted their work to the client. Damn, she was efficient. If the client didn't like the direction she'd given for the apparel campaign, then they were blind and he'd have to get with Molly to come up with a plan B.

"Austin? Your phone is buzzing. Want it?"

His phone? *What the hell?* Why was it making any noise?

He'd thought he'd turned the setting to silent. "I guess." He wasn't sure who'd be calling him and didn't really want to take the call. Truth be told, he preferred the quiet with Molly as opposed to anything else at the moment.

She strolled over to him with the device and plopped it in his hand. "For you."

"Thanks." He glanced down at the number. Melinda Trail from Aura. *Shit.* He scrambled off the bed and escaped onto the balcony. He watched the traffic below and listened to the waves lapping at the lakeshore. "Ms. Trail."

"Hi, Mr. Dean. I'm glad I reached you. I just opened my email and looked over this proposal. I have to say you and Ms. Neff work fast, but you're good. This is *exactly* what Ms. Sommerville wanted," Melinda said. "We'd like to meet to sign the contracts as soon as possible—say, tomorrow morning around ten?"

"I believe Molly and I will be available, but you'll have to contact Lee." He pumped his fist. He owed Molly big time.

"Of course," Melinda replied. "Now, the reason I'm expediting this is that the Aura Group is having our yearly gala to announce which charities we're funding. We'd like to announce the new ad campaign and possibly post a couple of these photos. Is that more incentive to get the contracts signed?"

"I— Yeah." Austin froze. Use the photos? Those were just for suggestion. "Molly used those as recommendations. I'm sure there are better models out there." Especially since the gala was the next night. Christ. He didn't want to see himself in poster form. Sure, he had a healthy self-image, but there was something intimate about what he'd done with Molly. He wasn't sure he wanted to share that intimacy with the world.

"True, but Ms. Neff did such a wonderful job it'd be a shame to waste them," Melinda said. "I highly expect we'll reshoot the photos for the actual campaign and have updated clothing in those shots, but for now, these are more than effective."

He agreed the images shouldn't be wasted, but he wouldn't give the green light without talking to Molly first. "I'd like to discuss that with my partner."

"Of course. I look forward to hearing from you before the morning. Good evening." Melinda hung up, leaving him in silence.

Austin gripped the railing and stared at the white cap waves on the lake. He and Molly worked fast, but the contracts never came through at that speed. Usually, they were on to the next project and almost done while the first job was finalized. He dialed Melinda's number and waited for her to answer.

"The Aura Group, this is Melinda Trail speaking. How may I direct your call?" she asked.

"Hi, this is Austin Dean. We just spoke." His hands shook. "I have a question or two. Number one, the gala is a black-tie affair, correct?"

"Yes. When the meeting takes place in the morning to sign the contracts, the invitation will be delivered. Consider it on the way."

He peeped through the glass doors to Molly. She'd rolled onto her side and clutched one of the pillows. His? He kind of hoped so.

"Question number two, are we to bring a plus one or only us?" He'd asked the question in the most awkward fashion. "I mean, Molly and I should arrive together, correct?"

"We want to recognize both members of the team but would prefer you not to bring a date," Melinda said. "Ms. Sommerville would prefer you to come alone."

He paused. Wait, didn't they want to recognize both members? "Ms. Sommerville? I thought you said we were both invited. I'd like to bring Molly. She did most of the work."

"We like to keep the security tight at the gala and to limit the number of attendees. It keeps the evening more quaint and exclusive. Who doesn't like exclusive?"

"I guess you're right, but I'm not sure why that means

Molly isn't invited." His heart sank. She was being left out again.

"She can come along, I suppose. I'll let the coordinators know."

How nice. He groaned. "Thank you. Ms. Neff and I will be there." Once he conned Molly into going along with him.

"This change won't pose an issue with the proposal or the contract?" Melinda asked.

"No. It should be fine once you've run it past Mr. Lee." His boss would be thrilled that someone from the company would be at the gala. He'd also love that they'd nailed the account. But Austin didn't appreciate Molly not getting the same rewards he'd been offered.

"Wonderful. Good evening," Melinda said and hung up.

Austin leaned against the railing and blew out a long breath. He'd have to tell Molly — not like he'd keep this kind of information to himself. They were going to a gala. He'd have the chance to see Iris again and Molly in a gown. He chuckled. Part of him wanted to see Iris, but the rest of him couldn't wait to see Molly all dressed up. Was he foolish for his interest in both women? Probably. He needed to make a decision and fast. If he tried to string them along, he'd end up on the losing end. Besides, he couldn't handle not having Molly in his life. He pushed off the railing and headed back into the suite.

Molly tipped her head and smiled. "I hadn't realized how tired I was until I stretched out." She waggled her fingers. "Gonna join me?"

"You bet. That's a comfy bed." He crawled onto the bed and tossed his phone onto the mattress. He didn't cuddle up to her. Instead, he rested against the headboard and crossed his arms. He wasn't sure how to tell her the good news. Why? He'd been the one invited — not her and not right away. He'd angled to get her in but he doubted she'd believe him.

"What?" She sat up and finger-combed the loose strands of hair from her face. "What's wrong? Having second thoughts?" She rolled her eyes. "I know. You've got a hot date or something. This was too good to be true." She scooted to the edge of the bed. "I'll go."

"No." He picked at the bedding and watched her. "Stay. I've got news and a big secret."

"That's not so bad." She shrugged but stood. "Spill. Which woman called you for a date? Do I have to play intermediary or bail you out?"

"No." He shook his head and clasped his hands together. God, he sounded so lame. How many times *had* she bailed him out? The more he thought about it, he realized she'd been his salvation too many times. He owed her. *Big time.* "I — *we* — are invited to the Aura gala. The big ball thing they throw when they want to let the world know who they're donating money to. We're in and you're coming with me." Wouldn't that make her day?

"How did you — *we* — get such an invite?" Molly tipped her head to the side. "From the campaign?" She sank onto the bed and stared at him. "Tell me."

His heart hammered. "Yeah, we got the campaign. Melinda opened the email and showed it to Iris. They loved it."

Her eyes sparkled and she sat up straighter. "That's awesome. I knew that would be a good angle for them." Pride shone all over her face. "I'm excited."

"We sign the contracts in the morning, but it's more or less a done deal." He should've been happy but he knew what was coming. He knew Molly. The invitation would've made anyone else's day, but she'd assume the worst. Not like she didn't have reason — he'd conned her into going to different events because he hadn't been able to go alone, and because he hadn't wanted her to be left out. Too many times the clients and their boss had assumed he did the lion's share of the work. Molly saved his ass routinely. He'd make sure she got the recognition she deserved.

"A contract now? That's fast." She hopped off the bed and did a silly dance where she bobbed her head and pointed toward the ceiling. "We got it, we got it. Whoop!"

He laughed and joined her. The dance reminded him of someone celebrating a touchdown. Truthfully, they had scored—getting the contract and working with Aura was a big deal. "There's more. They want to use your photos at the gala."

"They want to show you off." Molly stopped dancing and looked at him. She removed the elastic from her hair and fixed her ponytail then put the elastic back. "I understand." Her smile fell and the light in her eyes dimmed. "You're hot and they want to capitalize. It's a good fit."

"I don't agree." He tugged her onto his lap. Being with her calmed him yet had him on edge. He wanted to make her happy, not bring her down. "Molls, they want us. Not just me. I'm in the photo, but that's your work."

She stood and turned her back to him. "You've been invited. Have fun."

"I need you." He wasn't lying. She was more than his partner in crime at the ad agency. He liked her and wanted her by his side when he faced the firing squad at the gala. She was his rock.

"You need me to bail you out. I ran the extra yards to turn in the best proposal, but you wanted this campaign more than anyone because you wanted another chance with you. Well, you got it." Her tone changed. The pain in her voice was evident. She was getting screwed. He could do something about it—something beyond just insisting she was supposed to come along.

"No—yes." Shit. He'd fucked this all up.

"Which is it?" She faced him. "Am I your prop or your bail bondswoman?" No tears, but her voice cracked.

"Both—no. Fuck." He gritted his teeth. "You deserve tons of credit. The whole reason we got in at the gala was because of your photos. Yes, I want you there because you're my partner, but I said no because I know I'll need bailing out." He threaded his fingers into his hair. "I told them we weren't coming unless we were both included, because this

31

wasn't all my work. I can't do this without you."

Molly's shoulders sank. "Shit. Whose pussy did you fill and chill?"

"That sounds tacky." Not altogether unlike him, but he'd hoped he didn't have such an awful record.

"You're tacky. You jump from bed to bed," she snapped.

"I might have done that in the past." He wanted to be better. Wanted to settle down. But he couldn't decide who he wanted to settle down with. Still, he deserved every barb and nasty comment from her. He'd been just as guilty of using her.

"Austin."

"So I've made bad decisions." He held up both hands. "So what? I'm not perfect and never claimed to be." *Beg me to make up my mind. Force me to admit what you've already figured out.*

She shook her head. "Don't do this. Don't pander to my ego. I know the score. They liked my photos because the owner already has a thing for you." She wiped the tears from her cheeks and smeared her makeup. "You only told them I needed to come along because you felt sorry for me."

She was right, but he refused to let her know. Was he an ass? Yeah, he was, but he couldn't help himself. He'd tried to make things right, but nothing seemed to be going according to plan. "Is there anything wrong with me wanting you as my date?"

"No." She gathered up her things. "I'm not doing it." Molly tossed a twenty onto the table then shoved her phone into her purse. "Take the glory. Take the praise. I'm not interested."

Fuck. He balled his hands into fists. "I kind of told Mr. Lee we're dating." Not a total lie. He'd admitted to their boss he wanted to ask her out because he needed to know if they'd get fired for having an inter-office relationship.

"You what?" Molly's lips parted and her eyes widened. More tears slipped down her cheeks and her mascara smeared. "Are you kidding me?"

"No."

She pinched the bridge of her nose. "You did this because the relationship with Mr. Lee's daughter went south and she realized you're an ass, right?"

"I'm pretty sure she knows." Austin inched toward her. He wanted to gather Molly into his arms and make things right. "Go with me. You did the work and deserve the spoils. Hell, I should be staying home."

"But they expect you to be there." She arranged her bags on her shoulder then tucked her laptop under her free arm. She hadn't even unplugged the machine yet. "I'm not doing it."

"Come on." He crept closer. "Please? I'm begging."

"No." She started away from the table, but the cable on her laptop stopped her. She groaned as the connection fell away from the machine. Molly placed the computer on the table then unplugged. She tucked the cord into one of her bags. "I'm out of here. I can't stand being used — again."

Fuck it. Austin crossed the room and took her bags and the laptop from her. "I don't deserve for you to give a shit about me and Aura doesn't deserve to have you working for them. The whole situation is a happy, profitable accident and I'm benefiting, yes. The thing is, if I'm going to go to this event I need you. I can't do this alone — not because I'm hiding from a girlfriend. Promise. It's more complicated than that."

Everything was so fucked up. She knew him too well and wasn't giving him an inch. He needed to admit his feelings and be honest with her.

"Austin. You're just doing this because I'm the only woman you've ever slept with who still talks to you. I might be invited to this shindig, but the only reason you want me as your date is because I'm the one woman there who isn't a sexual threat or potential partner in the sack. I'm not trying to fuck you. God knows that won't happen again." She eased away from him and turned her back to him. Her voice cracked as she gathered up her things. "I'm the best you're going to hope for, right?"

She had him nailed and had cut him deep. They'd never sleep together again? Why? Because he'd kept his mouth shut for too long? *Duh.* He needed another chance to convince her to stick around. He placed her purse and shoulder bag on the table. "You're the only one I trust."

"Trust?" She reached for her purse but stopped and held up both hands. "Why now?"

"Molls, we can't lose this client. They're sending over the contracts in the morning. We get this sorted out, show up at the gala and smile a lot. You might have fun and if you don't, you don't have to talk to me ever again."

"Oh, I'm already on that." She grabbed the handle of her shoulder bag. "Just let me go."

He'd fucked everything else up. He might as well be honest with her. "Besides the fact that you're supposed to go because those are your goddamn photos they're excited about, you'll help me make the right impression. You won't try to climb the social ladder on my back. You've got heart and integrity. I need you there with me." To be honest, he was scared to go alone. Scared to admit he'd fallen in love with her and wanted her on his arm. She gave him strength, confidence and made him laugh. "I know I won't blow it if you're beside me. I'll help you pick out a dress and get you all dolled up. Just please say you'll come with me."

"This was supposed to be a good night. A fun time. We have a few drinks, work on this project and get it turned in. Watch a dirty movie, maybe end up making out, but having a good time. Now we get the account and are invited to a ball. I've never been to a ball." Her chin quivered and she closed her eyes. "You want me to go to salve your ego when Iris turns you down."

Austin sank onto the closest chair and rested his elbows on his knees. He dipped his head and stared at the floor. He'd been told a liar couldn't look a man in the eye. Was he a liar? No, but he couldn't face her. "I want you to accompany me because you're my best friend and the best co-worker I'll ever know. People like you, and I'm an arrogant ass. Maybe you can smooth out my rough edge." Knock some sense into him, make him admit the truth... only the impossible.

"You've got the ass part right," she snapped.

"I'm sorry, Molls." He looked up at her. She might've been arguing with him but she was still there. He had a chance. "I'm trying to do the right thing. Yes, they told me they wanted me there, but you did the lion's share of the work. I can't allow them to leave you out."

"Thanks, I think." She plopped onto the couch. "You annoy me so much sometimes. It's like you know exactly how to get under my skin, but how to be sweet at the same time. I should thank you, but I want to punch you in the arm." She swept her hair out of her eyes again. "It hurts, you know. Hurts to think the companies only see you."

"I know, Molls, and I'm sorry." He crossed the room and kneeled at her feet. "Come with me to the gala. Show Aura and everyone else you're a creative force to be reckoned with."

She swiped the tears from her cheeks again. "Let me think about it."

"I'm taking that as a yes." He rested his head on her lap. "We're going to have a great time."

"I never said yes." She stroked his hair. "I'm not convinced it'll be a good situation. I'm better suited as the silent partner."

"Well, the gala is tomorrow, so that doesn't give you much time to think. You're either in or out." He laced his fingers with hers. Her touch seared him to the core. "It's going to be very good and I'll get to see you in a dress."

"I hate dresses," she whispered.

"I bet Remy would go with you to find the right dress." He could see her now in something red, or maybe dark blue. She'd outshine the rest of the women at the gala and he'd have the honor of being her date.

"I should call Remy and get him out of himself for a

while. He's been lonely." She ran her fingers through his hair, massaging his scalp and soothing him.

"Why? He's not needed at the gallery?" He wound his arm around her legs and cuddled up closer to her. "I bet Saturdays are busy there."

"The gallery is closed until four on Saturdays, but I meant since he and Javier split he's not exactly busy."

"Oh." He frowned. "They were so good for each other. When did they end it?"

"Three weeks ago. It's still fresh." She sighed. "I can't see why they couldn't make it work. Maybe I'm wrong, but it almost seemed like Remy wanted it more. Javier wanted to be in a relationship, but he wanted to be free, too. I don't know."

Austin scooted off the floor and onto the couch beside her. He draped his arm around Molly's shoulders. Even he could see the parallels between him and Remy. She, like Javier, wanted something that could very well not be possible and why? Because he, like Remy, liked to roam. Remy might not want to change, but what if Austin did? The gala was his chance.

"Maybe you see things wrong," he said. "You never know. What you believe might be half the story." And he just might be capable of turning his life around. "What if Remy didn't realize the good thing he had until he lost it and he's willing to work to get that passion back?"

Molly stared at him. Her mouth opened and closed, but no sound came out.

"Can you trust me? For once? And not with an advertising account?" He rested his forehead against hers and kissed the tip of her nose. "You never know what could happen at this gala. People will see your photographs. You might be able to chuck the ad job and follow your passion. Other things could happen, too."

She didn't say anything right away. Molly's shoulders sagged and she folded her arms. "Show me you're not an ass and I might believe you."

"I can't guarantee I'll be perfect, but this could be good for us." She'd given him a chance. He wasn't worthy of her or another opportunity with her, but damn it, he was tired of screwing up. If he and Molly were meant to have a romantic relationship, then he wasn't about to tempt fate.

Chapter Three

Molly covered her face with both hands. A gala. How in the hell had she ended up being invited to one? She'd done her job. She rested her head on the back of the couch.

"So I'm going with you." She patted Austin's thigh. "I'm in a hotel room with you, I'm your ride home and I'm supposed to attend a gala. I'm so screwed."

"Why?" He clasped her hand. "I'm that awful?"

"You can be." But she'd been mean to him. "Did you tell them I'm coming along because you felt sorry for me?"

"Nope. I told them you were coming along because the photos are yours, the idea was yours and you deserve the credit. I fought for you."

She could accept that. "So, I need a dress. I don't have any. I never even had a wedding dress."

Austin sat up and faced her. "Wait, what? You didn't have… But you married Linc."

"At the courthouse." She shrugged. "He didn't want to wait and I couldn't find the right one. He said I didn't need one. I guess I was so wrapped up in not wanting to be alone that I gave in."

"Molls." He jumped up from his seat and paced the length of the room. "This is crazy. Nuts."

"You were happy. Our friend Aiden was happy. I was… alone." She left the couch and wandered out to the balcony. The chilly night air wrapped around her and sent shivers through her. She hated talking about her past, hated reliving any of it. But Austin deserved to know the truth. She wanted nothing more than to be in a relationship, just like her college friends, but Aiden had found a girlfriend and Austin had moved on long before she'd been able to tell Austin how she felt. Maybe she'd settled for Linc but she hadn't been alone.

"Molls." Austin joined her on the balcony. "Why didn't you tell me? Why didn't you talk to me and make me listen?"

"I was on my own. You and Carole just started getting heavy and I wasn't allowed into that situation. She'd slam the door in my face and hang up on me when I called. I gave up." She rested her forearms on the railing. "I let him talk me into expediting things. I hated the situation and, looking back, it was bad, but I learned from it. I gave up settling and focused on being happy."

Austin bumped shoulders with her. "Still."

"I know what I want and I'm not settling." She watched the waves crash on the jagged beach. Even when the world seemed to be falling apart, she took solace in her decision. She might not be in a long-term relationship with the man of her dreams but she was happy.

"Good for you." Austin tucked her close to his body. "But you still need a dress for tomorrow night."

"I do." She wasn't even sure where to start looking.

"Have you ever been to Erin's over in Avon Commons?"

"That's a bridal shop." She stared at him. "I didn't even go there while I was engaged, so yeah, no."

"Mom could set you up. I'll call her and ask for a favor." He frowned but continued talking. "She's always got a few dresses that might work." Austin steered her away from the balcony and back into the room. He strode over to the couch long enough to retrieve his bag then disappeared into the bedroom with his phone. "Every woman needs at least one nice dress." He turned his back to her and spoke into his phone. Less than a minute later, he faced her and grinned. "Done."

"Wait." Not that she had much of a chance to hold up anything. She stopped him and smoothed her hands over his chest. Here they were, him still in the underwear from the photo shoot, her fully dressed and they were discussing gowns as well as the past. Something was wrong. "Mom? What? Are you collecting parents? I thought Gretchen was down in Texas, or was it southern Ohio? She moved around so much."

"Mom hates staying in one place for long, but she's settled down for a while." Austin sat on the bed and tugged her onto his lap. "She had a bridal shop down in Oxford but decided to move it up here after I got the job at CDL. I like having her close — closer than Texas."

"But you never mentioned her coming back. I liked your mom and would've met her for lunch or something." Embarrassment washed over her. If good old Mom didn't really care for her then that would explain the disconnect.

"She has her thing and I've got mine, but she's always loved you. We've both been busy and I never got around to bringing her up." He twirled a lock of Molly's hair in his fingers. "Anyway, I called her. She put a few dresses aside and said to come in tomorrow morning after we sign the contract. She's got a friend who can do your hair and makeup. Hell, I bet even Dylan would help out."

"Why are you doing this?" Why did he feel the need to overwhelm her?

"Because I can." He brushed his nose against hers. "I want to make this night special for you. Both nights." He cupped the back of her head and feathered his lips over her mouth.

From her head to her toes, her body warmed and her nerve endings sizzled. She draped her arms around his neck. The desire to give in to him was strong. He wanted her. For right now? Forever? She wasn't sure.

Molly threw caution to the wind and ignored her better judgment. Austin had been her favorite mistake from the get-go and she refused to push him away again. She shoved her hand under his shirt and palmed his pecs. Damn, the man was strong. She pressed her knees together and moaned. He knew how to kiss, too. He alternated nips with longer kisses and sucked on her tongue.

"Molly." He shoved her blouse over her head and tossed the article of clothing onto the floor. "Sweetheart."

She curled away from him and wanted to hide. She wasn't perfect, slender or anything he normally went for in his women. Besides, she'd worn a sports bra.

"This is hot." He eased the straps of the bra down her arms. "I like it."

"Austin." She wished she'd worn something a little more fancy.

"Don't hide from me."

He moved the top of the lingerie over her breasts and bared her chest to him. He moaned then mashed his face into her boobs. His warm breath turned her insides out and when he sucked on her nipples, she whimpered. She threaded her fingers into his hair and tipped her head back. He was dangerous to her resolve and restraint.

"So good."

He scooped her into his arms and stood then placed her on the bed. The predatory look in his eyes scared and pleased her. She wanted to be possessed by this man. She sat up long enough for him to help her out of the bra then eased onto the mattress. Austin climbed between her thighs. He leaned over her and brushed her hair off her face. He kissed her until she couldn't catch her breath then licked a path of fire down her neck.

She wanted to protest, but why? Because she knew how this situation would end. Still. He was here and she wanted him. Why not give in and let nature take its course?

Molly didn't fight him when he popped the button on her jeans, or when he helped her out of the pants and her panties. She knew where this moment would lead and cherished what was about to happen.

Austin rested her leg on his shoulder and kissed his way down her inner thigh. She balled her hands in the bedding to hide the trembling.

He met her gaze as he nipped her belly. He trailed his fingers over her thighs then up her ribcage to her breasts.

She couldn't look him in the eye. The last time they'd fucked had been before her marriage. She'd been a different woman back then. There was no way he'd miss the changes.

"Don't hide from me." Austin dragged his tongue along her slit then grazed his teeth across her clit. The slight pain sent pleasure through her body.

Molly bit back a moan. Fucking balls. He knew what to do to make her soul sing. She writhed beneath him and planted her feet on the bed.

"Austin."

She squeezed her eyes shut. Each time he licked her pussy or sucked on her cunt lips, she cried out. The blood thrummed in her ears and the scent of his cologne wrapped around her. He swiped his tongue over her cunt and blew chilly air across her sensitive skin. He reminded her of velvet with each lick.

"Damn, babe." He buried his nose in her pubic hair and sucked hard on her clit.

"Austin," she bit out. The pressure sent pain-filled pleasure to her core. She opened her eyes and moaned.

"Love how you make noise when we're together." Austin speared his tongue into her pussy, mimicking sex, then rubbed her clit with the pad of his thumb.

She shuddered. This wasn't supposed to happen this fast—the climax washed over her and her legs trembled. Her world spun. "Austin."

"Fuck, that's sexy." He buried his face in her pussy again and licked until the bliss-filled post-orgasm glow settled around her.

She sagged against the bed. She caught her breath then whispered, "This puts a new spin on getting work done."

"It's not over yet." Austin stood and yanked the shirt up over his head. His chest glistened and his nipples beaded as he moved.

Molly had seen him a hundred times without his shirt and a few of him totally nude, but he still stole her breath.

Austin shucked the boxer briefs and stood before her.

He took his glasses off and placed them on the nightstand. "Been forever." He didn't give her a chance to think before he opened a condom wrapper and sheathed himself. He stroked his dick then crawled onto the bed. He paused over the top of her.

"I need this — need you." Austin captured her mouth in a kiss. He palmed her breast and moaned. She swallowed the noise.

Jesus. He overwhelmed her and had so much power. She needed to take some back — but not right now.

"Take me," she murmured between kisses.

"Mine." Austin slid his cock along her cunt lips, stroking her.

She drew her knees up around his hips and guided his dick into her pussy and groaned at the tight fit.

"God, that's good." He pressed his face to the side of her neck and nibbled between thrusts. He started slow but built speed within moments.

Molly gripped his shoulders. In and out, thrust for thrust she met him and melted. When he dipped his head, she tugged him closer and mashed her mouth onto his. She sucked on his tongue. She needed him everywhere.

Austin broke the kiss first and rested his forehead against hers. The muscle in his jaw tensed and he slipped his hand down to her hip. He dug his fingers into her skin as the orgasm swept over him.

"Fuck," he said from between clenched teeth. "Jesus." He shuddered and pumped into her a few more times as the trembling subsided.

Molly held on to him. She hadn't come a second time but she didn't care. She still couldn't quite move from the first orgasm. She looped her arms around his neck and basked in the delicious post-climax feeling.

A bead of sweat slipped down his temple and his shoulders sparkled with perspiration. "Missed that, babe."

She nodded. Having sex with him again hadn't been smart, but she wanted to keep making the mistake. He'd always been her favorite. She shoved her worry aside. For now, she'd allow herself to believe there was a chance she and Austin could make a relationship work. But just for now.

* * * *

Austin rolled over and watched Molly sleep. He'd forgotten how beautiful she was first thing in the morning. He breathed in the scent of her lotion, or was it her perfume? He wasn't sure and, really, it didn't matter. He didn't regret sleeping with her and never would. She might call their trying to have a relationship outside of work a disaster, but he didn't agree. She kept him sane. He wasn't giving her up.

Yes, he wasn't sure if they had a chance at forever and part of him still wanted to hold on to his freedom.

Molly sighed and sat up. She scrubbed both hands over her face. "Shit. What time is it?"

"Eight. You crashed shortly after we…" He wanted to say fucked, but sex with her wasn't fucking. He made love to her. "I held you and we slept. Best night of my life."

"I see."

"Hey, it was. I slept soundly, feel refreshed and cannot wait for tonight." He smoothed his palm over her back. "Can't wait to see you in some spangly dress and looking like a million dollars."

"That's right. I do need a little…work. You mentioned your mom, right?" Molly climbed out of bed and hurried into her clothes. She pulled her hair into a ponytail. She gathered up her tablet, laptop, phone and scooped them all into her bag, then yawned. "I need to call Remy, but if your mom's still got time, I'll go to the store."

"You will?" Austin couldn't get dressed fast enough. He scrambled into his shoes and snatched his keys and messenger bag from the couch. "Hold up. I need to make sure I have everything."

"I'm not in a hurry." Molly leaned her hip against the back of the sofa. "Where am I meeting you for this date to the gala?"

"I'd say your place." He rummaged through the couch cushions to ensure he hadn't lost anything then ruffled the sheets. He dug through his bag. "Keys, wallet, phone… tablet and notes. Looks like I'm good."

"Are you?" She rolled her eyes but smiled.

"You thought I was last night."

"That was last night."

"It doesn't have to end there." He followed her out to the elevator. "How about seven tonight? We've got to be there around eight."

"Okay." She nodded. "So I'm meeting you downstairs at seven."

"I thought I'd come up and get you. I'm calling a limo." He pressed the button for the elevator. "We should arrive in style."

"Right." She stepped into the car first. "A limo?"

"We're going to have a great time." He wanted to cuddle her, but the tension between them had returned and he didn't like it. "You'll see."

"Yeah."

When the elevator car stopped, she left first and strode across the lobby. She didn't say anything as she placed her things on the back seat. She eased behind the wheel of her vehicle. The drive across town went by in a blur — a quiet blur. He toyed with the strap of his bag but didn't try to talk. He wasn't sure what to say and he couldn't read her mind.

Molly pulled into the parking garage and stopped beside Austin's sports car. She gripped the steering wheel and sighed.

"What's wrong?" Austin asked. "Worried about tonight?" *Please let her be giddy about our date.*

"No." She flexed her fingers on the wheel. "What—what if this isn't what we're supposed to do? What if last night was a mistake?"

"Landing the Aura account was a mistake?" He knew what she meant but he wasn't ready to give up. "We rocked those pictures and we're going to make them proud. Mr. Lee will love that we got the account. We might even get a raise."

"For the love of God, you know what I mean. You and me. We're friends—not lovers." She dropped her hands onto her lap and closed her eyes. "You're going to go to the gala tonight, you'll find someone beautiful and you'll forget all about me. Stop building me up so you can stroll out with the next woman you see, okay? I know you. You're not meant to settle down. You can't even stick to a date for very long. I need commitment or nothing at all. That's not you."

He reeled from her words. She knew him too well and had nailed him again.

"I'd be lying if I said I wanted this to work out. You're my favorite mistake. You're the one I keep hoping will change, but that's not you." The corner of her mouth twitched as she tried to smile. "How about we forget about last night— other than the contract part, we focus on signing the papers today and get through tonight without issue?"

"Molls." He grasped her hand and kissed her knuckles.

"No strings. You're welcome."

"Molly."

"I'll see you in an hour, then tonight at seven." She didn't look at him. "Okay?"

"Sure." Austin climbed out of the car and watched as she drove away. He clicked the fob on his keys to unlock his vehicle. He'd fucked everything up. She was supposed to fall in love with him. Supposed to realize they weren't a mistake. But no. He sank behind the wheel of the car and groaned. How in the hell was she supposed to see they were meant for each other when she was right—he couldn't commit?

"Fuck." He pounded his fist on the steering wheel. He wanted more from life than simply sailing around and never quite landing anywhere.

Austin drove to his apartment. He parked and raced up to his floor then hurried through for a shower. As he stood under the hot spray, he thought about Molly. The way she fit against him, the way she'd moaned while they'd made love, the way her smile melted him to the core. The memory of her kiss lingered in his mind and he longed to have her there with him.

He leaned on the shower wall and lathered the washcloth. The suds slipped down his body and swirled around his cock. He wiped the soap off but paused. As he touched himself, he imagined her there.

"Molls," he whispered and stroked his dick. "Babe." He closed his eyes and imagined her in his shower.

Molly rubbed her bare breasts on his chest and threaded her arm about his neck. She curled her fingers around his erection and stroked. She punctuated each tug with a kiss on his lips.

The synapses in his brain sizzled. He moaned and picked up the pace. "Fuck, fuck, fuck."

"I love shower play." She turned and waggled her ass at him. "Soapy and slick."

Austin jerked himself off faster and gritted his teeth. She should have been in the stall with him. Damn it. The heat in his belly spiraled through his veins. He rocked his hips and fucked his hand. The muscles in his legs tensed as the orgasm crashed through him. He opened his eyes. Cum slid down his thigh and landed in the drain.

He groaned. The once-hot water cooled along with his need. He rinsed the soap and jizz from his body then switched off the faucet and left the stall. He'd never be the same until he either got Molly out of his system or married her.

Austin stopped, stark naked in his bedroom. Married. Jesus. He wasn't the type for such things. Why did Molly make him think that way?

Because she was right—she was the kind of woman a man didn't let get away. She was the one he cherished for the rest of his life.

She *was* the one he'd cherish for the rest of his life.

Austin dressed at lightning speed and hurried back to the advertising agency. He made a beeline for the office he shared with Molly. Once the papers were signed, he'd tug her aside and declare his feelings.

He switched on the lights and popped a pod into the coffee machine. When he turned around, Molly wasn't waiting for him. Mr. Lee stood in the doorway.

"Mr. Lee." Austin offered his hand. "Nice to see you this morning."

"It's Saturday. I hate working on Saturday."

"I know, but the deal came through." He shook hands with his boss then stepped back. "We didn't think waiting would be wise."

"It doesn't hurt that you were invited to the Aura gala." Mr. Lee closed the door and turned Molly's chair around. "Be honest with me. You've got a date for the party?"

"I do. I'm taking Molly." Austin poured the brewed coffee into his cup then filled a second one for his boss.

"Is that wise?"

"Offering you coffee?" Austin sat on the edge of his desk. "Or Molly? She worked on the project and should be there." He bobbed his head. "They weren't initially interested in her coming along, but I made them see reason. Why have one half of the team there? Both should be recognized."

"True." Mr. Lee sipped the coffee. "This is good. I've considered getting one of those machines."

"It was Molly's idea. She knows what I like." She knew plenty more than he'd ever figure out. "Anyway, she'll have fun at the gala."

"I'm sure she will." Mr. Lee sipped the coffee again. "But that's not what's bothering me. I'm worried about you. I'm your boss, yes, but I'd like to think you respect my point of view."

"I do." He kind of had to — Mr. Lee signed his paychecks. "What about me has you worried?"

"You don't give yourself time for relationships or time for them to develop. Once the woman gets her heart involved, you're gone. That might work in some situations, but not with Molly. Don't use Molly as a reason to go to that party or to hide from one of your various exes. You can't use her like you do other people. She's special."

"I'm not using her." Who was he kidding? He was. He'd figured out how to get her invited to the gala, but part of him was still interested in catching Iris' eye.

"Right. Danica will be there and so will Iris. I know Danica's still interested in you and Iris called my office four times last night to ensure this meeting would be taking place today." Mr. Lee shook his head. "She likes you and I suspect the feeling is mutual—or do you already have someone else in the wings?" He frowned. "You do, don't you?"

"I'm not saying." He didn't want to jinx things with Molly. They were a good team—in the office and in bed. He cared about her more than he wanted to admit.

"If it's not Iris, then I have no idea." Mr. Lee stood. He left his half-empty coffee cup on Austin's desk. "Here's the thing. You do good work for me. With Molly, you're dangerous. But that's it—you're dangerous to her."

"I'm not dangerous." Maybe to himself, but that was beside the point.

"Don't do this to Molly. If you've got any designs on dating her, stop. Be honest and let her kick you in the balls." Mr. Lee patted Austin's shoulder. "Understand?"

"Sir? I don't."

"Use your head, not your dick." Mr. Lee opened the door and left Austin alone in the office.

Austin sank back onto the edge of his desk and stared at the doorway. That was the trouble—he couldn't make up his mind about Molly. He thought he was using his head. He liked Molly and respected her—but he liked Iris Sommerville.

Maybe the gala would be a disaster and the magic from

the night before would be gone. Molly deserved more than a night of passion here and there. She deserved more than him.

He gathered up the paperwork for the contracts and glanced back at Molly's desk. Mr. Lee was right—he needed to leave her alone. He headed across the building to the main meeting room.

Melinda, Iris and Mr. Lee were already seated around the table. He sank onto a chair at the far end. Molly wasn't there. Running late?

"So?" Iris scooted her chair down the table and parked next to him. "You're coming tonight."

"I am." He smiled. Always treat the customer with care—or, as Molly would say, charm them into doing what you want. Molly was always right. Too bad the customer was caressing his thigh under the table.

"Good. I can't wait to see you in a tux." She licked her lips. "But in my boxer briefs was pretty good," she purred. "Such a nice, tight ass."

He tensed. This wasn't how he'd expected things to go.

"Are we ready to discuss the agreement?" Mr. Lee asked. He tapped the papers on the massive table. "Austin? Where's Molly?"

"Coming," Molly shouted. She burst through the door and her shoulder bag toppled to the floor. She smiled but blushed and averted her gaze. "Sorry." She gathered her things and sat on the closest chair.

"Terrible," Iris murmured. "Such a disaster."

"I wouldn't say that," Austin shot back.

Iris grabbed his leg again then slid her palm to his crotch. "You'd say something else."

He froze. Her actions were so wrong. He might have been interested in her but he didn't want to be mauled by her—especially not under the table. She leaned into him and nibbled on his neck.

"Stop," he muttered. He squirmed in his seat and nudged her away, but Iris didn't budge. She massaged his crotch and plunked his hand on her thigh. She'd hiked her skirt up, revealing her lack of underwear. He cringed. The wrong woman wanted his attention and the right one couldn't meet his gaze.

Molly's eyes widened and the apples of her cheeks reddened. She averted her gaze and fidgeted. The muscle in her jaw tightened. His heart sank. He'd let her down. This wasn't how things should've gone.

Mr. Lee pressed the button on the intercom. "Can we have bottled water in here? We need…water." He scrubbed his mouth with the back of his hand and rolled his eyes. "We need something."

"I'm fine." Iris smiled. She rested her arm on the back of Austin's chair. "Don't get me anything."

Austin shot a glance over at Molly. She didn't look at him. She signed the paperwork and nodded at the appropriate times. Once the meeting concluded, she hurried out of the room.

Damn.

Mr. Lee glared at Austin but kept his cool. "Thank you for your business," he said and shook hands with Iris. "We'll be in touch with the rest of the proposals." Once Mr. Lee had left, Iris scooted closer to Austin. "I wish the door was shut." She dipped her head and winked. "Don't pout. It crinkles your face."

"Don't what?" He hopped up from his seat and crossed the room to shut the door. He needed privacy in order to get the right words out. "Stop. I'm not comfortable with this." Truth be told, he wanted the hell out of there, but he needed to put an end to whatever was happening with Iris.

"So?"

"Iris. Molly is my partner. I do my best work with her. Now she's gone. There's no guarantee this will work." He pretty much knew anything between him and Iris would be a disaster.

"I'd rather you not work with her. She's a distraction." Iris pressed her body to his in the corner. "Now, where were we?" She tilted her head and dragged her nose along his cheek. "According to what I've heard, you're trying to get in good with me. It's working."

"Oh?" The closer he got to Iris, the more he wondered what he'd been thinking. Iris was beautiful, but she didn't stir him. There wasn't the tingle.

"Plan on having the time of your life tonight." She mashed a kiss to his lips. Her perfume curled around him and she slid her palm into his back pocket. She squeezed his ass. "I know *I* will."

"Iris." Melinda touched Iris' shoulder. "Time to go. We've got to get you to your fitting."

"Until then." Iris kissed him again then allowed her assistant to escort her from the room.

Austin blew out a long breath and scrubbed his forehead with the back of his hand. He was in deep. The woman he wanted wasn't interested and the woman he'd thought he wanted was. Now he had to make a decision. *Fuck.*

First, he needed to find Molly. He sprinted across the building to their office and stopped short. "Molly?"

He opened the door, but she wasn't there. "Molly?" He jaunted down to the restroom. He called into the room, but no one answered. Even when he pissed her off, she still talked to him. That was one of their bonds—they never went completely silent with each other.

Austin returned to the office and gathered his wallet, phone and keys. Maybe he'd catch up to Molly in the parking garage. He locked the office and bounded down the stairwell, taking the steps two at a time. He wanted to explain things to her, but what was he supposed to say? He wasn't seeing Iris but kind of wanted to. Then there was Molly. The sex had rocked his world and her smile brightened his life. She was his co-worker and should've been off limits. Still, he liked her and wanted to try to have a relationship with her. He hopped behind the wheel of his car. If he had any chance of fixing things with Molly, he had to find her. He drove around the level to look for Molly's car but didn't see it. *Damn it.*

He set his phone to speaker and dialed her number. The call went straight to voicemail. He thumped the steering wheel and tossed the phone onto the passenger seat. He'd try her number again once he got home. He might have given up easily before but not now.

Austin pulled out of the parking spot and navigated through the traffic until he reached his apartment building. Thank God only a handful of drivers clogged the normally busy streets. He wasn't in the mood for complications.

He shook his head. What was wrong with him? He lived a pretty boring existence. Parking garage to parking garage, office to his lonely apartment. Yes, he dated, but he wasn't happy and he had the gall to grouse about complications.

Once in his apartment, he flicked on the lights and dumped his bag onto the couch. He surveyed the view from his living room. Bland, beige walls, artwork original to the apartment, the furniture functional but boring. He only had a few photographs and those were of insects. He hadn't chosen the images — they'd come with the apartment. The place was not warm and inviting — not by a long shot. Things were brighter when Molly was around. Her smile, laughter and the way she knew how to snuggle up to him, she made the world a better place for him. She'd never spent much time in his apartment. Why? He'd never extended the invitation and she didn't expect to come over. He'd have to rectify that situation, and fast.

He left his bag on the couch and wandered into the bedroom. While he cleaned himself up, he'd work on his plan to win her over. He stripped down and stepped into the shower a second time. He didn't need another round in the shower, but the longer he stood under the hot spray, the more his ideas formed into a plan. The night would be original, he knew that for sure. They'd dance, laugh and he'd make sure she was given her due rewards.

He turned off the water and headed back into the bedroom. His phone buzzed on the dresser. Molly? He could only hope. Austin checked the number then answered and switched to the speaker. Not Molly. His brother was on the other end of the line.

"Hi, Dylan. What's up?" Austin strolled nude around the bedroom, sorting out what he needed for the evening.

"I hear you talked to Mom," Dylan said.

"I did." He yanked a pair of boxer briefs from the drawer and gripped the thin fabric. The underwear made him think of Molly. He'd never look at them quite the same. Her simple idea had brought them not only a new account and a bonus, but also closer together. He'd stripped down to his underwear, sure, but he'd also bared his soul.

"Who is the girl? I'm looking at her and she's beautiful." Dylan snorted. "Like out-of-your-league pretty."

"Looking at her?" He stepped into the boxers and pulled the underwear up his legs. "How? Are you at the store?"

"Where else do I spend my Saturdays?" Dylan asked. "Yeah, I'm here. She's sitting in her car. Seems scared to death. She's got a guy with her. Is this *the* Molly?"

"The?"

"As in the Molly Mom talks about and is practically giddy to see?"

"That's her." He'd forgotten how well his mother and Molly got along. Of all the women who had come and gone in his life, the only one his mother approved of was Molly.

"Okay, man. Don't screw this up," Dylan said. "Who's the guy with her?"

"That's her best friend, Remy. Nice guy." Austin flopped onto the bed. He and his brother weren't extremely close, but Dylan was usually good for advice. Too bad he had to take advice from his baby brother. "Do you have a minute or does Mom have you running ragged?"

"I've got a couple. Mom opened up just for Molly — if she ever gets in here. What's wrong?" Dylan asked.

"I'm — I fucked this up." He dipped his head and pinched the bridge of his nose. "Long story short, Molly is coming with me to a gala. Not as my plus one, but as an invited guest. I should be her plus one. Anyway, the woman throwing said gala… She's interested in me and I kind of am in her."

"So you can't decide. Jesus." Dylan groaned. "I'm guessing gala girl is gorgeous. A real rung on the ladder, but Molly — who won't help you advance — is sweet and reliable? Yes? No?"

"Iris is beautiful and yeah, she'd help my career. I don't want to be in advertising for the rest of my life. I could do more."

"You could also fly to the moon," Dylan said. "You like both but you can't decide, right? Then cut Molly loose. She doesn't deserve the headaches you're going to cause."

"You don't know that." He hated when Dylan had him figured out.

"Don't need to know. You're my brother. You're dangerous to the opposite sex because you have a way of getting women to fall for you, then when they do you end things." Dylan sighed and didn't say anything right away. "Gala girl — Iris — can probably manage if you break her heart. She's more than likely got half a dozen men like you waiting in the wings, but Molly doesn't. If you're not willing to give her your full attention then don't dick with her."

"You're probably right." He didn't want Dylan to be right, but he knew better.

"Who knows? I might make a play for her."

"Dyl?" A dull ache started behind Austin's eyes as an image of Dylan and Molly together formed in his mind. They would make a striking couple. But he didn't want her to end up with Dylan. She was supposed to be *his* girl.

"Hey, I'm just sayin' if you're going to fuck with her then get over yourself and leave her alone," Dylan said. "Gotta go. She opened the car door. Show time." He clicked off the line, leaving Austin alone with his thoughts.

Austin massaged his temples. *Damn it.* He didn't deserve a woman like Molly. He'd end up being another mistake and he doubted he could live with himself if he gave her the shaft.

He caught a glimpse of himself in the mirror and groaned. "You're an asshole, Austin Dean." He didn't want to end up as a scumbag but he wasn't sure even Molly could polish him enough to make him shine.

Chapter Four

Molly gripped the steering wheel. She'd opened the car door but wasn't ready to head into the bridal shop. She looked at Remy. He wasn't pushing her to get out of the vehicle, either.

"What's wrong?" Remy pried her fingers from the wheel. "Talk to me."

"I'm making a huge mistake. This isn't the place I should be shopping." She shook her head. "It's not me."

"Why? So Austin's mom and brother work here. So they're staring at us through the front window. So what?" Remy shrugged. "Brother Dylan is still fine." He whistled and stretched on his seat. "I'd ride that pole all night long."

"Remy Jack." She was used to his comments, but every so often he shocked her.

"He's hot. Sorry I noticed." Remy folded his arms. "Now tell me why you don't belong here."

"This is all wrong." She closed her car door. "I'm the girl who is happy in her sweatshirts and jeans. I keep things running behind the scenes. A red letter day for me is when I remember to wear makeup. I don't have any idea what looks good on me or even what colors I should wear. I'm a mess."

"That's why you have me here." Remy opened his door then rounded the trunk of the car. "You can stall all day if you want but you're going in there." He tugged her to her feet. "You're right. You're not a showy girl but you are going to a showy event. At least have fun and play dress-up." He nudged her forward then pushed the passenger door shut. "Lock?"

She pressed the button on her fob. "Done."

Remy wound his arm around hers. "We're going to find you a dress, get you dolled up and send you to the ball."

"You're so cheery about this." She allowed him to drag her into the store. "You have no idea how big this will be."

Austin's mother, Gretchen, strode up to her and Remy. "Molly, aren't you a sight for sore eyes." She threw her arms around Molly's shoulders, snatching her in a hug. "I've missed you."

"I've missed you, too." She wasn't lying. One of the few things she regretted about not pursuing the relationship with Austin was not keeping up the relationship with his mother. "Austin said he called you."

"He did." She grasped Molly's shoulders. "The Aura Gala. I'm glad you're taking him. Be right back." Gretchen left Molly alone with Remy.

"Taking him?" Remy snorted. "I don't get to go along." He twiddled with a fuchsia gown and ran his fingers over the sequins. "I get to hear about it once she gets home."

Molly sighed. If she'd had her way, she would've taken Remy along. At least he'd have kept her company. "I can call Austin. He's probably changed his mind about taking me as his date. Maybe I can convince him to make it a foursome."

"Foursome?" Remy grinned. "Honey, you know better."

"I do." Still, she could use her best friend at the gala for moral support.

Gretchen swept back into the room with three dresses draped over her arm. "Dylan and I sorted through the gowns and I think we've narrowed the choices down to these." She held up one dress and handed the other two to her son. "These should be the right size. It's a matter of what color you'd like and the shape. Austin said something about an old Hollywood glamor feel. I think these fit the bill. What do you think?"

Molly wobbled on her feet. She drank in the details of all three dresses. The red one featured sequins but a tight bodice. The skirt would be pretty when, and if, she decided to dance. She considered the navy gown. All satin and silk and delicate. She'd probably rip the form-fitting thing as she walked into the gala. She crinkled her nose. Neither dress was what she wanted but she didn't have the heart to tell Gretchen she was all wrong.

"Dylan, get me the burgundy gown." Gretchen put the dresses on a rolling rack. "Molly isn't impressed and neither am I."

Remy picked up the mint-green gown. "This one will emphasize the wrong parts." He held the dress up to Molly. "The mermaid skirt won't give you the right silhouette."

"Thank you?" She settled on the overstuffed ottoman. "See? I told you this wouldn't work."

"You haven't seen the best of what I've got." Gretchen tugged Molly to her feet. "Try this burgundy gown on. If it's not perfect then I'll give in." She nudged Molly into a dressing room and yanked the door closed.

"Mrs. Dean." Molly held up both hands. "I appreciate how hard you and Dylan are working. It's flattering, really, but I'm not sure I want to attend the function tonight. It's short notice, I can't find anything to wear and I'm not good in public. Why don't we call it a day?"

"Because you're not getting out of this. Strip down." Gretchen hooked the coat hanger onto the back of the dressing room door. "I've been in the formal wear business for almost forty years. I know a challenge when I see one."

Molly shrugged out of her sweater then shoved her jeans to the floor. She kicked out of her ankle boots and the denim. "I'm more than a challenge. I'm a disaster."

"You're a diamond in the rough." Gretchen eased the gown from the hanger. "The zipper's right here. Now this will look better without your bra, but for now I want to make sure it fits where I think it should."

Molly stepped into the silky red dress. She liked the way the slippery material eased over her hips. She stood still as Gretchen affixed the neckline around her throat then zipped her into the gown.

"I don't have a mirror in here but I think when you go out to the main room you'll like what you see." Gretchen opened the door. "Boys, close your eyes."

Molly groaned. She was being given way too much credit. She grasped the skirt and followed Austin's mother into the main shop room.

Remy opened his eyes first and his lips parted. For the first time in what seemed like forever, he didn't say anything. Molly shook her head and bit back a laugh. Remy talked all the time — even in his sleep — and if she had him reduced to silence, either she looked really good or really awful.

Dylan nodded once. "My brother will love it. He's crazy if he doesn't."

Gretchen grasped Molly's shoulders and angled her toward the mirror. "See for yourself. You were built for these vintage gowns. Old Hollywood has nothing on you."

Molly closed her eyes. She wasn't ready to see the monstrosity. Comments from her past came back in a rush. Her mother reminding her to put the fork down to ensure she'd have a good figure. Her father's constant comments about her filling out in the wrong places. Then there were the insults from Linc. He'd only loved her as a slender woman. He couldn't love a woman who wasn't perfect. Tears pricked behind her eyes. Austin wasn't much different. He thrived on beauty and setting the right image.

"I can't do this," Molly whispered.

"You haven't looked at yourself." Gretchen rubbed Molly's bare arms. "Come on. Open up and give yourself a fair chance."

Molly held her breath and did as told. When she saw herself in the mirror, the tears streamed down her cheeks. She wasn't sure how Gretchen knew, but the burgundy dress fit like a second skin. The halter top accentuated her chest without being tacky and the skirt showcased her curves. Gretchen was right — the old Hollywood style worked for her.

"Remy?" Molly wiped her face. "What do you think?"

"I'm speechless," Remy replied. "And jealous. You're beautiful."

Dylan leaned on the counter and grinned. "Like I said, if my brother doesn't like it...he doesn't deserve to be on your arm."

"Thanks." She needed to stop crying or her makeup wouldn't be right, but still. She couldn't believe that was her in the mirror. The dress hid the frumpiness and made her appear taller.

"Now." Gretchen eased up behind Molly. "I'm thinking something that'll show off your neck. Yes?"

"I'm not much into fashion. My idea of fancy usually involves a sweater and jeans," Molly said.

"There's nothing wrong with the right pair of jeans and a sweater, but you can't wear that to a formal engagement." Gretchen toyed with Molly's hair. "I'll call in my friend, Dasia. She'll know exactly what to do."

"I hope so." She stole a glance at Remy, who gave her the double thumbs-up sign. Molly turned her attention back to her reflection in the full-length mirror. She had no idea what Dasia would do with her hair or how she'd have her makeup done, but hope blossomed in her heart. A dress wouldn't change her life but it might show Austin she was a lady after all.

* * * *

Molly massaged her temples. With the exception of a break to grab some lunch, she'd been in the uncomfortable chair having her hair done and makeup sorted out. One day she'd figure out how to look beautiful without help, but that day wasn't today. The makeup artist had left her alone and the hairdresser hadn't come back yet.

Remy sat opposite her and folded his arms. "We've got five minutes when someone isn't making you beautiful."

"You're not jealous, are you?" She picked at the arm of the

chair. "I'm sorry. I dragged you along for this crazy train and never thought about what you wanted to do today."

"Are you kidding?" He laughed and leaned back in his seat. "This is better than sitting at home. Ever since Javier walked, I haven't been myself. Being here with you has inspired me."

"It has?"

"Yeah. I want to paint again and create some jewelry. I saw all those dresses, and stories to go along with them are filling my head. I want to put them on canvas. Hell, I want to create some fierce necklaces and bracelets to go with them, too." He pulled a notepad from his back pocket. "I can't wait to get some of these into my sketchbook."

"Good." She'd worried about Remy. When he loved, he went all in, too. "I'm looking forward to seeing them."

"Me, too." He stuffed the notebook back into his pocket. "Speaking of seeing again, I'm going to ask this before Momma and Dylan come back. You and Austin—did you? Again?"

The headache she'd been nursing came back stronger. She didn't have to hear the entire question to know what he meant. "Yes. We did. Last night."

"Girl." He grinned. "He was good, wasn't he?"

"He was." She bit back a sigh. She could still feel Austin's arms around her and his breath on her skin. "I'm crazy for trying, though. I keep telling myself we're not going to make it, but then he drags me in again. I should know better."

"You do." Remy met her gaze. He toyed with his thick watch—a gift from Javier. "Some things are meant to last and others not so much."

She remembered the moment Javier had gifted him with the timepiece last Christmas. She'd thought they'd be together forever. "What happened with Javier? What'd he do?"

"I caught him in bed with our friend, Thad. I should've known. I kept seeing them together and interrupting private conversations. I wanted things to be different, but wishing and hoping only work in pop songs."

"I'm sorry." She grasped his hand. "You loved him."

"I did—just like you love Austin." Remy nodded once. "Didn't think I caught on to that, did you?"

"I knew." How could she not know? "What are you going to do? Going to chew me out?"

"No," Remy replied. "What's the point in giving you hell? I've been in—I am in your shoes." He shrugged. "Yeah, I slept with Javier three nights ago. We needed each other and when I woke up, he was gone."

"Remy." She wasn't sure what to say.

"I thought I loved him but I see him for who he really is. He can't commit." He met her gaze. "Not like anyone we know."

"You have no idea. The only thing he'll commit to is his next conquest. I'm crazy for thinking I could be enough." Molly covered her face with both hands.

"Makeup!" Remy touched her arm. "Don't mess it up."

"Shit." This was another reason she wasn't meant for fancy dress anything—she even screwed up her makeup.

"You're fine." Remy patted the grips on his chair and nodded again. "Looks like the cavalry is on the way." He dropped his voice to a whisper. "Dylan makes my motor run."

"Then ask him out," she murmured.

"Nah. He's not interested." Remy winked then left the chair. "I'll be back in a few. I need to make a call." He strolled away, leaving her alone with Austin's brother.

"Hi." Dylan gripped the back of the chair Remy had just vacated. "Looks like the hairdresser won't be back. She had another job."

"Oh." Molly ran her fingers through her hair. "I can do something with it when I get home."

"No." He spun her around to face the mirror. Dylan smoothed his fingers through her hair. "Working here means I've had to learn things I never thought I could do."

He combed her hair back. "Give me half an hour and I'll make you more beautiful."

"You've got a long ways to go." She wasn't beautiful. Never would be.

"Are you done?" He tugged lightly on the ponytail he'd made from her hair. "You're a gorgeous woman who doesn't know how to use what she's got."

"I'd have to have something first." She squared her shoulders. "Think about the women your brother dates. Tall, thin with poise and grace. I trip over my own two feet."

"So?" He gathered her hair at the crown of her head. He didn't look at the style but at her. "Everyone is unique. You've got to embrace what you've got going for you — and before you ask, your smile, the way you make everyone laugh and feel welcome. You might not be conventionally pretty, but who is? I'm not conventionally handsome. I'll never be as tall as Austin or have his muscles, but I'm okay with that. I've got my own talents." He secured an elastic band around her tresses. "I was thinking something old Hollywood to go with that dress. Simple and elegant."

"You know an awful lot about making me pretty." She held still as he wound a curling iron through a hank of hair near her scalp. "I appreciate it."

"Hopefully my brother appreciates you." He curled another lock. "He's a good man, but sometimes he doesn't see what's right in front of him."

"I know."

"This is why we have to make him see." Dylan plunked the curling iron into the holder then sprayed the do with hairspray. "He might be clueless, but he's not heartless."

"Sure." She stared at her reflection. In a few moments, he'd turned her mass of unruliness into a slick, elegant ponytail.

"Austin is a difficult man to love. He might not think so, but it's true." He wound a barrette laden with white rhinestones around the elastic. "Perfect."

Between her makeup and the extra embellishments, she

agreed. She hardly looked like herself.

"What you've got to do is give that brother of mine something to miss. Make him see you're more than just his co-worker. I know him and you. If there was ever two people who should be together, it's you two."

"He'll never see that—but I'll try." She had a wonderful dress, her makeup appeared professional and her hair wasn't a frizzy mess. She'd do her best to have a great night and not waste everyone's hard work. She patted Dylan's hand. "Thank you."

"You're not even dressed yet." He leaned forward and hugged her from behind. "Before you leave me...Remy's not seeing anyone, is he?"

"Are you up for the job?" She turned in her seat to face Dylan. "He's asked about you, too."

Dylan bobbed his eyebrows. He might not have been as tall as his brother or as broad, but Dylan wasn't lacking in the appearance department. His blue eyes sparkled and his constant five o'clock shadow was endearing. He reminded her of a model, too.

"I need to get dressed, but Remy could use some entertaining," she said and scooted out of the chair. "Handle him with care and you won't regret it."

"I'm sure I won't." Dylan winked again and wandered into the main room.

Molly mulled over Dylan's words as she stepped into the dressing space. She yanked the curtain shut. *Austin...a hard man to love? Duh.* He knew how to leave at the wrong times and to keep her hanging. But how much of that was her fault? She could've let go at any moment. *Give him something to miss.* Like what? She wasn't sure. Austin seemed to need her but only at work. The sex was good—not great, but that didn't mean much. She shrugged out of her shirt then shoved her jeans down her hips. When she looked up, she noticed her reflection in the mirror. Geez, the place had a ton of mirrors... Dylan's words came to mind. Maybe it was time to get over herself, so to speak. If Austin couldn't see her potential then someone would.

Gretchen shuffled into the dressing space and yanked the curtain closed. She tugged a lacy corset from a plastic bag. "Before you can wear this, you're going to need some assistance. I'll help."

Undressing in front of people wasn't fun and now she had to go topless? *Big girl panties, time to put on the big girl panties.* She unhooked her bra and kept her back to Gretchen. Her feet hurt from wearing the high-heeled shoes, but if she didn't practice, she'd trip.

"Ready," Molly said. She exhaled and sucked in her stomach.

"Hon, be yourself. The corset will shape you." Gretchen angled Molly to face the mirror and helped her into the tight lingerie. "A little support never hurts."

Molly grunted as the corset was laced and tightened. She'd never worn such a thing before and had no idea how women wore corsets on a regular basis. She already couldn't wait to shuck it.

Gretchen unzipped the dress and unhooked the fasteners. "Here, step into the gown so you don't wreck your hair."

She wobbled but managed to wriggle into the dress. Gretchen stood behind Molly. She zipped and fastened Molly into the gown then stepped back and clapped her hands.

"You have no idea how beautiful you look." Gretchen smiled at Molly in their reflection in the mirror. "Honest."

"I'm sure you tell all the women that, but thank you." She smoothed the front of the gown and blew out a long breath. Although the corset kept everything slimmed down, she could still breathe. Good thing. Her heart hammered and her hands trembled. How in the hell was she going to get across town to her apartment to meet up with Austin?

"One more thing." Gretchen held a jewelry box. "I suggest pairings—baubles and gowns—all the time, but this dress needs something a little different. I've kept this necklace back because I wanted it to go with the right garment. It's time." She opened the box. Among the green velvet was a teardrop pendant.

"That's pretty." Molly touched the thick drop. "Silver?"

"Platinum. Here, let me put this on you." Gretchen eased the necklace about Molly's throat. "I only ordered one because it wasn't cheap, but with that dress you need something simple and elegant. This is both." She stepped back and smiled again. "I believe you have a gala to attend."

"I do, but I've got to get across town first." Molly smoothed her palms over the skirt again. "I'll have Remy drive me home — if he hasn't already left."

"No, he's here." Gretchen moved the curtain. "Your ride is here."

Molly stepped out of the changing room and strode out to the main room of the shop. Dylan waited at the counter, along with Remy. Molly turned around to show off her look and noticed another figure. Austin? The tips of her ears burned and her stomach roiled. He wasn't supposed to be there.

"Molls...wow." Austin held out his hand. "Look at you."

She gathered her wits and forced a smile. "I clean up pretty well, don't I?"

"You do." Austin's gaze swept over her. "*Very* well."

Remy and Dylan surged up to Austin and tugged him away from her. Both men spoke to Austin in low tones she could barely hear.

Molly could've sworn Remy told Austin to behave. She wasn't sure what Dylan said, but she couldn't miss Dylan grabbing Remy's hand as they stepped back.

"We should go." Austin offered his arm. "The limo's waiting."

"Limo?" Molly peeked around him. Sure enough, a black limousine waited in the parking lot. "Wow."

"Remy? Would you take Molly's car back to the apartment?" Austin asked. "I promise to bring her home and to take care of her."

"I can speak for myself," she said. "But yes, Remy? Help?"

Remy nodded. "You got it, babe."

Molly fidgeted, unsure of what to do with her hands. "What time is it?"

"Time to go." Austin wound his arm around her and waved. "Thanks, Mom. Dylan. You outdid yourselves this time."

"I had a great canvas to work with." Gretchen leaned against the counter. "Have fun."

The world moved by in a blur as Molly followed Austin to the gigantic black car. He opened the door for her and helped her into the back seat. She barely noticed the interior of the vehicle. All she saw was Austin in his tuxedo. He demanded her attention without saying a word. She folded her hands on her lap and focused on breathing.

Austin settled beside her. He draped his arm around her shoulders. "You look beautiful."

"Thanks." She wanted to relax but couldn't. She needed to get a few things off her chest first. "Ground rules."

"Oh?" He shifted in his seat and the corner of his mouth curled. "Shoot."

"Well, for one you don't have to tell me I look pretty. I appreciate the comments, but you tend to take flattery to the extreme." She shook her head. "Besides, I know the truth."

"Molls." His half-smile fell. "I mean what I say."

"Second, when we get to the gala you don't have to stick with me. I know your game. Play the field and leave a string of broken hearts in your wake. I'll be fine." There. She'd given him an out. "Even if Remy threatened to castrate you, you're off the hook."

"He did, by the way." Austin toyed with her hoop earring. "He mentioned something about also skinning me alive."

"That's Remy." She'd have to give him a big hug and a bottle of wine when she got her keys back later.

"Tonight isn't about worrying about who else is going to be there, who will skin someone alive and all the rest. We're going to have a blast and be recognized for our hard work—

especially you. You save my ass all the time." He tucked her to his side and pressed a kiss to her neck. "Wouldn't be where I am without you."

The words *don't say what you don't mean* teetered on the tip of her tongue, but she held back. The words of praise were nice, even if she didn't quite believe him. Yes, working with him was a challenge, but he wasn't a slouch in the advertising game. He knew a smart marketing ploy and could pump out the right words for a promo spot in seconds. She might make him look good, but he did just fine on his own.

The car stopped and the driver opened the door. Molly looked at the world beyond the limo and snorted. She wasn't sure what she'd expected to see, but not the back door of the dining hall. She held Austin's hand as he led her into the building.

"Gee. For being honored guests, we're not being very honored." Austin kept his arm around her. "But what do I know?"

"Me, either." She remained by his side as he navigated through the building to the dining hall. Just like he'd said, her photographs were the backdrop of the stage. Three banners, one of each photo she'd sent, lined the far wall. She bit back a gasp. She'd never expected to see Austin mega-sized. Even gigantic, the man grabbed her attention. No wonder the company loved the images. She fell in love with him all over again.

Molly held tightly to him, not because she thought he'd get away, but because the amount of people in the room scared her. Her heart raced and she could've sworn the walls were closing in on her.

"Are you okay?" Austin whispered. "We'll go out to the balcony and get some air."

"Thanks." She huddled against him until he led her through the French doors to the patio area. The chilly air helped to clear her thoughts and put her at ease.

"I have no idea how this night's supposed to go." Austin

gathered her in his arms. "I look at you and my thoughts blur."

"Oh." She fought the urge to roll her eyes at her ridiculous answer. Was he trying to be romantic? She wasn't sure.

"That's how I feel. I want to sound intelligent and it all falls apart." He curled his fingers under her chin. "I'm so proud of you and even more proud to be beside you."

"Thanks."

Austin leaned forward until his lips were a whisper away from hers. "You make me feel...shit." His eyes widened. "Double shit."

"I make you feel like shit?" She glanced over her shoulder at whatever he was looking at. As soon as she saw the reason for his shift in attitude, her mood soured, too.

Iris.

She should've known. She and Austin were having a good time. It stood to reason something or someone would get in the way.

Iris wound her way through the throng of people and zeroed in on Molly and Austin. She nudged Molly aside and clasped Austin's biceps.

"Look what the cat dragged in," Iris purred. "You strip down nicely and dress up just as well. I think I'm in love."

Molly groaned. She'd been down this road before. *Walk away with your dignity intact.* She'd earned her entry into the gala and refused to let one woman bring her down. She turned on her heel and blended into the crowd.

Chapter Five

Austin offered his best smile and hoped Iris didn't see through him. He gritted his teeth. The moment he'd spotted her he'd known she'd swoop in. He'd planned to make things up to Molly, not shove her aside. He surveyed the crowd and noticed she'd gone. *Fuck.*

Iris wound her arms around his biceps. "I'm glad you arrived. I've been lonely."

"I'm sorry to hear that." He disengaged from her. "I came with a date and she deserves my attention."

Iris' eyes widened then narrowed. "You should entertain her for a while, yes."

"I knew you'd understand." He didn't believe she did but he wasn't about to argue with her. He eased away from her in search of Molly. He never should've let her go in the first place.

Austin spotted Molly at one of the tables. She clutched the back of the chair. She stole his breath and sent happy shivers down his spine. Maybe she hadn't believed him when he'd told her he thought she was adorable, but she outshone the other women at the gala. She arrested his attention. All he could think of was getting her alone.

"Hi, pretty lady." He snaked his arm around her and kissed her temple. "Come here often?"

"Hi, and no, I don't." She gripped his forearm. "I can't sit down in this dress."

He frowned. "Why?"

"I'm afraid I'll ruin it. Your mom never said if it was on loan or anything and I'm sure I'll spill something down my front," she muttered.

"I'd tell you not to worry about it, but I know you. Worrying is your thing." He held her tighter. "I'm sorry about Iris."

"She's making her rounds. It's part of her job," Molly replied. "She's got a thing for you." She patted his arm but didn't pull away from him. "You don't have to stick around here with me. I know you're dying to get back to her. I understand. She's the beautiful one."

Austin turned her around and kept her in his arms. "I've already got a date. I might be an ass, and usually can't make up my mind, but I'm *not* abandoning you."

"I'm not your date. I'm your design partner and friend. Big difference." She smoothed her palms over his chest. "Don't worry about me."

Austin kissed her forehead. He needed to buy a few more seconds to think through what he wanted to say. *Fuck.* "You're my date and my partner. Much as you don't believe me, I refuse to ignore my date—meaning you. Let Iris push in again. I'm here with you and I'm going to have a good time with you."

She leaned back in his embrace and met his gaze. "I knew you had manners."

"You're shocked, though."

"A little."

When she touched him, even through the layers of fabric, she seared him to the core. She was his best friend but she also flowed in his soul. "Sounds like you're secretly pleased I'm using my manners."

"I am," she whispered.

"I'm glad." He held her closer and breathed in the scent of her perfume. "Dance with me."

"Absolutely."

She allowed him to whisk her away from the table. She snuggled up to him and swayed to the music. The more they danced and laughed together, the more he saw her in a different light. He was closer to her, sure, but that wasn't the change. They'd been close for quite a while. They worked long hours together, fell asleep on the couch in the office together and argued with gusto more times than he could count. He'd seen her naked and craved making love to her. He'd seen the various sides of her and couldn't see doing his job without her. He liked the way she fit beside him and in his arms. He wanted her to stick with him but he also wanted her to succeed.

Was he in love with Molly? He wasn't sure but he wanted to give their relationship outside of the office a chance. God, he'd become wishy-washy. Because of her? Could be.

"Excuse me." Iris wound her fingers around his wrist. "May I cut in?"

Molly tensed in his arms and met his gaze. The worry returned to her eyes. She eased away from him. "Ms. Sommerville."

"No, wait," Austin said. "We'd like to finish out the song." He smiled even when Iris shot him a dirty look and her lip curled in a sneer.

Although he'd upset Iris, she regained her poise in an instant. Molly was another story.

"You'd better go," Molly said. She toyed with the hairs at the base of his skull then let go of him. "She's the one paying the bills, and if she demands some of your time, you owe her. In some bizarre way, this is probably how she feels I owe her," she whispered.

"Molls." He hated having to play the game. Before, he wouldn't have cared but now he had someone special. Being with Molly trumped anything he had to do with Iris, but he understood Molly's position. Keep the client happy.

"Are you coming?" Iris snapped her fingers. "I don't have all night."

"I'll be right back. Promise." Austin feathered a kiss over Molly's lips. "Right back."

"Go." She poked him in the ribs. "I'm not leaving without you. I kind of can't—I don't have a ride."

"Smart aleck." He kissed her again then left her alone on the dance floor.

Iris sidled up to him and smoothed her palm over his ass. "Tired of your date? You should be."

"No, but you did request my presence." He cradled her hips and moved with her as Iris danced. She had rhythm and grace but she wasn't Molly. Where Molly would let him take the lead and work with him, Iris demanded his attention and expected him to follow her. Would that be his fate if he went out with her?

"I see great things in your future." Iris held him tighter. "You're the star of the campaign."

"I am?" He'd dreamed for half a moment about maybe being the center of the campaign but then he'd been knocked down to earth. He'd rather be happy in his own little corner than showing off his ass.

"You are so much more than you think." She nodded. "We want you to be the focal point. You sell my clothes better than the other models."

"Wow. Thank you?" He wasn't sure if he was flattered or appalled. He wasn't a model. He paused. The photos and the magic wouldn't have happened without Molly. "You're going to have Ms. Neff photograph the rest of the campaign, correct? She's the reason I looked good."

"I'd prefer one of my photographers to do the shoot." Iris eased the sides of his tuxedo coat apart and rubbed his abs. "I can't wait to unwrap these."

He gritted his teeth. He couldn't do anything without Molly. "I refuse." He was crazy and turning down a great opportunity but he wouldn't chase this dream without her by his side.

"You what?" Iris snapped. "You can't turn me down." She yanked him off the dance floor and to a quieter corner of the room. "I *own* you."

"Of course I can turn you down because you don't own me." Austin shoved his hands into his pockets. He gazed over to where Molly stood. Three guys were with her. Although he had no claim on her, he couldn't help the jealousy filling his brain. Molly smiled and laughed with the three men, and if he wasn't mistaken, the guys weren't slackers in the appearance department. He wanted to be the man who made her shine.

A raven-haired man turned enough for Austin to see the guy's face. He couldn't read the guy's lips but he got the general idea.

"Excuse me." Iris grabbed him by the chin and turned his head. "I'm right here."

"I need to go." Austin shrugged away from her.

"Why? Did you see those men?" She turned her back on him and rested her head against his shoulders. "They're models. They saw — like everyone else — the photos. I'm betting they're asking her to take their pictures, too. I'm using them for the campaign, too. Personally selected."

"You really think they want her to photograph them?" Austin asked.

"It was mentioned a few times. If she made an ad man look good, then she could do wonders with them." Iris wriggled against him, rubbing her ass over his crotch. "I told them it was a fluke. She can't do wonders every time."

"I disagree." He scooted back a bit to put space between them. "I felt comfortable with Molly. That's huge." Because Molly had made him feel that way.

"If I allowed her to take the pictures, would you do the campaign?" Iris whirled around and faced him. "I could convince you?"

"It's possible." The only way he'd wear anything by Aura was if Molly was there with her camera.

"Come over tonight and we'll discuss the details." Iris caged him in her arms. "All night long."

"I'm busy." Austin shrugged away from her again. "I've got a date."

"You're here with me. Forget her."

"No." Austin strode away from Iris. He'd wasted enough time with her for the moment.

"You'll lose the account," Iris called. "If you go home with me, I'll make sure you won't regret it."

Part of him wanted to chase the fame and everything Iris was offering, but the rest of him wasn't ready to walk away from Molly. He wasn't ready to trade his integrity and hard work in the advertising business for a romp in the hay with Iris. But what if they lost the account? What about Molly? He doubted she'd put up with him acting on impulse rather than using his head. She'd never speak to him again.

Which was he willing to lose—a fling and a short-term job with the woman he wanted to fuck or the friendship and connection with the only woman he'd ever been emotionally faithful to?

Iris stepped into his path and stopped him. "What are you going to do?"

"I need to take care of something." He'd left Molly alone for long enough.

"Here." Iris tucked something into his coat pocket. "I'll see you later when you've made the right decision." She walked away, wiggling her ass with each step.

Austin groaned. He doubted he'd see Iris later—at least not in the way she wanted. He maneuvered through the dancers to Molly. The models eyeballed him then left.

"What was that about?" Austin asked. He hoped the irritation wasn't evident in his voice.

"I was about to ask you the same thing." Molly smoothed his lapels and patted his chest. "I assume you're leaving. No problem. I'll get a ride."

"With one of the models?"

"You saw that?" She shook her head, but the corner of her mouth kinked. "It's nothing. They seem to think I can make them look the way I did with you. I told them it wouldn't happen." She squeezed his hand. "Have fun with Iris tonight. You deserve it."

As Molly eased past him, he snagged her in his embrace and escorted her to the foyer. He needed some privacy and the party wasn't going to be enough.

"What are you doing?" she asked and tumbled into his arms.

"Getting us a room." Austin ducked into the coatroom. He closed the door and flipped the lock into place. "Better."

Molly snorted. "What if someone wants their coat? You've put this place out of commission."

"They'll live."

"Brother." She sighed and brushed her hair from her eyes. "Look, it's no big deal. Iris is pretty and she's your key to bigger things. I get it. I don't know if it'll last beyond one of your famous quick turns, but if this makes you happy, then do it. I'll even stick around a while in case you need a backup plan. Seems that's my other strength."

"Nope." Austin held her to his chest and swayed with her to the muffled music coming from the main room. He hummed along with the tune. "I'm good."

"So I'm the plan until she's free." Molly pulled away from him.

He wasn't letting go so easily. He spun her around then tucked her to his chest again. She was his best partner.

"What are you doing? You're supposed to be going, not dancing with me." Molly laughed and fell into step with him. "Won't Iris be upset?"

"I have no idea, but she's probably pissed." He shrugged then dipped Molly. "I believe I said I was here with you. A man without integrity would leave his date behind in favor of another woman."

"Integrity?" She rested her arms around his neck as he swayed with her. "Or are you hiding from her?"

"Molls." He rested his forehead against hers. "I didn't beg for you to be invited because it was a good business transaction, or because I wanted a date. You deserve to be here. Those are your photos all over out there."

"I see."

"I like you, Molly," he blurted. His spirits lifted and his heart filled with desire for her. He'd finally been honest with her and that honesty felt good.

"Austin, you like me in the office and when you need an ego boost."

She'd cut him down to size, but he refused to give in. "I like you in my arms the best." He captured her mouth in a kiss and swallowed her moan. The passion he'd felt grew stronger, along with their connection. His cock thickened behind his zipper. He needed her. Right now.

Molly broke the kiss and put her hands on his chest. "We can't do this again. We work together." Her voice cracked. "I can want this to happen for the rest of my life but I'm practical. I know you. You'll find someone else and I'll be tossed overboard again. I can't do that."

Austin bowed his head. The full weight of his past decisions bore down on him. He'd treated Molly poorly and she deserved better. He checked the lock on the cloakroom then leaned against the door.

"Let me out." Molly reached for the lock, but he stopped her.

"I never said you weren't enough."

"Austin."

"I like when you say my name." He kissed her again. He'd never get enough of kissing her. "Love it," he murmured. She was his drug and he'd been crazy to think he could possibly give her up.

"How do you do that?" Molly wobbled in his arms.

"The lock?" He pulled her across the small room to the alcove. Even if someone barged in, they wouldn't see him and Molly right away. "I worked at a theater while I was in high school. Spent a summer here during college. We've got about ten minutes before someone checks." He pinned her between his body and the wall. "I might be the biggest jerk and unworthy of your attention, but you've got my heart in your hands."

Molly kissed him with gusto and popped the button on his tuxedo pants then unzipped him. Without breaking the kiss, she eased his cock out of his trousers.

Austin groaned into her mouth. Fuck. With her hands on his shaft, he'd come too fast. He palmed her ass and feathered kisses over her lips, cheeks, chin and neck.

Between nips on her skin, he said, "I've got a rubber in my coat. Inside pocket." God knew if he tried to retrieve the condom, he'd fumble.

"Always prepared?" Molly continued to stroke him but managed to locate the condom with her free hand. She held up the foil packet.

"Something like that—I wasn't a scout." He hiked her skirt up over her hips. The moment he touched her smooth skin again, his heart hammered. God, she was delicate, but so strong...and not wearing any panties. "You went commando?"

"Not at first." Molly stopped stroking him and her cheeks tinged red. "I had lines and took them off. You weren't looking." She shrugged and her eyes widened. "It seemed like a good idea at the time."

"It's a very good idea." He took the condom packet from her long enough to rip it open then sheath himself. "Wet for me?" He should've said to hell with the other women and followed his heart to Molly a long time ago.

She nodded. "I can't wait."

"Me, either." He turned her around and wrapped one arm around her to steady her. He nuzzled her neck and lined his dick up with her slick cunt. She hadn't been kidding. Damn, she *was* ready for him.

"Austin." She flattened her palms on the wall. "Hurry."

He eased his cock into her pussy and paused just a moment to savor the tight fit. He scraped his teeth over the side of her neck. "Yeah," he whispered.

Heat enveloped him as he started to push into her. His world spun and rational thought left his head. He should've been with her from the start. She met him thrust for thrust. He tingled from his head to his toes. Christ, she overwhelmed him. He moved her skirt out of the way and strummed her clit.

Molly whimpered. She kept up with his rhythm, making a more perfect cadence between them. She muffled her groans against her arm and arched her back. The slight change in angle sent him deeper into her body.

"I'm there," Molly murmured. "Right there."

"Then come for me, babe." He wasn't far behind her in the orgasm department. "Come apart for me."

Molly shuddered and tensed around him. She clawed at the wall. Although she'd muffled her whimpers, the moment the climax overtook her, he knew.

Austin pumped his hips. He couldn't hold on any longer. "Fuck," he bit out. "Jesus." He slammed into her and filled the condom with his seed. He shivered with her and managed to add a couple of extra thrusts as the orgasm washed over him. He panted against the back of her neck. He couldn't see her eyes but didn't doubt the love flowing between Molly and him. She owned his heart and soul.

He kissed her shoulder then eased his softening cock from her pussy. Her skirt fell into place around her hips and covered her most intimate areas. Good thing. He didn't want anyone else to see the special side of Molly—that was only for him. He removed the condom and shoved his dick behind his zipper.

Molly turned around. Her eyes widened again and her mouth opened and closed, but no sound came out.

He paused. God, she was beautiful. He'd seen her flushed and frazzled after a long project, deep in peaceful sleep and at ease in front of clients, but the flushed and glowing post-sex look knocked him off his feet. Her makeup had smeared a bit, but he'd never seen anyone more attractive. Being with her and making love was crazy, but right.

"Austin." Molly nodded and the color drained from her face. "Someone's trying the lock."

"Shit." Austin ensured her dress was back in place and that he'd zipped his pants before he flipped the lock.

The door opened. A man dressed in a tuxedo frowned in the doorway.

"Mr. Finch," Austin said. He grinned and looped his arm around Molly. "I'm glad you got the door open. Remember how it used to stick?"

"I thought I had it planed," the usher said. "How long were you stuck in here?"

"Not long." Austin clapped Mr. Finch on the shoulder. "My fiancée was upset and we needed a moment to talk. The window was already drawn, so I shut the door. Go figure, the locking mechanism decided to stick. I wasn't worried because I knew you'd come to the rescue."

"Is she— Are you okay?" Mr. Finch swiped his gaze over Molly. "Hon?"

"Austin was being a jerk, but it's worked out," Molly said. "Thank you so much for helping us." She eased away from Austin and left the cloakroom.

Was she being demure? Or just scared? Austin wasn't sure, but he'd use the rest of the night to make things up to her. He clapped the usher on the shoulder again. "Thank you." He winked. "Saved my life and my ass."

Mr. Finch shook his head and laughed. "I can't fire you now, but I swear, son, you'll get caught sooner rather than later."

Maybe I already am caught. Austin nodded. "Thanks." He strode out of the cloakroom to where Molly stood. "Why don't we head home?"

"They haven't done the presentations yet." Molly hesitated. "Or did we miss them?"

"I have the feeling Iris wasn't planning on recognizing anyone from CDL." No, she'd had other ideas and he'd refused to play along. "I'm tired of being here."

"I am, too." Molly tucked tightly to his side as he escorted her from the building. Once in the limo, she rested her head on his shoulder and placed her hand on his thigh. He loved how she could be sweet and romantic one moment then turn on the heat the next.

Austin breathed a sigh of relief once the limo started moving. He didn't want the night to end but he sure as hell wanted away from the Aura gala. "Come over."

"So I can play the role of your fiancée?" She patted his knee. "I'm not comfortable with that fib."

"I was thinking you could come over so we could talk."
And play engaged couple a while longer, yes. Mostly, he
wanted her with him.

"Oh." Molly sagged against him.

"I've got wine and we've got Sunday off. I thought
maybe you could come over. We'd talk, drink…see what
happens." Christ, he wanted to fuck her again, but not in
the limo. "Tomorrow we can do whatever we want—you
said you wanted to visit that little amusement park down
at the harbor. We could forget the world for a day and have
fun. Yes?" Anything to keep her in his arms a while longer.

"You're crazy."

"Probably," he replied. He'd been called worse over the
years. "The jury's still out." He rode in silence with her for
fifteen minutes until the limo stopped. He glanced through
the window and recognized the surroundings. "This is my
place. Care to join me for an adventure?"

"Austin."

He understood her hesitancy. He'd never invited her over
before. "I'm clean. Promise."

"I've already slept with you twice in the space of two
days." She twined her fingers together. "It'll probably
happen again."

"I'm being honest—I've been good and I don't want to go
home without you." He held out his hand. "Please?"

Molly met his gaze. After what seemed like an eternity,
she grasped his hand. She permitted him to escort her from
the limo to the apartment building after he paid the driver.

"You're finally allowing me to visit you at the new
apartment." Molly tucked herself into the corner of the
elevator car. "Seems nice."

"When we got the Ribbs Barbecue account and were given
the ginormous bonus, I put mine into the down payment for
this place." He pressed the button for his floor. "I wanted
something a little bigger than the last one and nicer, too."

"I see."

"Not yet you haven't." He grinned and reached for her.

He wouldn't be happy until he had her in his arms. "Molls. I made a mess of the evening and I'm trying to make it up to you."

The car stopped and the doors opened. Austin nodded. "I'm one of five on this floor. Last one's mine."

Molly eased out of the elevator and made her way down the short corridor. She didn't say anything as he unlocked the door. She wandered into the apartment, moving silently around the space.

"Well? Does it pass muster?" Austin shrugged out of his tuxedo jacket. "It's a little on the bland side."

"You have a balcony." Molly peeked back at him and grinned. She kicked out of her shoes. "I bet it's beautiful out there."

"I wouldn't know." He'd only been out there twice. "If you've got suggestions for making this place a little more homey, I'm all ears." He twisted the lock on the balcony door. "Wouldn't want to help me make this place better, would you?"

Molly slipped past him and stepped onto the balcony. "You can't see anything."

He eased up behind her and embraced her. "It's dark and my side faces the lake. We could try again in the morning."

"Deal." She shivered. "Chilly up here, isn't it?"

"Come inside with me." He led her into the apartment and shut the door. He still couldn't believe she was in his home. "Wine?"

"Please." Molly rubbed her bare arms. "I forgot how cold the nights get."

He draped his jacket across the back of the couch then headed into the kitchen. He popped the cork on a bottle of rosé and poured the wine into two glasses. He offered her one. "I have a few ideas to warm you up."

"Thanks. I'm sure we'll get around to that soon enough." She sipped the wine. "You need Christmas lights or something cheery around here. You're right—it's too plain."

"Christmas lights would look cool. They're good mood

lighting." He plopped onto the couch. "Sit." When she did, he relaxed a bit more. "Seems like forever ago that we first came to the city."

"Ten years." She tucked her legs up under her skirt. "We were so young." She sipped more of the wine and sighed. "I wish I'd brought a bag or my phone. I left all of it with Remy."

"He's trustworthy."

She toyed with the stem of the glass. "He is." She swirled the wine around the goblet. "I feel so out of sorts right now."

"Why?"

"This is not me." She swept her hand over her gown. "The hair, the makeup...this dress. You know me. If I'm not in my jeans and superhero T-shirts, I'm not happy."

"And you're not happy?" He took the glass from her and eased across the couch. "You still look fantastic."

"I feel silly." She groaned and stood. "I'm wearing a dress that's God only knows how expensive and I have no clue how I'm going to afford it." She glanced over her shoulder at him. "Then there's the fact I had sex in it. If this dress is a rental, I so owe more than the dry cleaning fee."

"Don't worry about the cost." He snagged her against his chest. "Consider it my gift."

"Gift?" She whipped around in his arms. "Have you lost your mind?"

"Depends on who you talk to." Austin shrugged but didn't let go of her.

Her eyes widened and she gasped.

He cupped her jaw in both hands. "Babe, you're fine."

She shook her head. "I'll never understand you." She shrugged away from him. "Why are you being so nice to me?"

"Molly." He sank onto the arm of the sofa. He didn't understand. Why wasn't she seeing his gift as a good thing? He wanted to treat her and show her a good time.

"Austin, you could have any woman. You could be on Iris' arm right now and have the world at your feet." Molly

84

toyed with the platinum drop on her necklace. "If you feel sorry for me, I need to know."

"I don't pity you. I paid for that dress because I knew you didn't have anything to wear to the gala. I know you. You're a denim and sweatshirt girl. There's nothing wrong with that—you like to be comfortable. But you couldn't wear a hoodie to the gala."

"I'd like my hoodie right now."

"Hold on." Austin scrambled off the couch and into his bedroom. He understood part of her problem. She wasn't comfortable. Truth be told, he wasn't either. He pulled one of his long-sleeved T-shirts and a pair of sleep pants from his dresser. "Molly?"

He listened for her footsteps on the carpet.

She peeked around the doorway. "What's up?"

"Thought you might like to change." He offered over the clothing. "Take my room."

"Thanks, but I need some help." She swiped her hair off her shoulders. "I can't undo the clasp or the start off the zipper."

"My pleasure." He popped the closure on the gown then eased the zipper pull down. He shouldn't push her but he couldn't keep from touching her. He kissed her shoulder.

"Don't go too far." She looked back at him. "Your mother put me in the world's tightest corset."

"Corset?" How'd he miss that?

Molly kept her back to him and covered her chest. "Sorry. I never had to try to get out of one of these things before."

"Nothing to be ashamed of." Austin unknotted the bow at the base of the corset. He loosened the ribbon, one loop at a time. He breathed in the scent of her perfume. "I love a woman in pretty lingerie."

"You love pretty much all women." She glanced over her shoulder. "Thanks."

"No sweat. Need anything else?" *Like my body covering yours? My arms around you? You in my bed tonight and every other night for the rest of my life?* He caught himself and hoped he hadn't said any of those things out loud—not because he regretted the thoughts but because he didn't want to freak her out. For him to change his mind…she probably wouldn't believe him.

"I'm good. I'll be out in a moment." She kept the dress and corset in place and flicked her fingers. "Please?"

"Anything for you." Austin closed the door and strolled back to the living room. He loved having her in his apartment. She made the place warmer. But he had to get past her shaky confidence and get her to open up to him. *Soon.* He unbuttoned his dress shirt and yanked the bow tie from around his neck, then picked his shoes up and put them in the closet by the door. He'd tried to make the evening memorable for Molly and wasn't done yet. Why? He'd never be done with the woman who made his heart sing.

Molly emerged from the hallway. The T-shirt nearly swallowed her small frame and the sleep pants rode low on her hips, but for the first time that night she appeared at ease. She shoved the sleeves up her arms.

"Feel better?" He unbuttoned the cuffs of his shirt. "You look happier."

"I can breathe now. Thanks."

"Give me five minutes to change and we can finish the wine." Austin ducked into his room and switched out of the remainder of his tuxedo. He'd been able to breathe the whole time, but he liked Molly's line of thinking. He switched into a T-shirt and sweatpants then wandered back into the living room. Molly sat on the sofa with her legs curled under her. She held the wine glass in both hands. She looked so right in his home—as if she'd been there all along.

"What are you staring at?" She sipped the wine. "Already bored?"

"Not at all." Now that he'd had a taste of his heart's desire, he wasn't about to let her go.

Chapter Six

Molly gripped the glass and met his gaze. Something in his eyes both unnerved her and sent shivers down her spine. He'd never looked at her quite that way before. She fought the urge to squirm under his appraisal.

"Do you remember when we went to that football game in college and forgot Aiden at the field?" Austin settled on the couch beside her. "I thought he was in the car and you thought he was in the bathroom."

"I remember." Like the moment had just happened. "He was so mad."

"He got over it." Austin rested his arm across the back of the couch. "You met Linc through Aiden, didn't you?"

"I did."

"You don't have to answer my next question, but if you don't answer it I'll probably needle you until you do." Austin grinned. "Sorry."

"I know you." She placed the glass back on the coffee table and folded herself up again. "Lay it on me. I'll answer."

"Why Linc? He never seemed to make you happy."

Molly bit back a groan and tried to hide her disdain. She hated talking about Linc, but Austin asked and she wasn't going to hide from him. Why? He'd be true to his word and pester her until she broke her silence.

"Sorry. He's none of my business." Austin swirled the wine around his glass then finished the pink liquid. "I push too much."

"You're fine." She cleared her throat and paused long enough to think through what she wanted to say. "During our last year in college, I was lonely. You had Jennifer,

Aiden was seeing Michelle and I was the fifth wheel. Then Aiden and Chelle introduced me to Linc. He was smart, amusing and seemed to like me." She shrugged. "It's funny. When I hooked up with him, the only experience I had was with you. Linc, for all the supposed confidence he had, was completely jealous of you. He saw you as the biggest threat and he was right."

"He was?" Austin scooted closer to her. "Molly?"

"I was seeing him but I dreamed about you." She paused to gather her thoughts. "Then I was forced to move on. You married Carole and I couldn't fantasize about a married man." Tears pricked behind her eyes, but she refused to cry. "I moved on."

"I—I don't know what to say." He smoothed a lock of her hair between his fingers. "I'm speechless."

"That's a first." She half-laughed. "Linc hated your guts, but once you got married, you weren't as much of a threat. You were my friend and we worked together sometimes. He hated Remy, too. He used to tell me a woman with only male friends was crazy or a whore." She willed herself not to cry, but the tears were there. "He once said I had to choose between Remy and him. I mean, Jesus. I couldn't do it."

"You're loyal," he murmured.

"Apparently not to the right people." She folded her arms and rested her head on the back of the couch. "Besides, loyalty doesn't keep you warm at night." Hadn't kept her warm or been the shoulder she'd needed to cry on. She'd spent more nights with her vibrator than she had with her ex-husband or dates. But it was her own fault—she'd never been able to get Austin off her mind.

"No, it doesn't." He tugged her onto his lap and held her. "I'm sorry."

"Meh. It's life. You were doing your thing and I had to figure out my own path." She clutched his shirt. The tears won out and slipped down her cheeks. "Part of me wished I never had to go through the whole shitty situation with him. I really would've preferred for him not to cheat on me but I learned. I grew up and realized I had to be happy on my own." She shouldn't have to be so strong all the time but she didn't have anyone else to count on. Remy was nice and a great friend, but he wasn't there when she needed more than a platonic relationship.

Austin rocked her on his lap. "Babe." He growled. "It's my fault."

"How?"

He patted her ass. She stood and he led her into the bedroom. He sat her on the edge of the bed and kneeled between her legs. "I screwed up."

"No, you followed your heart." She trailed her fingers through his hair. "It wanted the other women. I accept that."

"You shouldn't have to." He eased his palms under her shirt and caressed her belly. "You deserve better than me."

She wanted to agree, but her traitorous heart and body struggled accept life without him.

He eased the shirt over her head and pressed his face to her breasts. He kissed her chest and his five o'clock shadow abraded her skin. Each lick and kiss sent a frisson of heat through her. She balled her hands. If she reached for him, she'd fall even deeper in lust with him. If she kept some distance, maybe she'd keep her heart from breaking.

"Austin."

"Touch me," he said and kissed her. "Love your hands on my body." He placed her palms on his shoulders.

'Love'? He'd said the word before, but always in passing. She wanted to believe he meant more but didn't give in to that hope. She slid her hands along the sides of his head and threaded her fingers into his hair then moaned. Austin had such soft hair.

She whimpered. Once again his cologne wrapped around her and the memory of his kiss lingered in her mind.

He cupped her breasts. The chilly air curled around her sensitive skin. He gazed up at her then caressed and fondled her boobs. When he sucked on her nipple, she whimpered. He rolled her nipple in his teeth. The scrape and pressure turned her inside out. She gripped the sheets in her fists. Damn it. The sweet pleasure he created within her was almost too much to take.

Austin groaned and hummed against her breast. She sucked in a ragged breath. The man certainly knew how to please a woman. She couldn't deny the thrill.

She closed her eyes and basked in the heat of the moment. She could've sworn the temperature spiked.

"Need you." He planted kisses on her breasts. Austin helped her out of her sleep pants and left her socks on. He started at her ankle and pressed kisses to her skin.

Tingles ran the length of her spine. She covered her breasts with her hands and sank back onto the bed. A whimper lodged in her throat as he swiped his tongue along her inner thigh. He hadn't even touched her pussy and she wanted to scream his name.

"So good." Austin parted her thighs even more and nipped the very apex of her leg. He trailed his fingers over her labia, increasing her pleasure.

Need built within her. "Touch me."

She opened her eyes and stared at the ceiling. If she met his gaze, she'd melt even more. She wanted to give in to him — to allow him to have all of her, but she knew better. For now, she'd indulge in sex and foreplay with him. She moved his hands to her inner thighs and threaded her fingers in his hair to move his head.

"There's my inner goddess." He blew warm breath across her labia.

Another shiver wracked her body. She planted her feet on his shoulders and let go of his hair. She gripped the sheet again.

Austin traced small circles along the inside of her legs and dragged his tongue between her pussy lips.

She moaned from deep within her being. "Austin." She'd crumble. She knew now there wasn't much choice for her.

Her restraint wouldn't be enough to guard her heart from Austin — not this time.

He didn't answer her but instead he sucked on her clit.

"Oh fuck." She grabbed the pillow and propped her head up in order to watch him. She stuffed her hands under her butt to keep from reaching for him.

Austin met her gaze and grinned then resumed sucking on her sensitive skin. He closed his eyes and moaned on her clit. At the same time, he eased one finger into her cunt.

Her legs trembled and she writhed against his assault on her body. She needed to move. The climax blossomed low in her belly and churned. *Shit.* If he didn't give her the chance to come, she'd combust. She shuddered while Austin perfected his rhythm. He eased his finger in and out of her channel as he pulsed on her bundle of nerves.

She tensed. "Austin." She curled forward and grabbed his hair. She moved his face from her pussy. His lips glittered with her juices and his cheeks were tinged red. She gasped for air. "Fuck me." She needed hard and fast. Hell, she needed him.

"Yes, ma'am." Austin grinned then nipped her once more. He eased his finger from her pussy and stood. He licked her cream from his digit and groaned. "So good."

Molly covered her breasts again. The chilly air in the room curled around her. Shit. He knew how to tease her.

Austin whipped his shirt up over his head then tossed the garment out of sight. He shoved his sweatpants to the floor and stalked up to the bed. Instead of climbing onto her like she'd expected, he rummaged through the nightstand. She should've known where he'd keep his stash of condoms. Austin stared down at her with a predatory, hungry look in his eyes and tore the corner of the condom wrapper. He sheathed himself and rounded the bed then settled between her legs again. Without breaking the connection, he pushed inside her with one slick move until he buried his cock to the hilt. He leaned over her and kissed her.

The kiss and his possessiveness stole her breath. He

overwhelmed her. She grasped his shoulders, digging her nails into his skin.

Austin bit her bottom lip. "Still so good."

He brushed his nose against hers. His thrusts started slowly but grew in intensity in an instant. Warmth slid through his body while he pumped his hips and braced himself on his knees and shins. *Oh shit. This feels good.* He grasped her thighs, forcing her to let go of his shoulders. Austin draped her right ankle onto his shoulder. The change in position gave him an easier glide in and out of her pussy. He massaged her from within and nudged her closer to coming apart.

She met his gaze again. She'd tried to resist him for too long, but her heart knew what she'd finally figured out—she loved Austin.

He palmed her breast and pinched her nipple. The combination of him moving inside her and pleasuring her body on the outside knocked her orgasm right to the edge. Her restraint and resistance shattered. She tensed as he continued to thrust into her body. She arched her back and met him push for push. No way she'd be able to hold back any longer. The climax washed over her. She shivered and her legs trembled. From head to toe, she felt weightless.

Austin clenched his teeth. "Got me right there." He leaned over her and pumped his hips. His heavy-lidded gaze churned her insides to mush. A bead of sweat slipped down his temple and the crinkles deepened in his forehead. His hair brushed against her forehead.

He tensed within her and groaned. Austin stopped moving and his cock throbbed in her pussy. "Jesus, fuck." He kissed her. "Fuck." Laughter bubbled in his throat. "You. Wiped. Me. Out." He panted and closed his eyes. He braced himself on his arms and knees. His dick slipped free of her body.

She threaded her arms around his neck once more and dragged him on top of her. She bumped noses with him. From head to toe, he'd wrung her out. Being with him was bad but so right.

"Give me a moment." Austin patted her hip. "Be right back." He left her long enough to remove the used condom, then moved the blankets and helped her crawl between the sheets. He settled beside her and draped his arm across her belly.

Molly basked in the boneless feeling. A million thoughts rushed into her head. The good feeling and connection wouldn't last. She knew him—she'd end up being a fuck friend, just like the other women who'd passed through his life. But after the gala and the passion they'd shared... she wasn't so sure. Still, she crumbled inside as the weight of the situation settled on her. They'd ruined the working relationship and the friend version. She'd never be able to look at him the same way again, especially not once he moved on. He was her biggest weakness. Before she might have been okay with saying at least she'd been with him more than once, but not now.

Austin snuggled her to his side and kissed her temple again. "This is better than the first time we slept together. We've gotten better with age."

"Oh?" She snorted. "I thought you avoided me in the bedroom because I was that bad."

"No." He tipped her chin, forcing her to look him in the eye. "You can't keep cutting on yourself. I don't know why you do. Is it me? Something I said? Linc? Talk to me."

So he wanted to go there after sex... She studied the smattering of hairs growing on his cheeks and noticed the three gray hairs at his temple. Time had certainly changed them. Was she ready to talk about her issues? Might as well.

"Molly?"

She exhaled to fortify her nerves. "I've never been skinny. Even back in college and I worked out with you, I wasn't thin. I like to eat—I like chocolate. You might not have said anything, but each time you'd pick our other friends for stuff, like the time we played spin the bottle during the last year of college. You chose every other girl there but me."

She placed her fingers over his mouth. Of all the things she wanted, an apology wasn't on the list. "Then there was Aiden and Linc. Aiden flat-out told me I was one of the guys but not hot. He'd rather watch football with me than kiss me."

"He said that?" Austin closed his eyes and groaned. "Asshole."

"It stung less because I wasn't interested in him. Just hurt because it seemed like you agreed with everything he said," she added. Back in the day, Austin and Aiden had been like twins — when one had done something, the other had followed.

"There was a lot I did agree with, but not everything." He twined their legs and bumped noses with hers. "Aiden acted sweet, but he wanted every woman in his bed. He stepped on so many people."

"Is that why you're not friends with him any longer?"

His eyebrows rose and a smile curled on his lips. "You knew?"

"He emails me every so often and asked me one time if you were still working with me at CDL." She shrugged. "I told him we were and doing great things."

"You built me up." He brushed her hair from her face. "I think I'm in love."

"You are full of shit." She sighed. This was why she didn't believe him. He used the word love sparingly, but the few moments he did, he didn't mean the sentiment. He could be so sweet and yet, he scared her away from embracing the possible emotion behind the words.

"I'm usually full of shit, but not right now. Molls, you're very important to me."

"You're important to me, too." For different reasons, but she wouldn't get into that. "Anyway, Linc was just like Aiden. I was pretty while we were dating and good marriage material, but that's when it all went south. He never hit me but he cut me down to size all the time. I found out how many times he'd cheated on me. He told me the only reason he'd married me was because he was afraid he'd be alone. Then he bulked up and fixed his hair. He dressed better and women noticed. How could you not?"

"Easily. He had the attention span of a gnat—which is insulting to the gnat—and a prick attitude. You can be good-looking but have an ugly personality."

"Bingo." She rolled onto her back and sighed. She'd cried herself out over Linc years ago and wasn't about to fall apart again, but talking about him hurt. "I was so happy Mr. Lee paired you and me up."

"I'm honored and humbled." He squeezed her. "And horny."

"You're always horny." Always trying to redirect her attention, too. She snuggled against him. Screw it. She was there with him and the sex was good. She wasn't running away just yet. "But I like it."

"Good."

She hesitated. "I know you're trying to be nice to me right now. You're trying to build me up. I'm not sure if it's because you feel indebted or what, but you don't have to. Just don't be like Linc or Aiden, okay? Let me keep my dignity."

"Molly." He tipped her gaze again. "I promise. I might not be the best man for you and this could all implode before we know it, but I will do my best not to break your heart. You're smart, funny and adorable. Any man who doesn't see any of that about you isn't looking hard enough."

Although every cell in her body screamed not to trust him, she believed him.

"Aiden was right—we always saw you as one of the guys. Why? Because you knew football stats better than any of us did, you weren't afraid to speak your mind or to cut us down to size. Where he was wrong was him believing that's all you were supposed to be. You're so much more than you even know."

The words *you're delirious* teetered on the tip of her tongue, but she kept her mouth shut. She liked his praise.

"Sleep, babe. We've had a long night. I'm not going anywhere," he whispered and closed his eyes. "I'm right here as long as you want me to be."

She settled on her side and spooned against him. Sleep overcame her and she sighed. For the first time in what seemed like an eternity, she was happy.

* * * *

Molly wasn't sure how many hours had passed when she flopped onto her back. She knew exactly where she was—in Austin's apartment. She reached for him, only to touch a chilly spot. When she did, she sat up and peered around the space. She dragged the bedding around her body. The night before she hadn't noticed her surroundings—she'd just existed.

His closet had been left open. Molly tugged the sheet with her as she left the bed. She covered herself and strolled over to the closet. He'd organized his suits and dress shirts according to color. Thank God he wasn't a monochrome kind of guy. The godawful Hawaiian shirts were still there. He could've ditched them years ago but kept them around. She wondered why. He liked to hold on to a tiny piece of the past?

The scent of bacon wafted into the room. She paused. Was he cooking for her?

"Molly?"

When she whipped around, the sheet slipped from her hands. She grasped the door of the closet. Her skin burned from her hairline to her toes. "Austin."

"I should've given you something to wear besides that awful shirt." He strode past her, clad in nothing but his boxer briefs. "How about this?" He tugged one of the dark blue dress shirts from a hanger. "It's your color."

Austin held the piece of clothing open for her to slip her arms through the sleeves.

"Thanks," she murmured.

He embraced her and breathed her in. "Made you breakfast."

"I can smell it. Smells good." She sagged against him. "You'll spoil me."

"That was the idea."

Molly shrugged away from him and wandered down the short hallway to the kitchen. He'd plated eggs and bacon and poured juice. She looked back at him. "You're seriously going to spoil me. I'm a milk and cereal girl."

"So?" He pulled out the bar stool for her. "This isn't my normal breakfast either, but we're celebrating." He grinned. "Eat."

She watched him while she nibbled on the eggs. The food tasted good, but he looked better. Fresh from bed and with his hair disheveled, he could've been ready for another photo session. She could see him lounging in the clothes from Aura. If he decided to get into modeling, he could make a go of it. But she wanted him there with her. Damn, she'd become possessive of him.

Austin finished his breakfast first and carried his plate over to the sink. With his back to her, she noticed the mark across his shoulder. A tattoo? She dropped her fork and tried to regain her poise. He'd once told her he hated ink. How had she missed the tat? Because she hadn't seen him without his shirt—not from the back anyway.

"When—when did you do that?" she blurted.

"Huh?" Austin glanced over his shoulder. "Do what?" He dunked the pans and his plate into the sink then faced her.

"Your back." She folded her hands to keep from pointing at him. "You got a tattoo. How did I not know?"

"Oh." He shrugged and dried his hands. "That. Yeah." Austin crossed the expanse to her and leaned on the counter. "I hadn't planned on getting inked, but a year ago I changed my mind."

"What was her name?" She nudged the empty plate away. "I'm sure it was because of a woman." Everything he did was because of a female.

"No." He shook his head and folded his arms. "Remember when I went to New York and got mugged on the subway? My life flashed before my eyes and I flipped out. I had a midlife crisis."

"You're only thirty-three." He was way too young for a midlife crisis already. Maybe a not-quite-ready-to-be-thirty crisis… That was possible and understandable.

"I thought I was going to die and I was scared, if something happened, no one would know who I was." His voice rose an octave. "No paper ID, and anything else crazy, I needed to know I could be identified. What if someone pulled out my teeth or cut off my head?"

"You're getting a tad overdramatic, but I see your point. You're planning ahead. It's smart." He could've told her or hadn't he been planning on her knowing? "Who did you tell? I mean, so they could identify you – if something traumatic happened."

"Yeah, about that. I didn't. I got the thing done and it hurt like a bitch, so I didn't say anything."

"That month you complained about your shoulder? You said you messed it up at softball practice."

"I lied." He shrugged again. "You always give me shit about everything – and rightly so – so I kept my mouth shut. Being held up scared me, but coming clean to you was worse. Doesn't feel that great right now." The muscle in his jaw tightened. "Anyway, it's script that says *no regrets*. I might not be the best man, but I don't regret anything I've done."

"Smart." He was afraid to tell her stuff? She should've been upset, but a twinge of pride swirled around in her brain.

"And now you know." He drummed his hands on the counter. "If you're done, I'll soak the plate and we can shower."

"I'm done." She scooted the plate across to him. "You didn't have to worry about me giving you a hard time. I'm not that awful."

"You can be, but I tend to deserve it." He dunked the plate then headed out of the kitchen. "Doesn't take long for the hot water."

She followed him down the hallway to the bathroom. He switched on the water and closed the glass stall.

"I've got plenty of towels, shampoo, conditioner and stuff. No flat iron. I know you like using yours." He tugged a couple of extra towels from the cabinet over the toilet.

"You've always been worried about your hair." She unbuttoned the shirt and let the garment slide down her arms. He faced her and she closed the front of the shirt over her body. Being with him was freeing but did a number on her confidence.

"What's wrong?" He shoved the boxer briefs down his hips until the underwear landed on the floor around his ankles. "Don't tell me you're going to hide from me now."

"Maybe." She held her breath as he strolled around her. The man was a specimen—all muscle and perfect skin, save for the tattoo. She felt so inadequate around him.

Austin removed the elastic from her hair and the crystal barrette Dylan had used. He eased his fingers through her tresses, massaging her scalp. "Water's hot." He nudged her into the shower stall. "I'm right behind you."

She kept to the back of the shower and damn near drooled as the water sluiced over his body. He had no idea—no, he knew his own attractiveness—but the moment he wasn't trying to be someone else, that's when he made her want him the most.

Austin stepped under the spray. His hair plastered to his head and the water droplets slid down his taut abs. His cock bounced with each movement. He turned his back on her, and she fought the urge to grab his toned ass. Being that handsome was criminal—had to be.

"Here." Austin held a bottle of shampoo. "May I?"

"Sure." She eased around him long enough to dampen her hair.

Austin tugged her to his chest and her knees buckled.

Being with him was crazy and overwhelming.

"I've always wanted to do this." He massaged her scalp again. "Wash my woman's hair. It's oddly soothing."

Suds slid over her shoulders and his cock nestled between her ass cheeks. *His* woman? He needed to stop teasing her, but yeah, having someone take care of her was indeed soothing.

"The longer I have you in my apartment, the more I realize it's been lonely around here." He eased her under the spray. "Close your eyes while I rinse this out."

She did as she'd been told. "How can you be lonely? You've always got a date."

"Easy." He turned her around to face him and worked the rest of the suds from her hair then picked up the bottle of conditioner. "I don't invite them over."

"No?" She doubted that. He had too many girlfriends not to have one or more of them inhabiting his space for at least a few nights.

"Nope. We meet at her place or a hotel." He added the conditioner to her hair and sighed. "But I haven't even done that in a while. I swear, I'm becoming a hermit."

"You can't. You go to work. A hermit doesn't leave the house." She picked up the washcloth and poured shower gel onto it. The suds formed quickly when she squished the cloth. She kept one hand on his hip and smoothed the lather over his upper body. She'd touched him during sex, but this was different. She met his gaze and her cheeks burned.

"Did I mention, besides looking like you belong in my apartment, you look better in my clothes than I do?" Austin turned her around again and rinsed her hair. "Damn sexy if you ask me."

"I doubt that." She wiped her face then handed over the cloth. She'd smeared soap and makeup into her eyes. "Shit."

"Hold still." Austin cleaned her face, slowly wiping away the makeup and soap. "I hate when that happens. Stings."

"It does." She blinked as the soap dissipated. "Thank you."

"Of course." Austin gathered her in his arms. "I'm sorry I overlooked you and made you feel less than desirable. I'm sorry I've been a dick."

"You're fine." Not really, but she wasn't sure what else to say. "Can—can I shave you?"

"I'm that prickly?" His eyebrows rose.

"Nah, I've just always wanted to shave someone."

"The shaving cream's behind you. Go for it." He kept his hands on her hips. "Be careful, but I'm warning you, I only trust you to do this." He notched his chin in the air while she spread the cream over his cheeks and neck. "I'm rather fond of my face."

"Think I'm going to slash you?" She ran the razor under the water. Shaving him wasn't just an act of trust, but intimacy. He'd never let anyone do this for him before? She sucked in a ragged breath and moved the razor over his skin. She slicked away the tiny whiskers and foam. He swallowed and his Adam's apple bobbed.

"You're about the only person I know who won't slice me open." He swallowed again. "When I'm with you, I feel like *me* again. Our arguments in the office, disagreeing on football teams and scores, falling asleep together after too many hours spent on one campaign and all those conversations over takeout, those are the moments I live for." He trailed his fingers over her spine. "That and last night. You're… I'm in awe."

"Please." She sucked in her stomach and wished she hadn't eaten all of her breakfast. Being raw with him exposed everything and she wasn't thrilled. She cared about her appearance but she knew her limits. "You're all muscle and hotness. I'm not." She was all hips and ass. "Now hold still. I'm almost done."

She worried she'd cut him because he kept talking and wriggling. Shaving him was harder than it looked or seemed.

"You're beautiful." He grinned and water dripped down his forehead. "Nothing to be ashamed of."

"Uh-huh." She swiped the last of the shaving cream from his throat. "You're perfect. I'm just the sidekick. Rinse."

"Don't you start the embarrassment stuff. You're sexy, beautiful and you make me laugh. I had the time of my life last night and things only got better once we came back to my apartment." He feathered a kiss over her lips. "The only reason I liked the gala was because I got to see you all dressed up. The rest could've taken place right here and I would've been happy."

"You really had fun?"

"I did." Austin turned the water off and shook his head. Water droplets flew around the shower stall. "Now, we've got today off and I'm not ready for you to go home. Do you trust me?"

She eased out of the stall ahead of him. "If I didn't trust you, I wouldn't have worked with you all this time." She yanked the towel off the hook. "What did you have in mind?"

Austin dried himself off and stood before her. "We go down to the lakeside, the little amusement park. All day, just you and me—commando." His eyes widened and a wicked smile curled on his lips. "Yeah?"

Commando? She'd done that last night, but this was—well, not really any different. But last night she'd worn a dress. Right now she didn't have clothes of her own at the apartment.

"Well?" He dropped his towel. His cock thickened and his nipples beaded. "What do you think?"

She allowed her towel to slide to the floor. Two could play his game. She wanted to hide her imperfections, but fuck it. "I'm game—but I need to stop at my apartment. I'll go commando all day long, but I'd like to wear my own clothes and shoes." She liked the dare and she liked him—win-win.

He narrowed his eyes and grinned. "I knew your secret adventurous side wasn't a one-time thing. You might not want anyone to know you're not always tightly laced, but I

102

like seeing the different sides of you."

"The same goes for you." She followed him back into the bedroom. "Mind if I steal your shirt and those sleep pants until we get to my place?"

"I said you looked better in my clothes than I do."

She sighed and dressed. Her hair needed brushing and she wasn't even wearing her own clothes, but the adventure he wanted to go on sounded fun and exciting. How could she tell him no when she wanted to cut loose with him? Easy—she'd go along for the ride and accept whatever fate had in store.

Chapter Seven

Austin replaced the towels then dressed. As he buttoned his jeans, Molly strolled into the bedroom.

"You got ready fast." He unballed his socks and sat on the edge of the bed. "I should take lessons from you."

"It's not hard when you don't have much to wear." She handed over his phone. "This rang twice while I was in the living room. I didn't answer it, but that number has called a dozen times since yesterday."

He swiped his thumb across the screen. Sure enough, he had sixteen missed calls—most of them from one number. He recognized another number from the list. "Remy's been looking for you. Why don't you call him and let him know you're not dead?"

"He worries too much." She accepted the phone. "But then so do I."

"It's endearing." He put his socks on and stepped into his running shoes. "Ready?"

She nodded and pressed the phone to her ear. Molly padded barefoot across the apartment. She looked down at her high-heeled shoes then put them on.

He'd get her back to her place so she could wear something more comfortable. He scooped up his wallet and keys then eased his arm around her as they left the apartment. He paid little attention to her phone call. Remy was a nice guy and a good friend for her. After the work he'd done to get her dolled up, maybe he'd even possibly won Remy over again. He doubted it, but he could hope.

Austin held Molly's hand and headed into the parking garage below the building. He opened the car door for her and once she settled on the passenger seat, he rounded the hood. He eased behind the wheel.

"Here you go." She rested the phone on the middle console. "I forgot you had this car."

"Remember my hatchback?" He engaged the engine and navigated his way out of the garage. "That thing was ugly but reliable."

"Well, you've certainly gone all-out since. This is a nice car." She trailed her fingertips over the stereo system. "Really nice."

"I like 'all-out'. It's fun." He glanced at her. "You don't. You're happy to be in check. That wasn't you when we were in college."

"Things changed since then." She scooted down in the seat. "After Linc, I had to—I had to ensure I was in control."

"Just because one guy was a douche, doesn't mean we all are." He blended into traffic. "I'm not saying I've always been the best example, but still."

"You're honest. That's hard to come by."

"I'm with you. I want to be honest—it's easier to be me than it is to be that image everyone seems to have of me." He slid her hand into his. "You're one of the very few people who can cut me down to size and build me up at the same time. How do you do that?"

"I don't know." She shifted in the seat and faced him. "But I'm glad I can do it."

"Me too."

"I guess it's because I've seen the real you." She rubbed the top of his hand with her thumb. "You're only really happy when we're in the middle of a project or when you smell blood in the water. If there's a deal to be made, you're there."

"That's business."

"You'd have to settle down with a woman in order for me to see the relationship side of you."

"You're the longest relationship I've ever had."

"We aren't really a couple." She laughed and squeezed

his hand. "You made up a story about me being your fiancée and we slept together three times. That's not much of a relationship."

"We've had sex four times," he corrected.

"A day and a half of trying to be more than friends."

"Fine, but in this last day and a half, we've been through more than a lot of people. Besides, the thing about you being my fiancée wasn't supposed to be a farce." He pulled to a stop in front of her building complex. He might have lived in a fancier building, but he liked being able to park closer to her actual townhouse. "We're here."

"Thanks. I'll be a minute." Molly climbed out of his car. "I need to stop by Remy's first to grab my keys."

"I'm not sitting out here that whole time." He killed the power to the engine and opened his door. The sunshine warmed his skin, but not like when Molly held him. He followed her into the building and to Remy's door.

Remy answered and eyeballed Austin. "Funny seeing both of you here. Come on in."

Austin started into Remy's townhouse, but his phone buzzed. Christ. "I'll be right there. Let me get this — whoever keeps calling won't leave me alone."

Molly nodded. She and Remy disappeared into the apartment. Austin strode over to the short staircase and peered out of the window as he answered the call.

"Hello?" He shoved his free hand into his pocket. "Who is this?"

"You don't recognize my number?"

Austin gritted his teeth. Iris. He should've known she'd call — not once, but close to fifteen times. "I didn't. I'm sorry."

"Well, now you know," she said. "Seems you're hard to reach."

"I am when I'm not at work." He wouldn't get nasty with her but he wasn't up to being her buddy. "Did you need something?"

"Other than your tight little ass in my penthouse? Yes.

I have an offer for you," she said. "One you can't refuse."

"I'm not so sure about that." He looked back at Remy's door. Either he hadn't seen Molly leave, or she was still in there. *Fuck.*

"The more I look at your pictures, the more I agree with you about Ms. Neff's work. It's fantastic. Did she mention she'd talked to the models?"

"No, I lied because I didn't want to get into it with you." He pinched the bridge of his nose. He didn't have time for this. "What's your point?"

"No need to get bitchy with me," she snapped. "But she was rather engrossed in their mundane chat. She probably left with one of them. God knows those guys will fuck anything in a skirt."

He resisted the urge to correct her about Molly. Right now he just wanted to get off the damn phone. "You said something about Molly's photos." Maybe a little redirection would get the conversational ball rolling.

"Yes. If I contract her as the principal photographer, are you interested in doing the modeling for the Aura fall campaign? She'd be photographing other models, in addition to you, and there would be other photographers there, as well. The financial gain for you would be substantial. Five thousand for each of the three sessions."

"Hold up." He opened his eyes. Today wasn't about business talk—he was supposed to be having fun down on the beach with Molly. "I can't speak for Ms. Neff, but I would consider doing some modeling." Fifteen grand would cover his bills for two months, with a little extra left over. "But *only* if she's *my* photographer."

"Discuss things with her. I can't seem to get in touch with her. Not good if she's going to be a professional." Iris sighed. "The faster you let me know, the faster we can get things going."

"Yes, ma'am. I'll see what I can do." He hung up on her, knowing full well he was being rude. Screw it. His heart hammered. Fifteen grand was more than three months' salary at CDL. A thought occurred to him. If Molly was taking the photos, what would her cut be? She'd better be paid handsomely. He'd worry about that later.

He turned on his heel and headed down the short hallway to her townhouse. If she wasn't there, then he'd try Remy's. He knocked. "Molls?"

"It's open," she called.

He tried the knob and opened the door. Molly stood in the middle of the living room with her back to him. She'd brushed and curled her hair but had gathered her tresses in another ponytail. Her jeans contoured to her frame like a second skin. When she bent over, his mouth watered. Damn, she had a nice ass.

"Is your call finished?" She finished tying her tennis shoes and looked back at him. "Anything important?"

"It was, but I don't want to talk about it right now. We're supposed to be going on a date." He offered his arm. "A *real* date, not a contrived fancy dress bullshit thing."

"You're so sweet." She shook her head. "Let me grab my sweater and we can go." She picked up the cardigan she'd slung over the back of the careworn couch and shoved her phone into her back pocket. She wound her hand around his arm. "I'm ready."

"Cool." He didn't say anything as they headed down to the parking lot. He had so much he wanted to tell her but needed to sort out *how* to say it. Christ. He could scare her away, make her hate him or bring them closer together – if he didn't fuck things up.

"I know you're trying to be sweet so we can have a good weekend, but I can't *not* say this. I keep expecting this sweeter side of you to disappear. I hope it sticks around, because I like it. But you've got a track record. You get close enough to build up emotion and then disappear when things get tight." She allowed him to open the car door for her again. "That's bad, though, isn't it? I'm an awful friend."

"No. I deserve that." He rounded the trunk and ended up behind the wheel. "I'm sorry I've been such a dick."

Molly toyed with the thick silver band she wore on her middle finger. "Since we graduated from college, you've only ever taken enough of a personal interest in me to keep tabs on me. Other than the times you've needed me to bail you out or to serve as a pick-me-up, I don't seem to mean much to you. Now we've had a crazy fun night together that was like before. I'm not sure how to feel—happy or to expect it to all fall apart."

Jesus. He'd been a dick to her. A few of the times he'd called her to come to the bar because his then-date hadn't worked out came to mind. He expected her to fix things, but she had no control over the situation. He wanted her to be his backup and available, but he'd treated her like crap. He clenched his fist tightly. *Damn it.* He'd fallen head over heels for her, but instead of saying how he felt, he screwed her over.

"I hate feeling used, but I'm addicted to you." She sighed. "God. I'm nuts. I've got to be. I know I'm going to get hurt but I keep happily snatching up the breadcrumbs you leave for me. I want things to be more but I know there's a dead end coming. Always a dead end." She didn't look at him, but he could hear the cracking in her voice and knew she wasn't far from coming apart. How she'd managed to stay strong all that time amazed him.

He hated himself for stringing her along. Hated himself for not telling her how he felt a long time ago, and hoping she'd agree to the photo shoot. He wanted her to shine and wanted to be the man at her side. He also wanted to try his hand at modeling. A dull ache built behind his eyes. He was fucked up—not sure of what he wanted and unable to explain himself.

"Sorry. I'm ruining our date and it hasn't even started yet." She wiped her face. "I'm even crying. I'm a mess."

She wasn't the problem. He and his past decisions were the issue. He hated what he couldn't change and wished he knew how to fix the future. First things first, he needed to get a few things out of his system.

"You never should've married Linc," he blurted. He'd wanted to tell her that all along but hadn't found the right time. Somehow, he doubted right now was the best moment, but the words tumbled out. He didn't regret speaking his mind, though.

"You could've mentioned that a whole lot earlier — like before I went through with it." She faced him. Her cheeks were ruddy and her eyes a bit puffy from crying, but she still knocked his socks off. She folded her arms. "But that's you. You don't clue me in until after the fact."

She was right. The moment she'd married Linc, he had known she'd made a mistake, but he'd been so wrapped up in his own life that he'd kept his mouth shut. But part of him had been jealous of Linc. The guy hadn't deserved Molly. Austin had known they'd never make it, but he wasn't sure he'd be a good match for her either. What made him think now he could be what she needed?

"Got any other bombshells you'd like to drop?" she asked. "I'm raw but I'm listening."

"I was always jealous of Linc. He had someone special — you." Austin reached for her and laced his fingers with hers. He needed to touch her. Needed her reassurance. "He liked your free spirit but couldn't handle it. You closed up because of him."

"It's hard to let loose once you're all tense like that," she whispered. "But thanks for being honest." Tears shimmered in her lashes and the blush on her cheeks accentuated the blue of her eyes. "I don't know how to relax."

"You did pretty well with it last night." He kissed her knuckles. "You allowed yourself to have fun and so did I. We made a good team — with the campaign and in bed." Hell, having her around made his life brighter. She knew how to bring out the best in him. He'd work on relaxing her as long as she wanted because he needed her in his life.

"True." The corner of her mouth lifted in a smile. "You've ruined sex for me. You're just that good."

"Nah. You're pretty awesome already. I'm arm candy."

He drummed his fingers on the armrest. Although he'd made a breakthrough with her, he had a hundred questions and wanted answers. Did he deserve the answers? Not really, but wanting and deserving hadn't stopped him before. "What did Linc have on you that you stuck around that long? You said he cheated. Why not leave his ass high and dry as soon as you found out?"

"Well...he was my first—kind of." She shrugged. "I'm serious. I had, like, no experience until him."

Austin frowned and held her hand again. "I thought Reyland was your first. You two were tight and he told everyone about you and him in your bedroom."

"Uh-uh. He chickened out and drove me home."

"But he told everyone—" Austin didn't finish his statement. He knew what he'd been told, but as he gazed into her eyes, he knew the truth. Well, part of the truth anyway. "Then what happened?"

"He lied and I didn't correct him because I didn't want to be mean." She rested her other hand on top of his. "He seemed so proud of what he'd done—what everyone thought he'd done—and I didn't want to steal his thunder. It worked out. The guys who wanted to get in my pants because they thought I was a virgin left me alone and the others simply ignored me because I wasn't gorgeous like Joann."

He disagreed with her assessment. He'd kept most of those guys at bay and had refused to allow them to hit on her. He'd been a jerk, but he'd thought he'd known what had been best for her. Unfortunately he hadn't been able to prevent the Linc fiasco.

She pulled away from him and grabbed the door handle. "Let's go for a walk. It's a nice day and I need to move around."

"Sure." Austin left the vehicle and locked it then fell into step beside her. He stuffed his hands into his pockets. He wanted to hold her, but she kept her arm between them. When she wanted to get closer, he'd be ready. He noticed a couple at the bus stop. The guy held on to his girlfriend and they were completely absorbed in each other. Austin wished he had the same with Molly. He glanced at Molly and a thought occurred to him.

"Wait. Linc can't be number one." He paused. They'd slept together before she'd fucked Linc. He knew so and cherished the memory of their first time. "I came before Linc." The sex had been frantic but good.

"That's true. You were my first time, but he was my first relationship. I thought when I was with Linc we were making love, not fucking. Then I was with you the first time. It was fumbling in the dark and awkward because I didn't have any experience." She covered her face with her hands. "I was so goofy back then."

"You were fine. I liked it." Correction—he loved being with her. "Everyone needs to start somewhere."

"You started at perfect." She patted his thigh. "I was so out of my league."

"Never." He draped his arm around her and held her close. "You just needed to bloom."

Molly sighed and rested her head on his shoulder. "You asked why I stuck around with Linc. Truth? I thought I could love him enough to convince him to stop cheating. If I stayed strong and put up with his crap, maybe he'd see I was worthy of him. Looking back, I see he was the unworthy one, but I wanted my marriage to work."

"Molls." He loved her tenacity. The odds could be stacked against her, but she always refused to give up.

"Everything changed the moment he mentioned kids. I refused to bring a child into a situation where one parent can't stand the other parent's job and work partner, let alone the other parent can't keep his dick in his pants." She clutched Austin's arm. "He hated you so much and wanted me to stay home. I like being a homebody but I need something to do."

"Sounds like a winner." He gritted his teeth. The more he learned about Linc, the more he wanted to rearrange the bastard's face. His heart bled for Molly and for his own stupidity. "Why didn't you tell me all of this before? I'd have helped." He liked to think he would've helped. He'd never cheated on his various girlfriends and couldn't understand why anyone would, especially on Molly.

Molly chuckled. "You sound so noble, but it's a joke. I know you and you wouldn't have done anything. It didn't involve your dick or Joann and eventually Carole. Remember? And besides, if I spent time with you, Linc went ballistic."

He bit back another growl. He'd been the world's worst friend. Not that her ex-husband had been any better. "He didn't trust you."

"No kidding. I've only ever slept with three guys in my life, but he was convinced I'd been with way more. Christ." She laughed and collided with him, stumbling forward. "Would you believe he hated you because you were competition?"

"I believe it." He steadied her and rubbed his cheek on the top of her head. "Who were the other two? Linc being one and me being another."

"Joe Handleman," she whispered. "It was one time and not that good, but yeah, him."

"I'm in an elite group," Austin said. He sounded like a prick but he rather liked knowing there hadn't been many men in her bed.

"You always were special."

He caught the snarky tone of her voice and didn't mind. He'd take all the tongue-lashing she could give him in order to make up for the things he'd done in the past.

"Special competition." She tugged Austin forward. "Let's head back."

He stopped walking and stared at her. "Wait. Linc knew us all in college. He knew I was involved with Joann then Carole. How'd he realistically think I was competition? Once you hooked up with him, I behaved. We didn't flirt like we always had and I'm not a cheater."

She bridged the gap between them and grasped both of his hands. "You know that and so do I, but Linc thought he knew everything. When I wasn't fucking you, he was convinced I was having sex with Remy." She shook her head. "I'll be honest. I never stopped hoping I'd get a chance to be your girl, but I never said anything like that to him."

"Molly?" He couldn't believe what she'd said but desperately wanted her words to be true.

"I never stopped thinking you could be the one." Molly tried to pull away from him, but he refused to let go. Her cheeks tinged red again and her eyes sparkled. "Austin?"

"Maybe I *am* the one." He certainly wanted to be. He gazed into her eyes but he swore she saw straight through to his soul. He'd bare everything to her. No one else mattered — no jobs, no other women, nothing except Molly existed.

Molly sighed and eased away from him. "As much as I want this to work, I know the truth. You're a mistake and this was a mistake. All of the times we've had sex were — mistakes." She shook her head. "I can't do this." She started away from him and threaded her fingers into her hair.

"No." As she put space between them, his heart sank. His world seemed to be falling apart. "No, babe. None of this was wrong." Being with her was beautiful, peaceful... destined. The goddamn cosmos had finally lined up and allowed him to have the chance he'd always wanted with her. No fucking way he'd give up now.

"I know you. You'll get bored or hold out just to prove me wrong. You've done it before and told me about it — maybe not with me, but I know your track record."

"I could surprise you." No 'could' about it — he'd shock the hell out of her.

"I doubt it," Molly said. "Ever since college you were the guy everyone wanted but I could never have. Being friends with you was good, but I wanted more. I saw all those other girls with you and wished I was them. Then Aiden reminded me I was one of the guys. That's when I knew."

"Knew what? If you wanted to date me, you should've

said something." He pressed his lips together. He was getting her to talk and snapping at her wouldn't help his cause.

"You never saw me. I disappeared as soon as your girlfriends showed up." Her voice cracked and she whipped around to face him. "I was the chunky friend who made you laugh and was willing to take you in after your date imploded, but I wasn't good enough for you to ask me on a date."

He wanted to tell her that's not how he'd felt, but he'd have been lying. Back then, yeah, he'd seen her as his reliable pal.

"Did you ever look at me before last night and see a hot woman?" She shook her head. "Last night you saw me as a conquest. I was the one person you fucked but hadn't fucked with."

"That's not fair or true." He reached for her, but she stepped out of his grasp.

"The first time we had sex — way back in college — you told me it was because you wanted me to get some experience with someone who wasn't Reyland." Tears slipped down her cheeks again. "Fuck. I don't cry this much, but you bring out my overactive hormones."

"You have a lot of scars that needed ripping open in order to heal, and I needed to have my ass kicked more than eight times over." He caught Molly and enfolded her in his arms while he caressed her hair. Goddamn it, he'd fucked up.

"I'm not in the mood to have my heart stomped on, okay?"

Her words were muffled against his chest, but he caught everything she'd said. Austin held her and wished he could keep from hurting her. He wished he hadn't been such an ass all those times he'd wanted to tell her he loved her. He closed his eyes and exhaled. "Babe, you don't know how I see you, because you never heard me say the words. That's fucked up on my part and I'm sorry. I'm not good if I have to bare my soul. I'm my best when I'm with you — at CDL and right now. You've always grounded me and been my rock."

"Don't worry about it."

"Bullshit. I will worry about it and you. Christ, I had — have — the most loyal, sweetest, adorable woman by my side and I jacked it all up because I didn't want to admit I liked you." There. He'd said the words on his heart.

"What?" She stared up at him and her eyes widened. "What did you say?"

"You freaked me out back in college." The more he talked, the more he needed to be completely honest. "You've always been so smart and quick with ideas. You're confident, too. When you're on the job, you're the force to be reckoned with — not me. Guys are scared of you because we know you'll chew us up and spit us out if we fuck up. I had the added pressure of not wanting to lose you as my friend. I didn't want to lose out."

"Oh."

"Come back to the car with me. I owe you a day down at the lake. Please?" He swiped the tears from her cheeks and rested his forehead against hers. "I like you so much." *And I'm scared it's love. I'm scared I'll fuck up and lose you.*

"Okay." She blew out a long breath then wound her arm around his. "Maybe us being together isn't a mistake. Maybe."

He fell into step with her again and headed back to the parking lot. He hadn't noticed the scenery along the way — still hadn't. The only thing that mattered was Molly. She'd thought their relationship was a mistake? Not a chance. He'd been foolish not to morph what she saw as a problem into a solid partnership. Was he in love?

He nodded. Yeah, he loved her. Always had, but until now he hadn't been ready to admit that fact, even to himself. His spirits buoyed as Molly accompanied him to the lakeside amusement park.

The park wasn't much more than a Ferris wheel and a rickety roller coaster surrounded by food stands and games of chance, but he didn't care. To him, the place was paradise because he had Molly by his side. He bought an elephant ear to split with her.

Molly sat on his lap and nibbled on the sweet treat. He smeared powdered sugar on the tip of his nose and laughed. When she kissed the sugar off his skin, he melted a little bit more. He'd become putty in her hands and she had no idea how much control she held. His heart beat for her.

"Ferris wheel?" She tugged him across the dirt trail to the bottom of the attraction.

Austin bought the tickets and waited with her in line. Molly squealed as she climbed into the car. The paint peeled and the Ferris wheel creaked but seemed stable. He settled on the seat with her and yanked the safety bar across their lap.

"You can see everything from up here." She gripped the bar. "I've only ever been on this ride once before. Remy dared me to ride it."

"You did and I bet you had fun." He draped his arm around her. "Wonder if we'll get stuck at the top."

"Probably. We're the only couple on the ride." She squeezed his thigh as the car stopped at the top of the wheel. "The view is so pretty. You can see forever."

"You can." He noticed the expansive view around them but he also saw so many things much clearer. He and Molly had fun together. They laughed and the sex was off the charts. She outsmarted him but was his equal. He should've admitted the attraction long before. He'd wasted too much time.

Austin kissed her. He wasn't about to lose any more time. He tangled his tongue with hers and smoothed his palm across her belly. He was the luckiest man alive because he'd found the love of his life — even if he'd taken an eternity to figure that fact out.

Molly whimpered and eased back from him a bit. "This is fun." She bumped noses with him. "Private, but public, too. People could see us."

"Who cares?" He wanted to tug her onto his lap and make

love to her in the Ferris wheel carriage. "There's no one else I want to be stuck up here with. I've never been this relaxed or happy in my life."

"Me too." Molly rested her head on his shoulder. "Austin?"

"Right here." Everything was perfect. If he had a ring, he would've proposed to her. Yeah, he wanted her forever. Now that he'd had a taste of Molly and knew what he wanted from his life, he refused to look back. No regrets and no more mistakes.

"Your pocket is buzzing." She patted his thigh. "Your phone. You'd better answer it."

"Fuck it. I'm here with you. Work or whoever wants me can wait." He kept his arm around her as the carriage moved around the wheel and until it stopped. He didn't bother to check the phone, but it buzzed in his pocket again. He reached into the side pocket of his jeans and silenced the device.

"Molls, would you ever get married again?" He needed to know. No point in getting his hopes up if she wasn't interested.

"Why? Are you offering?" Her voice was wistful, almost as if she wasn't taking him seriously. Why should she? He only got serious at work.

"You never know." There. He'd volleyed the possibility. Would she take the bait? "Would you?"

"I don't know. I'd have to have the right guy come along. The job is vacant and I'm accepting applications — if you're interested." She tipped her head to meet his gaze. "But only serious applicants are being taken into consideration."

"I'm serious." He slid his phone from his pocket and checked the screen. He didn't recognize the number and put the device away.

Molly snuggled against him. "Just answer it." She clutched his shirt. "Want me to? If it's someone from CDL, they'll get one hell of a surprise."

"It's not work." The people at CDL liked their days off as

much as he did. "I don't know who it is."

"What if that's your mom? Or Dylan?"

He shook his head but slid his phone from his pocket. He doubted his mother would call and knew better than to expect Dylan on the other end of the line.

"Well?" Her eyes sparkled and the blush infused on her cheeks added to her beauty. "I'll be over at the railing if you want to answer." She pulled away from him and glanced over her shoulder as she strolled to the boardwalk.

He gritted his teeth and checked the screen again. Twenty-seven missed calls. He didn't recognize the number and he knew the last four digits of Iris's personal cell. *Fuck.* Who in the hell wanted him that badly?

"Austin?"

He looked up from the phone, expecting Molly. His blood ran cold. Iris Sommerville stood before him. She folded her arms and tapped her foot on the sidewalk. How'd she know he'd be at the park? She'd had him followed. *Well, fuck.*

Chapter Eight

Molly breathed in the cool lake breeze and gripped the railing. The wind whipped her hair and the sunshine sparkled on the water. The moment couldn't have been more perfect—except to have Austin holding her. She snorted. That man and his phone. The thing should've been surgically attached to his head.

He'd been so sweet to her and so un-Austin. As if he cared about her as more than a friend. His question came to mind. Would she ever get married again? What a loaded thing to ask. After Linc, she hadn't thought anyone would want to marry her. Austin certainly made her rethink her anti-marriage stance. He'd been her perfect vision of the man she'd spend the rest of her life with, but did she really want perfect? She wasn't without her flaws. Her lack of self-esteem and her self-effacing tendency weren't fun, but he seemed to see past her problems.

She chuckled. He'd always been her Prince Charming, even when he hadn't been so charming. He'd hinted about marriage and her. He claimed he was serious. She wanted to believe him, but the same niggling worries came to mind. He wasn't the type of man who settled down.

She peeked over her shoulder. If he was still on the phone, she didn't want to interrupt, but she did want to ask a few questions.

Where'd he go? Molly left the railing and crossed the boardwalk. The moment she stepped onto the concrete, she wished she hadn't gone hunting for him.

Austin stood locked in deep conversation with Iris Sommerville. What in the hell did Iris want? Probably

Austin in her bed. Molly shored up her courage and eased up to Austin.

"Molly." Austin eased his arm around her shoulders. "Iris is here."

"I can see that." Molly offered her hand to Iris, only to get a dirty look in return. "Nice of you to join us."

"Austin, have you explained the deal to her?" Iris folded her arms. Her blazer accentuated her narrow frame and her high heels served to make the woman seem to tower over everyone.

"I haven't." Austin bowed his head. "Sorry."

Molly glared at Iris then stared at Austin. Where was this shift in attitude coming from? He was normally such a strong, confident man. "What's going on? What should I know about?"

"I talked to your partner about a business proposition." Iris waggled her fingernails and the bright red sparkled in the sunshine. Her sunglasses concealed her eyes, but the venom in her voice was evident. "He must not have mentioned anything to you."

Molly looked at Austin for a split second before turning her attention back to Iris. "Go on."

"Aura and I liked the photos you created for the intimate wear campaign. We'd like to bring you on — on a temporary basis — to finish the photography for that line. The models you spoke with last night are the ones you'll be capturing." Iris smiled. "I'll have you take a few shots of Mr. Dean as well. That was one of his requirements before he'd agree to pose for me. The particulars are being emailed to you as we speak. You'll find the reservation number, your passcodes and anything else you need in that email."

"I see." She wanted to sock him in the arm. Why hadn't he mentioned any of this? Especially if he already knew he was thinking about doing the campaign.

"I've already spoken with Roscoe Lee. He's more than happy to loan the both of you out for this project. I'd like to start tomorrow. Ms. Neff, I have the suite at the Seven downtown booked for the session. I expect you there tomorrow morning at five." Iris brushed past Molly and grabbed Austin by the arm. "Now you." She dropped her voice to a whisper.

Molly didn't hear everything that was said, but she caught enough bits and pieces. Something about being naked, caressing him and making love to Austin all afternoon. She'd have her driver take Molly home, but Austin was all Iris' for the duration. *What the hell?* Molly blew out a long breath and pinched the bridge of her nose. The opportunity to photograph the models was huge. Hell, she'd never planned on taking her hobby to the next level, unless she had Austin involved, but something about the whole situation didn't feel right. Besides, Austin wasn't acting like himself.

A man in a business suit and sunglasses strode up to her. "Ms. Neff? Ms. Sommerville asked me to take you home."

"Just a moment." Molly crossed over to Austin and touched his arm. "I need to talk to you real quick." She didn't give him a chance to protest, or for Iris to intervene. Molly yanked him from her and ducked with Austin behind a food stand.

"Molls." The muscle in Austin's jaw tensed and he shook his head. "I meant to tell you. I wanted to—but things happened too fast."

"Okay." She dragged a deep breath into her lungs and let it out slowly. "What exactly is going on?"

"At the party, Iris demanded I be in more of her company's photos. I was flattered. Hell, you know me. I like to show off. I wanted to do it—but I swore to her I needed you to do the pictures. Without you, I can't." Austin scrubbed both hands over his face. "She assumed I was in and that I'd get you onboard. What she didn't expect was for you and I to get close."

"Oh, I think she saw that coming." Molly folded her arms and rocked on her heels. She needed to think fast. On one hand, she wanted to do the photography session.

The offer was a great one. On the other hand, she could see Iris pulling Austin in her direction. He had always wanted fame somehow. He liked being the center of attention.

"Molls." He dropped his hands. "I—I'm sorry. I wanted this to be more of a team effort."

"I understand." Not really, but she wasn't about to argue right now. "Want to tell me why you're being docile all of a sudden?" She met his gaze. "You like her, don't you? You saw this was a good experience and one where you'd get to be famous—even if only for a little while—and jumped at it, didn't you?" She flattened her palm on his chest. "I know you. You've always wanted something more and I'm smart enough to know I'm not that person who can give you more. I loved what we had today and last night. Hell, you got me thinking about trying at love again. But I'm not about to stand in your way."

"Molly." His voice broke. "I want you there because I can't do this without you—any of it. I meant what I said. I've fallen for you."

"But getting these pictures done is more important." She patted his chest. "Go. Have fun with her. I need to see Remy and sort out what I want to do for tomorrow morning, since it seems everyone's making decisions for me. Call me if you want to talk." She blinked back tears and left.

"Molly, wait." Austin stopped her and ducked behind a balloon cart. "Don't do this."

"Don't do what? We've been moving at warp speed. I went from lusting after you, to photographing you, to hopping into bed again in a matter of a few hours. My heart wants one thing, but my head is saying to slow down. Maybe this is the slow-down we need. You figure out if you really want all the things you said, or if you want to try something with Iris." She brushed the tears from her face and kept her head held high. "I love you, Austin Dean, but I'm not going to hold you back." She turned on her heel and headed away from him again. This time she didn't stop.

Molly settled on the seat of the luxury car and stared

at the front seat leather as the car sped off. "I'm over on Clarendon. The Lakeway condos."

She didn't watch the scenery or allow herself to cry. She had a job to do and a day to prepare for. She might not like the job, but fuck it. She'd make the photos look great.

Ten minutes later, the car pulled to a stop in front of her building. She thanked the driver then headed up the walk. She didn't go to her condo. Instead, she stopped at Remy's and knocked.

"Hold on to your shit. I'll be right there." A moment later, Remy opened the door. He stopped short and his eyes widened. "What? There's a story." He ushered her into his condo. "What's going on?"

"I need your help." Molly strode past him and collapsed onto the couch. "I've got so much to tell you." She loved her best friend, despite his overly colorful greeting. At the moment, she needed to decompress.

"Dish, dish." Remy shut the door then joined her. "Where's Mr. Wonderful?"

"First things first, I got a job offer—for my photography." She wasn't ready to talk about Austin just yet. "For Aura Sportswear. They want me to photograph the intimate wear line. I'm still in shock."

"This is sudden." Remy stared at her then frowned. "Since when did you decide to become a professional photographer? Not that I don't think you can do it—you can and will rock it—but you said taking pictures was a hobby. Are you quitting the ad game?"

"Austin sort of forced my hand, but I'm taking it as a positive and no, I'm not quitting CDL." She held up one finger. "Things are so complicated."

"Sounds like." He picked at the fuzzy edge of the pillow he'd tucked onto his lap. "Lay it on me."

"Long story short, those pictures I took were a hit and Aura wants me to do more work for them. It was even okayed with Mr. Lee—before I could come to terms with what was going on."

"No shit." Remy shook his head and sighed. "Bet Austin knew all about it. He's smooth."

"Yeah, he is." Molly kicked out of her running shoes and sagged against the couch. "Tomorrow morning I'm photographing three models — male models — at the Seven."

"Like the Seven, the downtown chic hotel that you can't get a room in because they're booked up for like the next five years?" Remy blurted.

"Yes." She turned her phone around and flipped through the emails. Sure enough, the one from Melinda pertaining to the Aura photo shoot was there. She skimmed through the email then handed over the phone to Remy. "Read it for yourself."

He met her gaze then turned his attention to the email. He sank back on the couch. "Holy shit." Remy looked back at her and snorted. "These guys are like freaking gods. Drool-worthy."

"I know. That's why I want you to be my assistant. Me alone in a room with these three is probably not bad, but an assistant is always welcome and you're the only one I trust."

"No Austin?" Remy frowned again. "Where's the rat bastard going to be?"

"So I'm told, he'll be there, too, but I saw the way Iris devoured him with her eyes. If he's allowed in the room, I'll be shocked." She crossed her arms again. "Will you help me? We'll have to get there at least an hour before Iris demanded I show up. If I have to do this all by myself, it'll be a disaster. Think you'd be willing to help take pictures of hot men tomorrow morning?"

"How early? I like my beauty sleep."

"Five in the morning, but I say we get there at four." She held her breath and awaited his response. She loved him like a brother and needed him for the project, but if he decided to be moody, she could be screwed.

Remy narrowed his eyes and cocked his head. "Austin was okay with this? I saw the way he looked at you at the store. It wasn't the same way he looked at you last weekend."

"I have no idea how he feels about it, but Iris set it all up. I should've given him a chance to explain himself, but it was too raw. That's part of why I need you around. I don't know if I can face him. Something tells me it was tame and nothing to worry about, but I've been jacked over by him before." She wasn't proud of that point, but she had little control over her advertising partner. "If you're willing, you're in."

"I'm willing. It's not like I had a date tonight anyway."

"No? Why didn't you ask Dylan out?"

"I never got the chance. We talked, had some wine and he bought takeout, but it was so awkward." Remy flopped back onto the couch and held Molly's hand. "I thought there were sparks, but who the hell knows? I thought Javier and I would work out and he's got his dick buried in Hart's ass."

"I'm sorry." She understood how he felt. She'd fallen hard for Austin years ago and the weekend had only strengthened her feelings, but he wasn't available. "Well, we can either worry about the men in our lives, or we can get ready for the photo shoot."

"Deal. I'm tired of giving my heart to guys who only want a quick fuck." He patted her thigh. "Let's gather up whatever you need and I'll set the alarm."

"Sounds like a plan."

* * * *

The rest of the night flew by in a blur. Molly flopped onto her bed and stared at the ceiling. She went through a mental list of what she needed to bring. Her portable lights, camera and laptop were bagged up and sitting by the apartment door.

Remy snored beside her.

With him making so much noise, she'd never get any sleep. Truth be told, she wasn't going to sleep much anyway. Not with Austin on her mind. Although they'd only been together for twenty-four hours, she missed the way he'd held her when they'd slept and the taste of his kiss. She wanted to call him, or send a text to check on him, but why? He was holed up with Iris…probably.

She grabbed her phone. The light blinded her for a few moments as she typed out the text. She couldn't ignore him.

You okay?

She held the phone to her chest. She didn't expect a response. He was more than likely to be naked with Iris and nowhere close to his phone. She checked the screen again. A message popped up. Her heart skipped a beat. *Austin.* Well, she hoped the person on the other end was him.

Not okay. I miss you.

Her hands shook. He missed her? What was she supposed to say to that?

You'll see me tomorrow.

Not the smoothest text she could send back but she had to be cautious.

Bet your ass I'll be there. Want you in my arms, he wrote back.

Hope blossomed in her chest. She shouldn't give in to the hope but she didn't have much of anything else left.

Who are you with?

Remy.

She pressed the buttons to return the text when another popped up.

I'm sorry I let you down.

She typed out another message and sighed.

You can make up for it later.

Molly glanced at the clock. She had to be awake in a couple of hours in order to set the staging for the shoot. Time to get some sleep. She switched her phone to silent and placed it back on the nightstand.

Molly closed her eyes and a vision of Austin came to mind. He curled up beside her and held her as she slept. With him, she was safe. She buried her nose in the pillow to muffle the whimper. But she missed him so much. Austin brought out a different side of her and sent delicious shivers through her body.

Soon she'd get out of this predicament and be able to go on with her life. If that meant a life with Austin, then great, but if not…she'd deal with that consequence later.

Molly flopped onto her back and opened her eyes. Once the numbers on the clock came into focus, she bolted upright. *Shit.*

"Remy, it's three-thirty." She shook him awake. "Remy."

He grunted and rolled over. "I'm up." His dick tented the blankets.

She nodded. "No kidding." Molly climbed out of bed and into the bathroom. If she rushed, she'd be able to shower and do her hair before they had to leave.

"Don't flip out," Remy said. He marched past her and raked his fingers through his hair. "Give us fifteen minutes. You'll be fresh and I'll get clean clothes. No sweat."

"Whatever you say." Molly hurried through a shower and tucked her hair into a towel. Ten minutes later, she'd dressed and put on some makeup. She wasn't going to win any beauty pageants but she was passable. She used the blow dryer on her hair and pulled the tangle of curls back into a ponytail.

"Cinderella's gown officially poofed," she muttered.

"Cinderella didn't give up," Remy called. "She got all emo when the spell broke, but she tried to get the prince's attention. You can't give up on Austin."

"Sure." She gathered up her bags and the lights. "Ready?"

"I should be." Remy slung the camera bag and her computer bag on his shoulder. "You go. I follow." He tagged along behind her to the car and helped load the gear into the trunk. He didn't say anything for the lion's share of the ride.

Molly looked at him a couple of times to make sure Remy was awake. He wasn't big on being quiet and his lack of conversation bothered her. She pulled onto the drop-off lane in front of the hotel.

She swatted Remy's arm. "Stay here."

"I'm awake."

That's what she'd thought. She closed the door and headed into the hotel. The three models stood by the counter. Molly squared her shoulders. "Boys." She strode past them and up to the receptionist. "I'm here for a photo shoot. The paperwork should be in order. We're supposed to be in one of the penthouses. I'm Molly Neff."

The receptionist smiled and pushed a piece of paper across the counter. "Sign this. The room is ready and under the name of Iris Sommerville, correct?"

"Yes." She scanned the form. According to the paperwork, she wasn't liable for any of the damages — if there were any. She signed and handed the page back to the receptionist.

"Here are your key cards." The desk clerk slid the cards to her. "Good luck."

"I'll need it." She turned to the models. "I see three of you. Are the clothes up there?"

The blond nodded. "Iris and Austin already went up there."

"You're kidding." She bit back her frustration. "Okay. I need to get my things and park the car. I'll be right back." She headed out to the pickup lane and her car. Remy snored in the front seat. She opened his door and thumped his arm.

"Hey, you. I need your help. I've got three hunks at my bidding. Get up so I can get through this."

"Sorry." Remy eased out of the seat and stood. He scrubbed both hands over his face. "I so want to kick Austin's ass."

"Why?" She retrieved her things from the trunk and handed her keys over to the valet. The idea of relinquishing control of one of her prized possessions to someone she didn't know bothered her. With Remy in tow, she made her way back into the hotel. The models followed her to the elevator.

She shook her head as Remy eyeballed the models. He could've looked a little less obvious. She elbowed him twice before the car stopped on the seventeenth floor. When the doors opened, she strode ahead of the others to the suite doors. She tapped her key card on the reader.

Austin opened the door and eased into the hallway. "Everyone in." He stepped out of the way as the models filed into the room. Austin waggled his fingers. "You too, Rem."

"Asshat." Remy trudged past Austin then peeked back at Molly. "If he does something stupid, scream and I'll kick his ass."

"That's why I love you." She met Austin's gaze and considered his wince a small victory. *Good. Let him feel a little uptight.* She waited until Remy had disappeared with her gear into the suite then faced Austin. "I'm not allowed in?"

Dressed in a white T-shirt that left little to the imagination, faded blue jeans and running shoes, he looked every inch the model. Austin wound his arm around her and headed back to the elevator.

"Seriously, I'm not allowed in there?" she asked. "I thought—"

"You're fine," Austin whispered. "I wanted some privacy and there's none in there." He stopped in front of the closed elevator doors. "Molly, I'm sorry."

"Don't need to be." She folded her arms and faced him.

"This is what you wanted—a pretty girl, a job where you don't have to do much and can make a shit ton of money. I'm happy for you." *Liar*.

"You aren't happy." Austin groaned and scrubbed the back of his hand across his forehead. "Here's the thing. When I texted you last night, I meant what I said. I wanted you with me."

"You were with Iris."

"She locked me out on the balcony. The only thing that saved me was it wasn't that cold last night."

"Why?" Molly met his gaze. "I thought you were her new boy toy."

"She's younger than me."

"Whatever."

"That's just it. She thinks I am, too. The whole bursting in on our date and suggesting you be driven home was all her. I turned her down at the gala. You're the one I wanted to be there with. Still are." Austin enfolded her in his arms. "I screwed up. Yes, two hours before the gala I wasn't sure if I wanted to go home with you or her. Yes, when she mentioned doing the modeling shoot, I jumped at it—but my main condition was that you were there. I'm not letting the other guy photograph me. I can't do it."

"What do you mean, other guy?" She leaned back in his embrace. "There's someone else here?"

"The only way she'd agree to have you here today was if I agreed to have a second photographer." Austin shook his head. "I thought I was helping."

She wasn't sure what to think. Another person there. *Good God*. How many people were in the suite? "Then what's my role?"

"At the moment, everything's stopped. There are three suites within that one. Iris has one, the main one is where the photography is taking place and the other is for the models to change."

"Except you," she added.

"Except me." Austin rested his forehead against hers.

"This is a freaking mess."

"Why are you losing your edge with her?" She needed to know.

"Because I suck." Austin bumped noses with her. "Okay, it's because I dug myself a hole. I came on to her before we were tapped to do the Aura campaign. I didn't know how you felt and I went with my dick instead of my gut."

She shrugged away from him. "Okay. I'll see what I can do, but if that guy pushes in, I'm not sticking around. I know what I would do with this shoot and how I'd handle it. If you can work with me, we'll get through it."

"I'll do whatever you want." Austin slipped his arm around her and pressed his belly to her back. "I dreamed about you last night. Fantasized you were with me. Christ, I nearly blew my load on the balcony."

"You're terrible." She sighed and leaned into him. "I slept with Remy."

"What?" He turned her around. "Really?"

"Yeah. He snored beside me and I tossed and turned." She smiled, despite her frustration. "Let's get through this. We'll figure things out. Oh, and I need some time to set things up. I don't suppose Iris had breakfast planned for any of you."

"No, but I can see what I can do." His eyes flashed and he smiled finally. "Molls. I'm not me without you."

"Or you're a colossal mistake." She shrugged then left him alone in the hallway. She'd get through the shoot and on with her life. All of his sweet words and kisses turned her on, but she needed a man who could make up his mind.

Austin followed her into the suite and snapped his fingers. "All those ready to model, meet me in the next room. I'm ordering room service for breakfast." He corralled the models then looked back at her and winked.

Iris appeared in the doorway to the other suite. "What's going on?"

"I'm feeding the models." Austin shut the door to the third suite. "Why don't you join us? You've got to be hungry.

Besides, Molly and Remy need time to set up. Nelson did a wonderful job photographing you, but for the photos you want, you need to give Molly the chance to work her magic."

Iris glared at Molly and narrowed her eyes but allowed Austin to escort her to the third suite.

Once the door closed, Molly sighed and met Remy's glance. "Where's the other photographer?"

"He got the hell out," Remy said. "She wanted nudes." He shuddered. "The female form is beautiful. Truly. But if you're not expecting to see it, it's a shock."

"You don't want me to strip down?" She snorted. "Okay, so he's gone?"

"He's outta here." Remy took the light stand out of the bag. "What's the game plan?"

She surveyed the layout of the room. The first rays of sun crept over the horizon. Once the sun rose a bit higher, the warm glow would enhance the models. She yanked open the curtains to the balcony the rest of the way.

"Mess up the sheets. I don't want a made bed." She rested her hands on her hips. "Let's move this lamp and find a newspaper."

Remy nodded and sprang into action. "The models aren't bad."

"Oh?" She arranged the pillows for a more lived-in look. "You got to know them?"

"We talked. They're just as confused by all this as you are. You weren't kidding. Iris got this ball rolling in record time." He turned his attention to the adjustable light. "I'm sure there were ulterior motives. The guys seem to think she picked her flavor of the month and wanted to show him off."

She snorted. "I'm not shocked."

"Well? How was he? I can see it all over your face, Moll." Remy sat on the edge of the bed. "Was he worth all this trouble?"

"Great—no." She sighed and sank onto the mattress

beside him. "Better than I expected and a far cry from the first time. Rem, I'm screwed."

Remy bowed his head. "You told him, didn't you?"

She didn't have to ask for clarification. She knew what he wanted her to say. "I blurted it right out. I love Austin Dean. I've lost my mind."

"Nah." He rubbed her back and his voice dropped an octave. "You've had a crush on him for as long as I've known you."

"It's so fucked up and complicated. We danced, laughed, fucked in the coatroom and it was so good." She glanced over at him and grinned. "Yeah, I did that."

"Roar." Remy chuckled. "I thought that was just my thing. Go you."

"We went to his apartment and talked some more. Had sex again. Snuggled in his bed." She flopped backward on the mattress. "His sheets. I could live in his sheets, just to smell him. He was better than my dreams."

"But?"

She closed her eyes and covered her face with her hands. "That's where it gets sticky. We went to the lakeshore to the park. He knew the way to my heart."

"Bought you an elephant ear, didn't he?" Remy laughed. "I could go for one right now."

"We rode the Ferris wheel and he asked if I'd ever get married again." She propped herself up on her elbows. "Do you believe it?"

"Fuck." Remy's eyes widened and his eyebrows rose. "Really? What'd you say?"

"I said I'd consider it, but the right guy had to come along. For a split second on the top of that wheel and then on the boardwalk, I actually let myself dream he could be the one." Saying the words out loud to Remy gave the whole situation a finality. She could want Austin all day, but in the end he wasn't hers for the taking.

"He still could be," Remy said. "I wouldn't, but he's not my type."

"If Iris has her way, it'll be impossible." Molly stood and crossed the room to her camera. She need to keep her hands busy. "It's like she rules the world and there's no way for me to overtake her."

"I know how you feel. I'm a rush-in-and-fall-in-love kind of guy and I seem to keep ending up alone. Normally, I'd tell you to kick her ass or something and demand what you want, but I think you should take things slower."

Molly pieced through what he'd said and nodded. So much made sense. She'd only been with Austin—if being with him was what they were defining the relationship as—for twenty-four hours. She was close and he loved not having to do much chasing.

She snapped her fingers. "Proximity."

"Huh?"

"I was the one with Austin at the gala. I was right there. Think about it. In the whole time you've known him, he doesn't go after the girl. She chases him because he's lazy. I was close so I got the golden ticket," Molly said. "He falls in and out of love in an instant. I should've known."

"No." Remy opened her laptop on the counter and shook his head. "That's not it."

"I've expected a lot out of him in the last twenty-four hours. I'm moving at breakneck speed like I always tell you not to do." She blew out a long breath. "If whatever happened with Austin is meant to happen again then it will. If not, I'm not out much. Until then, I'm not moving on assumption. If he wants to be with me then he'll decide when he's ready." Although saying those words out loud didn't reassure her. She knew Austin. He could talk a great game and fuck with the best of them but being honest with his feelings, he sucked.

The blond model opened the door between the parts of the suites. "Ready for us?"

Molly pasted on her best smile. She didn't have much choice. She'd been given the opportunity of a lifetime and refused to screw it up because she was too wrapped up in her nearly non-existent love life.

"Sure am," she replied. "Get the others and get dressed."

Chapter Nine

Austin marveled at Molly's ability to get the models to work with her. He'd just finished listening to them all complain about having to work with a new photographer, but when she'd told them what to do and how to pose, they'd cooperated. If he wasn't mistaken, the blond kept undressing her with his eyes. Austin's possessive streak reared its ugly head. He wanted to step between Molly and the blond specimen. But what in the hell was he going to say? She's mine. Not hardly. He'd fucked that up before the relationship had had a chance to start.

"Okay." Molly motioned for Austin. "You're up."

He clasped his hands in front of his cock. She had no idea how right she was. The thin boxer briefs weren't going to hide much of anything and if she kept grinning and waving her ass, he'd lose his shit.

"Austin?" Iris strolled into the room. "I see it's your turn."

"Yes." Molly nodded. Tension filled the space and she winced. "Did you have suggestions? I saw the list."

"I do." Iris shrugged out of her robe. She stood before them in nothing but a pair of skimpy panties. "I was thinking some couple photos would enhance the overall feel of the shoot."

He nearly choked. Jesus. Iris wasn't lacking in the looks department. She could walk the runway with ease and fancy clothing worked on her lithe frame, but her attitude was the killer. She knew she had the goods and wasn't afraid to show off. Then there was her belief everything and everyone belonged to her. He wasn't her toy.

Who was he kidding? He'd treated the women in his past

like playthings. Once he got bored, he moved on. Except with Molly. She'd been the one to hold his attention and how had he treated her? If he managed to get her to tell him she loved him again, he'd never leave her side. Talk about a big if.

"Of course." Molly's smile faltered for a split second before she regained her composure. "We'll do those first."

Austin shuddered. *Fucking hell.* He didn't want to pose with Iris. He wanted to be with Molly. Modeling wasn't his best idea. He belonged in the damn office with Molly, working on jingles and how to best sell sliced bread and peaches, not whatever he was about to do with Iris.

"Austin." Iris snapped her fingers. "You stand here." She tugged him over to the bed and eased up behind him. She wrapped her arms around him and gazed over his shoulder. "Snap this. It's sexy."

"Yes." Molly nodded, but her smile never wavered. She crouched behind her camera. "Looks good."

God, she was skilled at lying. He tried to appear as if he enjoyed Iris' hands on his body, but the emotion wasn't there. Iris had too much makeup on, too much perfume and her touch didn't draw out the bone-deep need within him like when he was with Molly.

"Is this good?" Iris wrapped her leg around Austin's and ground her crotch against his ass. "I love it."

Austin wished he could've seen Molly's expression, but she hid behind the camera.

"Well?" Iris growled. "Don't you talk?"

"Iris." Austin glanced back at her. "She's concentrating. If you want these to be right, then you've got to let her do her job." Christ. How in the hell this woman remained the head of her company and a force in the business world blew his mind. She demanded everything and thanked no one.

"We need to get this done. I've got other things to do before I can relax tonight." Iris swatted his butt. "Like you."

"I've got a slew of that pose and have room on the memory card for a few more," Molly said, interrupting Iris. "Did you have any others you wanted to do?"

"That's better and yes." She shoved Austin onto the bed. "Turn around and sit up, darling. This'll be the coup de grâce photo. Ultimate sexy and great for selling panties. Now shoot it from the side and make sure you get me in the best light."

"Sure." Molly ducked behind her camera as Iris arranged herself on Austin's lap.

Iris draped her arms around Austin's shoulders and straddled him. The bones in her butt dug into his thighs. He bit back a groan. Iris did nothing for him, but when he caught sight of Molly his dick reacted. She licked her lips then tucked a stray lock of hair behind her ear. He wanted to trade Iris out for Molly. Hell, those pictures would be sexy because he'd have the woman in his heart in his arms.

"Ooh, you're hard for me." Iris leaned forward, a whisper away from his lips. "So hot."

"Iris?" Molly touched Iris' arm. "May I rearrange you a bit? Just to fix the composition."

Iris narrowed her eyes. "How?"

"Well, you want sexy, but you're not permitted to have nudity in your catalog—not as much nudity as you're willing to show. Melinda let me know in no uncertain terms in the email." Molly moved Iris' arm. "So, if you move just a little, the viewer still knows you're topless and about to have sex with him. We just won't see your breasts." Her voice cracked on the word 'sex'. "It's tasteful but steamy."

Austin met her gaze. He wanted to apologize and beg her to forgive him. Molly slipped behind the camera again. He had no idea how she managed to get through the shoot, especially when he wanted to scream and get the hell out of there. She maintained her composure so well.

"Jesus, she's demanding," Iris hissed. "These had better be the best fucking pictures or I will *so* fire her."

He ground his teeth to keep from replying. If he did, he'd say something he'd regret and he wouldn't do anyone any favors.

"That's better," Molly said. "Ready?"

"As I'll ever be." Iris rubbed against his crotch. Something burned in her eyes — passion? Desire? The need to fuck? He wasn't sure and didn't want to find out.

Austin held still until Molly snapped the last shot. She'd used harsher lighting than the last time and his shirt stuck to his back. He needed to move and strip out of the shirt, but not with Iris in the room.

Melinda opened the door a crack. "Iris? You've got a call. The California office has some questions I can't answer."

Iris crooked one eyebrow. "Fine. Send the boys back in, but don't let Austin leave." She climbed off his lap. "I'll be right back, baby."

'Baby'. Fucking hell.

"I'm almost done," Molly said. "A few solo images with Austin and we'll be out of your hair."

"Fine." She waved her hand and snorted. "Clean up and get the hell out, then." Iris sashayed out of the room and disappeared into the adjacent suite.

Austin fell backward on the bed and groaned. When in the hell would the day end?

"That was interesting," Remy said. "And one of the most awkward things I've ever witnessed. Would you like me to start cleaning up? Or what?"

"I have to do some solo work with Austin." Molly sighed and shook her head. "I just want to get this over."

"The magic isn't there." Austin stood and crossed the room to her. "Rem? Can I have a minute? Maybe lock the door to the other suites and check out the balcony. It's a nice balcony." Austin fought the urge to reach for Molly. "Please?"

"Sure." Remy flicked the lock to the adjacent suites then broke out in a fit of laughter. "I don't care what you do, just don't get caught." He disappeared onto the balcony and tugged the door shut.

"You didn't have to kick him out." Molly twiddled with the camera. "He's harmless."

"I'm not worried about him," Austin said. He toyed with a lock of her hair. "But the magic only happened when it was you and me."

"True."

"I don't want to do this alone." He slid his hand into her back pocket. Just touching her helped to right his world on its axis. "We need to talk."

"We need to get this done." Molly eased away and turned her back to him. "Over and *done*."

"Molls." Her curt tone cut him deep. "I'm sorry." He deserved a tongue lashing from her but still. He wanted things to get better, not worse.

"You're following your dream." She scratched her forehead then nodded to the clothing on the table. "I believe she wanted you in the black shirt and gray shorts. You're supposed to look like you're spending a lazy afternoon with a book. Did you bring your glasses and a book?"

"No." He'd had enough. "I'm not doing it."

"That's helpful." She rolled her eyes. "Iris could come back at any moment. We need to do what she wants, so I can leave."

"Don't." He wasn't ready to give up on the special connection they shared. "Where's your phone?"

"In my bag," she replied. "Why?"

Austin whipped his shirt over his head then retrieved the phone from her shoulder bag. "If we're going to do this, I know what images should be captured." He tucked Molly to his chest. "The theme should be a lazy afternoon with the woman he's seeing." He couldn't say the word love and not out loud just yet. He sat on the edge of the bed and dragged her onto his lap. "Straddle me."

"Austin—she could walk in at any time." Molly collapsed onto his thighs and faced him. "What are you doing?"

"She won't. If Remy locked the door then she's stuck over there." He brushed her hair from her face and cupped the back of her head. "I'm sorry."

"Don't worry about it."

"I will." He breathed in her scent. She was his drug and he needed a fix. "Take this off." He toyed with the hem of her shirt. "Please? She won't walk in on us and Remy isn't watching."

Molly hesitated then yanked the tunic over her head. Her hair fell around her shoulders and her skin flushed. She covered her chest with her arms.

"You have no idea how much you turn me on." He curled his fingers under her chin and angled the phone to take a photo.

"Austin." She tensed again. "What are you doing?"

"Taking the photos that were meant to be in this campaign. Pictures for later." He dropped the phone long enough to arrange her arms around his neck. "Better."

"I don't know how these are better." Goosebumps rose on her skin. She opened and closed her mouth a couple of times but didn't say anything.

"Babe, your idea for this campaign never involved a ton of models or an overzealous owner sticking her nose in. It was always meant to be intimate—two people or maybe one—but very everyday and casual." He brushed his nose against hers. "I get it."

She tugged the hairs at the base of his skull. When she met his gaze, his heart shattered all over again. She was holding on to her restraint with the thinnest thread. One more pull and she'd come apart. He refused to do that to her.

"I want these pictures of us because you're very important to me. I don't care if no one else sees them. What matters is that you know how I feel." He kept his gaze fixed on hers and tugged her closer. He pressed the button to capture the moment over and over. Molly didn't fight him. She bowed her head and closed her eyes.

"Show me the innocence, babe." He'd use up the memory card in her phone before he quit taking pictures of her. "Let me see your sweetness and the sexiness you want to hide."

"Austin." Her lips parted and her voice cracked. "I meant what I said. I love you."

Hell yeah. He mashed his mouth on hers and pushed between her lips. He needed to taste her. She made him complete. He splayed his hands on her back and held her closer. His life wouldn't be the same without her.

"Oh fuck," Remy shouted.

Startled, Molly broke the kiss. Her eyes widened and the color drained from her face. "We've been caught."

"No, but you're about to be." Remy locked the balcony door then ran to the main suite door. "Get dressed," he growled.

Molly scurried off Austin's lap and yanked her shirt back over her head. "Stretch out on the bed and hide that." She nodded to Austin's erection. "Please?"

"This isn't over." He crawled onto the bed and rested on his belly. He didn't have his glasses but he grabbed the newspaper anyway. "Go for it."

Molly shoved her phone into her back pocket then grabbed her camera. She moved around him, clicking away. She gripped the camera tightly. The worry lines etched around her eyes.

Fuck. He'd added to her stress.

"Three, two, one..." Remy darted out of the way as the door to the suite opened.

Iris gripped the front of her robe and notched her chin in the air. "Time to vacate." She strode up to Austin. "I'm sorry, baby, but you're going to have to go, too." She patted his ass. "But you'll be going with me tonight to California. I want to show you off at the movie premiere."

"What premiere?" He knew nothing about a trip, or being her arm candy. "I can't. I have to go to work tomorrow."

"Correction. You're accompanying me. As far as CDL is concerned, you're no longer an employee. Ms. Neff? According to your boss, you've got tomorrow to finish my photo spread." Iris narrowed her eyes. "Say your goodbyes to Austin. After tonight, he's not coming back to Ohio for a long time."

Iris sashayed out of the suite, leaving Remy, Molly and

143

Austin alone. Austin stared at the door for a long moment. What the fuck had just happened? *Say your goodbyes?* He wasn't going anywhere and certainly wasn't leaving Ohio for a *long* time. Who did she think she was to order him around? He didn't want to go anywhere, especially not with her.

Remy hefted the light bag onto his shoulder and ducked out of the room.

Molly tucked her camera into her bag then shut down her laptop. Although she appeared calm, her cheeks paled and a muscle in her jaw tensed. One more word from just about anyone and she'd blow her top. She didn't deserve to be treated like shit. He had to do something to keep her there and to fix the situation. He couldn't stand to see her upset. Beyond that, he couldn't handle knowing he'd cut her so deeply.

"Molly, hold up." Austin eased up behind her and massaged her shoulders. "Just...give me a second."

"What for?" She placed the laptop into her messenger bag. "You got your wish."

"No, I didn't." He slipped her phone from her back pocket and scrolled through her messages. He sent the photos he'd taken of them together to his phone. He wanted something to remember her by until he got everything straightened out.

"I have things to do and a life to lead. You've chosen your path." She took the phone from him. "I don't blame you. Ever since college, you wanted more than Ohio had to offer."

"I didn't have you." He clasped her hands in his. "Babe, I messed up."

"You went after what you wanted."

"Molly?"

"I'm never going to be Iris—I don't want to be, but if you need me, I'm always a phone call away." She paused. The smile on her lips didn't quite shine in her eyes. "Just don't forget about me. Mistake or not, you're my favorite." Molly wriggled free of him and hurried out of the suite.

When she left, his heart went with her. Being with her wasn't wrong, but letting her stroll out of his life was and he'd never be the same. He shouldn't let her go so easily but he'd done too much damage. If he kept pushing, she'd never give him another chance. Then again, she'd given in pretty quickly, too. Why? Because he'd hurt her so many times. He'd teased her in the past into thinking they had a chance at a relationship. Now that he knew who he wanted, he was in a tight spot with Iris. *Christ.* Was the world out to get him?

Austin raked his fingers through his hair and headed into the other suite. Two of the models had gone, but one lingered behind. Austin snatched his clothes from the bed and glanced at the guy.

"Did you enjoy the shoot?" Austin asked. He wasn't sure what else to say to him but the silence was deafening.

"I did. I'm Clint, by the way." Clint offered his hand. "I've seen more than my share of these circuses. I've posed for book covers, print campaigns, underwear campaigns for online venues and nothing was like this."

"Oh?" Austin narrowed his eyes. *Just try to tell me Molly did a bad job. You'll regret it.* "How?" He shrugged into his shirt and ditched the underwear in favor of his original boxer shorts. "I enjoyed it."

"It was good. The photographer knew how to get the best out of us. Some can't do that. She's a natural. She's also hot as fuck," Clint said. "I heard you know her. Think you could snag me her number?"

"For professional reasons?" He stepped into his jeans and straightened to his full height.

Clint shrugged. "She could do my next set of headshots, sure, but I was thinking more along the lines of dinner and dancing. Somewhere hip, happening and with a throbbing base."

"Unless you're taking her to a metal concert, she's not into throbbing base." Austin yanked his socks then shoes on and stood. "She's also not single." *Fuck you, asshole. She's mine...once I get things sorted out.*

"Huh. I didn't get the in-a-relationship vibe from her. More the lonely, single and hoping to mingle one." Clint waggled his eyebrows then frowned. "I thought you and Sommerville were a thing. God knows you suck ass when it comes to posing."

He wasn't that bad. *Asshole.* "Sommerville thinks we're a thing. We're not."

"Not a thing is the reason she's taking you to San Fran? To show off her not-boyfriend? Come on." Clint stepped toe to toe with Austin. "You suck as a model and as a boyfriend. She'll get bored with you like she did with the rest of us. Either don't get involved with her and give the photographer what she wants or keep playing Iris' lap dog. Women like Ms. Neff won't wait around forever."

"You're right." Austin strode past Clint and out of the suite. He still wasn't sure where he stood with Iris, but he sure as shit wasn't going to California. He'd give Molly a few hours to decompress, but he wasn't taking no for an answer tonight. He needed his woman.

* * * *

Molly bobbed her head to the music and roved her gaze over the bevy of muscle-clad men on the dance floor. She hadn't wanted to go out initially, but once Remy had mentioned free beers and admission to Clutch, his favorite bar, she hadn't been able to refuse. She hoped Remy would find a partner — if even just for the night. He deserved a roll in the hay after the shit he'd been through with Javier.

Remy wandered back to where she stood and finger-combed his hair from his forehead. "Struck out again."

"You'll homer sooner or later." She downed a swig of her beer. "Or you're destined to live out your life with me and we'll both be single."

"That's not a horrendous thing, you know...you and I

146

ending up together." He took the beer from her and drained the bottle. "Maybe that's it. You and I were supposed to go through all this together and realize we were the couple all along."

"You really believe that?" She snorted. "Remy, you're not *that* desperate." He wasn't interested in her, unless she miraculously sprouted a dick.

"Javier used to say attraction knew no sex."

"Words to live by—except they came from your ex who was out fucking someone else." She bumped shoulders with him. "You'll find a guy who makes your blood heat, your cock hard and the rest of the world disappear. He's out there."

"Then where in the hell is he?" Remy laughed and shook his head. "Probably with Austin."

"Probably."

"Let's head back to the townhouse. There's nothing here I want." Remy tossed the beer bottle into a garbage can. "Ready?"

"Yep." She linked arms with him and headed out of the bar. The chilly night air wrapped around her and sharpened her senses. It also got her thinking. "Rem? How would you describe me?"

"Hmm... Caring, stunning and smarter than I'll ever be," he said. "Why? How'd Austin describe you?"

"I have a bright smile, a sweet personality and I'm loyal." She refused to tell Remy how Austin had complimented her breasts and cunt. That could wait for later.

"Well, it's true. All three. You're the only one who's stuck by me all this time. Ten boyfriends, two townhouses and one big-ass move. Yeah, when I ever get married, you're going to be my best person."

"Why is it the moment I want to call you an ass, you say something sweet and make me change my mind?" she asked. Cars whizzed by on the street and the headlights flooded the sidewalk. She clutched Remy's arm. "You're such an ass."

"No, I want ass. Big difference, but I do have my charms." He grinned. "I'm sweet because if I don't have you in my life, I'm lost. Kind of like Austin, and speaking of him, why do you think he put you down?"

"He wants to be with Iris. Wants the popularity she can give him. The only thing I've got going for me is I'm sweet and loyal." She held up her phone. "He and Iris made the gossip sites." She swiped her thumb across the screen and pulled up the page. "See? As of three days ago, they're the new power couple."

"I didn't get that vibe from him, but I did see the website. He doesn't look thrilled." Remy turned onto their street. "Have you heard from him since you left the suite?"

"No and I don't want to. He knows how to reel me in. He pushes me away and screws with my head then gets me to come back. That's all that shit was—his way of keeping me around. She'll ditch him and he'll be on my doorstep." She shivered. "I can't do this any longer."

"So you'll dodge him in order to prove you're not his go-to girl?" Remy shook his head and groaned.

"Remember when we were in the third grade and I declared to everyone I was going to marry you?" She rested her head on his shoulder. "I was so certain."

"Who could forget? You stood on the table in the cafeteria."

She'd also earned her first detention, too. At the time, she'd thought the world had been ending. "Even though I said it, I knew in my gut it wasn't going to happen. I knew you were gay before you did."

"I remember that, too. That time we watched the music awards and we both ogled the boy band. You told me to stop drooling."

"I did." She laughed. The memory came back fresh. She'd begged her mother for him to come over and they'd sat in front of the television together. Remy had mentioned the lead boy-bander had a nice ass. She'd agreed and noticed Remy wiping his mouth. At the tender age of fifteen, she'd figured out his sexuality.

"What's my past got to do with Austin?" Remy opened the door to their building and ushered her inside.

"Plenty." She waited until she and Remy were in his townhouse. She flopped onto the couch. "Austin and I were in design class during our sophomore year and I had this grand idea that I'd end up with him. I kept my mouth shut because he was with Jessica at the time. I was so out of his league, but even then I had the same feeling I had with you. I can want him all night long, but as soon as the daylight comes I'm not good enough."

"Bullshit. You're beautiful and if he can't figure that out then that's his loss," Remy growled.

"Doesn't matter. I should've kept things platonic with him. The moment I make it romantic, reality hits me upside the head. I'm not going to end up with you or him."

"You're a romantic at heart." Remy poured two fingers of whiskey in two glasses then handed her one. "You love him and have since I've known you."

"It's not true any longer." Who was she kidding? She still loved him but she knew the truth.

"You expect me to believe you've gotten over him? I don't because I can see it in your eyes. You know he could be the one—once he gets his head out of his ass—and that scares you. What if it does work out? Your self-esteem might be in the pits, but if he truly loves you, he won't care. He'll build you up."

"I'm being realistic. Guys like Austin don't want women like me. They marry women like Iris and move to the suburbs to have two-point-seven children."

"Who has a point-seven kid?" Remy downed the whiskey. "Disregard."

"You know what I mean." She was trying to explain away her hurt, but it wasn't working.

"Shockingly, I do understand." Remy tapped his ring on the glass and didn't say anything for a few moments. He glanced at her then averted his gaze. "Look, he messed up. All guys mess up. It's in our DNA. That said, you can't keep

149

discounting yourself. There's no rule saying he can't be interested in you and falling for you. Give Iris a run for her damn money and show Austin what he's missing. You're a wonderful person with a hot bod and gorgeous eyes. If he passes you up then that's his loss and you're the wiser."

"You almost sound like you like me."

"I've always loved you, Molly, but until you grow a cock or we're both forty and unmarried, I'm not hopping in the sack with you. It would be too weird."

"I love you, too."

"You can't dodge Austin for the rest of your life. He'll come back to CDL eventually."

Molly sighed and sipped the whiskey. She considered Remy's words. He was right. If Austin couldn't make up his mind then boo on him. Her confidence, though still in tatters, lifted a bit. She'd never be five foot eight inches tall, but she needed to start embracing her positives and her flaws if she wanted to move forward. She stood and finished the whiskey.

She didn't have to go into work in the morning, but she had over a thousand photos to sort through and she wanted the Aura fiasco over with as soon as possible.

"I wish Dylan would've called me back. That rat bastard said he was interested and he couldn't fucking call." Remy groaned. "I wasted time waiting on him and nothing happened."

She stared at him for what seemed like an eternity. Remy had taken the initiative with Dylan? Nice, but the guy hadn't returned Remy's call? *What an asshole!* She leaned over and hugged Remy.

"Just like you said with Austin, if he can't see the hot guy with a heart of gold when he looks at you then he's not worthy." She kissed Remy on the cheek. "I'm sorry, I'm heading home. Sounds like we don't deserve to be alone tonight, but I've got to work on those pictures tomorrow."

"I understand." Remy waved but he didn't smile. "Call me if you need me. Call me if you don't. Hell, just call me and make sure I'm still alive." He didn't seem like himself and she wished she could've stayed with him a while longer. Remy's luck with men wasn't working out lately and what did she do? Crab about her jacked-up love life.

"I will, so don't do anything you'll regret. I'll call you tomorrow and we'll get lunch. Deal?" Once he nodded, Molly headed down the hall to her town home. She stuffed her key into the lock and twisted. Her phone rang as she opened the door. Good God. Now what? She tucked the phone between her ear and her shoulder. "Hello?"

"Molly, it's Roscoe."

She nodded, although her boss couldn't see her. Talking to him never ceased to put her on edge. Partly because he had the power to fire her, and partly because she worried he'd changed his mind about her working with Aura and Austin. "Mr. Lee, hi. What can I do for you? I'm sorry I wasn't at work today. I thought Ms. Sommerville explained the situation."

"She did, and that's why I'm calling. Loaning you and Austin out has been a good move for CDL. I've seen the initial photos. You should be doing photography instead of your ad work, but I shouldn't tell you that because I don't want to lose you as part of the team."

"Thank you." She hadn't seen *that* coming. The last she knew, Mr. Lee wanted his people to stay within the company. This was an extraordinary circumstance, but she'd still kind of expected to get into trouble.

"That said, I'm not loaning you out again. This was a one-time deal. The results were phenomenal, but I can't risk my best people. Speaking of my people, Austin is leaving us."

"Leaving?" she blurted. "Since when?"

"Since this morning. Because he's being let go from CDL, I'm pairing you up with Tyson."

She wobbled and sank onto the arm of the sofa. Yet another thing she hadn't seen coming — Austin succeeding in getting fired. Or had Iris speeded up the process?

"Your new partner is eager to get up to speed. You will be

ready to go come Wednesday morning, correct?"

She massaged her forehead with the tips of her fingers as she replayed her boss' words. She needed the extra few seconds to understand what he'd said.

"Working with Tyson?" She didn't have anything against him but she preferred working with Austin. "I should be able to get things rolling." She paused. "Some of my work is with Austin. Is the rumor true? Did he quit or was he reassigned?"

"He's moving on to new assignments."

"I see." She bet she knew what assignments, too. She'd hoped Mr. Lee would've been more forthcoming, but no. "I'm sorry he's leaving, then." '

For the first time since she'd started working in the advertising game at CDL, she didn't regret her partnership with Austin or the work she'd done with him. She closed her eyes. She wanted Austin back.

"When you come in on Wednesday, I'll move Tyson into your office. Sound good?"

She didn't have much choice. "Yes, sir." She nodded again and opened her eyes. Her life wasn't working out quite the way she'd planned. *Go figure.*

"I'll see you at the office on Wednesday, then. Good evening," Mr. Lee said.

"Sure." She swiped her thumb across the screen to end the call then dropped the phone. No Austin, but a new partner. What the hell? She stared off into space and simply existed for a few moments. Her head ached and she needed a stiff drink.

"Molly?"

She sat up straighter. Austin? She had to be imagining him. He wouldn't be there. Couldn't. He was on his way to California or something. Iris wanted him close by and probably had him holed up in another suite or penthouse somewhere.

"Molly."

Damn it. His voice was too strong and clear. She looked

back at the door. Was it possible for him to be in the hallway? She'd never forgive herself if she didn't check. "Austin?"

"It's me, babe. Let me in."

Molly stood and smoothed her fingers through her hair. For a split second, she hesitated. This could be a trap or something to embarrass her. It could be the big goodbye she swore was coming. She'd never get closure if she didn't give him the chance. She crossed the room and peeked through the security hole. Austin stood alone in the hallway. She opened the door a crack—just enough to be sure he was really there and not a figment of her overactive imagination.

"Just me." He opened his arms. "Got some time for me? Maybe some sugar, too?"

Against her better judgment, she opened the door. "I'm out of sugar but I'm not afraid to help a friend." Closure or another night of passion with Austin, she needed answers or hot sex and she'd take both.

"That's all I am now, isn't it? A friend." Austin's shoulders sagged as he strode into her townhouse. "I've got it coming." His eyes widened. "But look at you. You're a sight for sore eyes."

"I went clubbing with Remy. Kind of. He clubbed and I kept him out of trouble."

"He had the best date out there tonight, then." Austin smoothed a lock of her hair between his fingers. "I'm jealous."

"And I'm confused." Molly snicked the lock and leaned against the doorframe. A million questions flooded her brain, but she wasn't sure what to say. She wanted to run into his arms or slug him for not making up his mind. The ache behind her eyes intensified. *Damn it.* "Why are you here?" she blurted. "I thought you were going to California."

"I am, but first I need to talk to you." Austin cupped her jaw in both hands. "And kiss you until I change my mind about leaving."

Chapter Ten

Austin dragged his nose along hers and breathed in her scent. He was crazy to leave her and nuts about her. She owned his soul and held his heart in her hands.

"I don't understand." She didn't pull away from him but didn't kiss him back. "Don't you have to go?"

"I do. The contract states I'm property of Aura for the next two weeks. Whatever promotional needs they have, I'm their man." He grasped her hands and tugged her to the couch. He needed her close. He collapsed beside her and pulled her down onto his lap. "Better." Being with her relaxed him. He'd made the jacked-up decision to follow his opportunistic dreams. He never should've signed the contract. Never should've agreed to break from CDL for a while, or to implode the relationship with Molly before he'd given them a chance.

She rested her arms around his neck. "I heard you lost your job at CDL. Mr. Lee called. I've got a new partner. Didn't want one."

"I know. He told me they gave all my work to Tyson — sounds like they gave him my partner, too. Trust me, I'm not happy about that. I thought the agreement was me being loaned out, not me getting canned and you getting a new partner." The thought of her working with someone else soured in his brain. They were a team. He lived by the theory of no regrets but he wished he'd never seen the underwear campaign. No, the campaign had been the catalyst to bring him together on romantic terms with Molly. He regretted nothing of his time with her.

"Tyson isn't a bad guy, but he's not my ideal partner."

She shrugged and half-smiled. "Are you happy?"

Not ideal? No shit. The guy had a wife and kid, yet he hit on every woman at the firm. Austin trusted Molly's judgment and knew in his heart she wouldn't fall for Tyson, but still. He wanted to be there with her — and not just at work.

"Austin? If this is what you've always wanted, then say so. I won't stand in the way of your dream."

"No." He met her gaze. He'd been raw before but nothing like when he looked into her eyes. "I thought I knew what I wanted from life. Ever since college, art and advertising were secondary. I wanted to be famous." He placed his finger over her lips. "I succeeded — kind of. Your photo of me is going onto billboards. I'll be in magazines, but it's not what I want. Not any longer." The taste of her kiss and the feel of her body around his lingered in his mind. She'd imprinted herself in his memory.

Molly straddled his lap but folded her arms. Her eyes shimmered with unshed tears. Everything was so fucked-up and he had fourteen days before he could fix anything.

"I've got two weeks before I'm free of Aura and Iris. Two weeks until I'm back here with you and figuring out where in the hell I'm going to work. Two weeks of my heart breaking because I'm fond of you." He kissed her. He'd never get enough of her and didn't want to leave her. What was he supposed to say to get her to give him another chance? "Can you give me that long? It's not forever, but it's nothing I can change." Christ. Why wasn't he telling her he loved her? Fear hit him hard. The idea of committing scared him shitless. Could he be faithful to her? Yeah. She made his heart beat. But what if he messed up? Would he be the right man for her in the long run?

"You'll get out there and find someone else, so don't worry about me. You'll be just fine." Her chin quivered. "Tyson isn't you, but I've got to keep working. I've got bills to pay and a life to live."

Fucking hell. She wasn't fighting for them. She was giving him space and allowing him to walk away. *Hell no.* He refused to give up on them, not now that he finally knew what he wanted from his life. "I'm coming back to you. There's too much unfinished business between us."

"Sure." She didn't sound like she believed anything she or he said. "Remember that later at the movie premiere and Iris showers you with gifts."

"You're making me sound like a gigantic ass." He swiped the tears from her cheeks. "I've been a dick, yeah, but come on. Give me a chance. I'll only be away for two weeks. For Iris, that's nothing. Besides, she means zilch to me. I've had my issues before but not since we started this. You're the only one for me. Please? Don't walk away from me now. I'll beg. Whatever you want. I'm yours. What do I say to convince you this is for real?"

"I'm trying to believe but I know you."

"You do." He didn't want Molly on that list. She deserved more. He met her gaze again. The redness in her eyes brought out the blue in her irises. Jesus. He'd hurt her and done so many times. He needed to stop the bleeding, so to speak.

"What are you thinking, Molls? Let me in. I'm dying here and it's my own fault."

She snorted. "Dying. You're overdramatic." She sighed and averted her gaze. "Something Remy said came to mind. He just told me tonight that I needed to give you something to miss."

"He's a wise man." He already missed her and knew exactly what Remy wanted to get through his thick head. Why screw around and mess up the good thing he had? All he needed to do was look at the photos on his phone. He'd never again have a connection like he shared with Molly. Once he got out of the contract, he belonged to her.

She unfolded her arms and draped them around his neck. She toyed with the hairs at the base of his skull and sent shivers down his spine. "He also said, if whatever we've got between us is meant to be, then it'll work out. I don't know if he's right, but I don't disagree."

"Makes sense. No one knows what fate has in store." But he didn't care. He wanted her. As long as she loved him, he could face the shit storm he'd created and make it back to her. "Did you mean what you said when you told me you loved me?" Christ, he hoped she still cared about him that much. He loved her.

Molly nodded. "It's not the same as back in college. It's more mature and stronger, but yeah, I'm still crazy about you." She didn't look him in the eye. "I've lost my mind. I want something with the one man I can't have."

Fuck, fuck, fuck. "You've got me, babe. I'm right here with you. All night if you want because I've got a lot of making up to do and nowhere else I'd rather be. Let me stay and show you how I feel about you." He brushed his lips over hers. The more he kissed her, the more he needed her.

"You don't love me," she whispered. "You don't love anyone."

"You don't know that." Austin scooped her into his arms and carried her to the bedroom. He wasn't going to waste any more time. "I belong to you. Heart and soul." The confession not only freed his mind but lifted his spirits. He'd never been so brutally honest with anyone, not even himself. "I think about you when I'm not at work and I wonder what you're doing. Once we slept together again, I remembered just how much I needed you. I'm happiest right here."

"But—"

Austin kissed away her words. She didn't trust him and shouldn't—he'd screwed with her good nature and now he saw the error of his ways. Maybe he couldn't say the word love out loud to her but he could show her.

He carried her to the bed and arranged her on the mattress. He kissed her, imprinting her sweet taste on his brain. He wanted every nuance etched into his memory. He kissed along her neck to her earlobe then across her cheek to her mouth. Each touch and nip sent shivers along his spine and heat to his cock.

Austin crawled on top of her and brushed her hair from her face. He gazed into her eyes. Damn. He'd seen her so many times but never really appreciated her in the way she deserved. Molly sucked in her stomach and held her breath. She pushed her knees together.

"You don't have to be something you think I want." He settled beside her and parted her legs. "Be yourself."

"There's a lot of me." She blushed from her cheeks down to her chest. "I'm embarrassed." The muscle in her jaw twitched. "You're perfect and I'm...not."

"So?" He smoothed his hand across her belly. "I like you the way you are."

"You're aiming low with me." She averted her gaze. "God."

"Enough." He popped the button on her jeans. "You cut on yourself too much."

"I'm being honest."

"I'd say you're being too hard on yourself." He dragged her jeans and panties down her legs. "I don't care what anyone else thinks. You're beautiful. I'm attracted to the woman on the outside, and especially the one on the inside."

"Austin." She sat up and stilled his hands. "Stop."

"You're making foreplay difficult." He curled his fingers under her chin. "I'm not going anywhere."

"Sorry. My confidence—it's..."

"Babe." Fuck. He'd been part of the problem. He'd have to work twice as hard to build her back up and damn it, he'd do it. She mattered that much. He eased her shirt over her head. Her breasts strained against the lace of her bra. She still wore the teardrop pendant and the platinum sparkled on her skin. She covered her breasts with both hands.

"Don't hide, babe." He eased her back onto the bed and stretched out, fully clothed, beside her again. He cupped her pussy and speared his middle finger between her cunt lips. Her tiny gasp sent his senses reeling. He pressed her clit in order to get another whimper from her.

"So wet," he murmured in her ear. She might've been

irritated with him, but her body wanted him. She responded so well and thank God. He craved her.

Austin buried his face in the curve of her neck and kissed her. He tasted the bit of perspiration on her skin and memorized her. He massaged her pussy, rubbing her cream over his fingers before he slid his middle finger into her channel.

Her heat and excitement turned him on. She moaned and spurred his desire. Every nerve ending in his body stood at attention. His cock throbbed behind his zipper and the blood coursed through his veins. Shit, he needed her.

Molly planted her feet on the bed and writhed. "Austin." She slapped his belly then caressed down to his denim-covered cock. She worked him into a frenzy. "Austin," she murmured. "Oh."

"Love hearing you say my name." He didn't want to leave her but he needed to get naked. Now. He scooted off the mattress long enough to shuck his shirt and shove his jeans and boxers down his legs. The garments wadded up at his feet. "Fuck." He wobbled and kicked out of his shoes and the tangled up clothes. He stumbled forward and landed on Molly. He managed to break his fall with his hands to keep from crushing her. "Sorry."

"It's nice to see you're not always smooth." She draped her arms around his neck. "You're human."

"I'm not a superhuman or anything like that." He wondered what she meant. He'd made plenty of mistakes in his lifetime. "Happens to all of us." He braced his knees on either side of her legs and toyed with her hair. "Why?"

"You're perfect." She pressed her lips together then sighed. "Sorry."

"Sweetheart, you're fine. I love you the way you are." He kissed her lips, neck and down to her breasts. Power radiated through him as he eased the cups of her bra down and exposed her nipples. God, she had beautiful nipples. He sucked one tight bead in his teeth and pinched the other.

"Damn." She threaded her fingers into his hair and

tugged. "Austin."

"Tell me what to do." He scraped his teeth across her sensitive skin. He loved her moans and whimpers. The noises told him he'd pleased her. All he wanted was to make her happy.

"Don't stop." She held his head to her breast. "I forgot how everything feels when you're playing with my tits. I feel it to my core."

"Beautiful." He sucked on her nipple again as she pulled his hair. Pleasure-filled pain shot from his scalp to his dick. *Fuck, yeah.* He surfaced for air long enough to meet her hungry gaze. "I need you."

"I'm right here." Molly let go of his head. "Love me?"

"You bet I do." He wasn't sure if she'd asked a question about his devotion to her or if she wanted him to make love to her but he didn't care. He wanted to lap at her cream and bring her to orgasm before they had sex but he'd do that later. Right now, he needed to be inside her. "Got rubbers?"

"In my dresser." She rolled him over and pinned him beneath her.

Her nipples grazed his chest and his nerve endings tingled. He palmed her ass. She had such a perfect ass — more than enough to grab, and so soft.

Molly crawled off him and strode across the small room to her dresser. Her bra straps slid down her shoulders. She glanced back at him before she unhooked the lingerie.

"Yeah." He crossed his ankles and propped himself up on his elbows to improve his view. "You have no idea how sexy you are." She embodied every one of his fantasies. Austin stroked his dick to prep himself — not that he'd need much help. He wanted her on top of him.

She grinned then retrieved a box of condoms from the drawer. Molly returned to the bed and ripped the cardboard. Condoms tumbled onto the bed and floor. The tips of her ears tinged red and she met his gaze. Her smile melted.

"Gives us a reason to make love a hundred times tonight." He picked up one of the wrappers and tore the corner.

She had nothing to be embarrassed about—he loved her clumsiness and the way she blushed. He sheathed his dick and patted his thigh. "Come here."

She wrapped her fingers around his erection, stroking him.

He arched his back. Desire filled his brain. "Love that." He groaned and grasped her wrists. "Ride me."

Her smile returned as she crawled onto his lap. She straddled his thighs. Inch by inch, she sank onto his erection. When he filled her completely, she winced.

Austin cupped her jaw in both hands and eased her flush against his chest. He kissed her. The way she overwhelmed him…he'd never be the same without her. "I can't tell where you end and I begin," he murmured. "Feels so good."

"Feels full." Her hair slipped in front of her eyes again before she tipped her head back. She sat up and palmed her breasts, tweaking her nipples.

Seeing her so comfortable with her body and pleasuring herself kicked his desire up another couple of notches. "Do that again. Rub your titties."

Molly met his gaze and her lips parted. She rolled her nipples between her thumbs and forefingers. Her sharp intake of breath echoed in the room. She rocked her hips. "Do you like that?"

"I do." He held onto her waist and braced his feet. The better grasp helped him increase his leverage. The deeper he surged into her pussy, the closer he came to climax. He pumped his hips. Damn.

Molly closed her eyes and moaned. "Yes." She stopped rubbing her breasts and tensed. She slowed his thrusts. "Fuck." She slipped off his lap and propped herself up on her hands and knees. "Like this. Harder."

He didn't need more instruction. Austin scooted off the bed and embraced her. He filled her cunt again and grasped her hips. The moment he sank balls deep into her, his restraint splintered. He swatted her ass.

"Oh, fuck," she blurted.

"Like that?" he asked. He'd acted on instinct but hadn't been sure if she'd go along.

"Love it. Harder." She backed into him, meeting him thrust for thrust.

Fuck, yeah. There was her adventurous side. He built a steady rhythm and moved with abandon. Each time he slapped her ass, she moaned and writhed on his cock. The sound of her and skin on skin echoed.

"Oh, my God. Yeah." She flipped her hair over her shoulder. "More."

Austin wrapped his hand around her tresses and tugged. He swatted her ass once more with his free hand. Molly required his full attention and he refused to deny her anything. He loved every moment of being with her.

Molly trembled beneath him. "Austin." Her movements turned ragged and she panted.

"Come for me, babe." He teetered on the edge of orgasm, too. The heat spiraled through his body and desire overwhelmed him. His thoughts blurred. All he saw was her. Austin slammed into her body. "Come for me."

The orgasm was so close. Just a few more thrusts and he'd tumble over the edge.

Molly tensed and clawed at the sheets. She clamped down on him from within. "Oh, fuck," she said and drew out the words. She bowed her head and buried her face in the bedding. Her pussy spasmed as she climaxed.

Austin gave in to his orgasm. He'd held himself in check for too long. He buried his dick to the hilt and groaned. "Fucking balls." He added a couple more thrusts as he emptied his seed into the condom. "Jesus."

The room spun and when Molly collapsed on the bed, he settled on top of her. He kissed her shoulder. "Babe." He'd have to move, but he didn't want to—not yet.

"Stay with me tonight." She laced her fingers with his. "Stay with me."

"There's nowhere else I'd rather be." He eased out of her pussy and managed to stand. He needed to ditch the rubber before he fell asleep beside her. He scrubbed his face with the back of his hand until the room righted. Once he had his bearings, he removed the spent condom.

Molly crawled between the sheets and patted the mattress. "Join me."

Austin tossed the rubber into the waste basket then stretched out beside her. He gathered Molly in his arms. He'd have to leave her in the morning, but for now, he'd bask in the perfection of the moment. Once he sorted out his life and finished his obligations to Iris, he'd spend the rest of his life with Molly. He belonged with her.

* * * *

In the morning, Austin dressed and checked his watch. Shit. If he wanted to make the flight, he needed to get moving.

He found her in the kitchen and snagged her in his arms. "It's almost time."

"I know." She rested her hands on his. "I expected this."

Fuck. He knew he'd have to leave, but his heart refused to cooperate. "Walk me to the door?" *To the airport? Convince me to stick around?*

"Sure." She threaded her arm around him as he made his way across her apartment.

"I have to go, Molls," Austin said, more to convince himself than anything. He lingered at the doorway. When he left, she'd have his heart with her. Christ, he wasn't going to be able to get through the next fourteen days. "I don't want to go."

"You made a commitment." She smoothed the lapels of his shirt and patted his chest. "Follow through and before you know it, it'll be done."

"You're taking this well. I'd be a wreck." He sighed. He had no idea how he could let her go if the roles were reversed. Shit. He'd probably beg her to take him with her. But the roles weren't opposite and Iris would never approve of him having Molly along for the ride. "I promise. I'll call you." He'd make time and get in touch with her. Screw Iris and her rules. He'd fallen for Molly and needed her. He'd do the photo shoots and the obligatory press if only to get back to the woman in his heart.

"Just get through it and get back. How about that?" She kissed him. If her heart was breaking, he couldn't tell. Damn, the woman had a strong will. He envied her.

"Bye, Molls." He held her close and kissed her once more. He swiped his tongue across the seam of her lips and pushed the connection deeper. He groaned. He'd have to go through withdrawal. She was his drug.

Molly nudged him and broke the kiss. "Go, or you'll never leave."

"Still might not." He grinned then stood tall. "I'm out."

"Not yet. Bye, Austin." She paused. "Love you."

"Always. Bye, babe." He peeked back at her once then headed down the hallway. He could do this. He could leave her and be with the woman he didn't like in order to get back to the one he loved.

He ambled down the rest of the stairs and out to the street. He slipped behind the wheel of his car. Was she watching him? He hoped so. If Remy had told her to give him something to miss, well, she'd succeeded. He longed for her already.

He drove across the city in the direction of the airport. He had to go. Had to. He swept his gaze across the skyline. The building housing CDL caught his attention. According to Iris, he was fired. He turned onto the exit and made his way down the main roads to CDL. He wasn't just giving up on his career—the modeling gig was just that, a gig. Not permanent.

He parked in the visitor lot and strode into the foyer. The receptionist smiled. She allowed him into the main portion of the building. He navigated his way down the corridors to Mr. Lee's office. He'd grovel if he had to in order to get his job back once he returned.

He knocked on his former boss's door. "Mr. Lee? Do you have a moment?"

Roscoe Lee looked up at him. "Austin." He narrowed his eyes. "What brings you in to CDL?"

"Well, I'm not sure I want to leave."

Roscoe jumped up from behind his desk. Instead of the warm welcome and handshake, he shook his head. "You and Molly were my best team. I could count on you no matter what, but now? I can't trust you. Yes, I agreed to loan you out. I loaned her out, too, and you both did great work, but she never really left. I've already got her proposal for W whiskey. I have no idea what you're going to do. It's all very wrong."

He stared at Roscoe. *Shit.* He'd thought he could waltz in on his way out of town and return to life at CDL with no questions. Now, he wasn't so sure. He sighed. "Which wrong are you talking about? The wrong in considering Iris might have my best interest at heart or allowing Molly to push me away?" He wasn't sure why he mentioned the falling out. They'd patched things up — at least he hoped so. She'd told him she loved him. That had to mean something, right?

"Are you kidding me?" Roscoe growled. "You got involved with her?"

"Iris? No. Molly...yes." Why lie?

"Austin."

"You encouraged me to ask her out." Austin widened his stance and gripped the back of the closest chair. "I'm confused."

Roscoe sat on the edge of his desk and bowed his head. "Molly needed to get out of that office. She spends — spent — so much time with you and I thought she deserved the chance to be happy. You've got tons of friends and I hoped you'd set her up with one or two of them. I never expected her to hook up with you. God knows working with you cannot be easy."

Austin pinched the bridge of his nose. "I did what you

said — except I didn't hook her up with my friends. We went out and had a great time. Hell, I had the best time and if Iris hadn't butted in, we'd probably still be together. The work we did was off the charts and the rest was even better."

Roscoe met Austin's gaze. "Wait. Iris?" He shook his head and groaned. "Explain the whole thing, but use the short version. I don't have all day."

"Molly and I hit it off. We have since the beginning, but when we worked on the Aura account, we realized we were better together than being just partners. It was going well until she decided the only reason she was invited to the Aura gala was because of me begging Iris. Me using my charms, so to speak."

"Tell me you didn't do that."

"No, I didn't. I'm not going to lie. I thought about it. Thought long and hard about climbing the ladder on Iris' back. I'd date Molly but dump her in favor of Iris." He put both hands up. "But I changed my mind. I'm a jerk but not *that* big of a jerk."

"Why would you do that to Molly?" Roscoe asked. "You work together. If you and Molly split, then what? I'm out two of my best people."

"I know." He'd thought about that very point quite a bit.

"You weren't thinking," Roscoe snapped.

"Actually, I was. I looked at her and all of the times I'd said no, I'm not getting involved or I'm not attracted to her, all those reasons meant nothing. I swore I wouldn't fall for her. But the longer I spent with her outside of CDL… I didn't have an ex in the way or a random girlfriend bothering me. I had no excuses." He turned the chair around and settled on the thick plastic seat. "Then when Molly walked out of the dressing room at the dress shop, all the emotions I'd kept in check spilled out." Well, he'd fallen hard for her long before and showed her in the hotel suite, but he wasn't going to tell Roscoe that. "I remembered why I fell for her back in college and realized the feelings weren't dead — they were stronger."

"Then why didn't you chase her back then?" Roscoe crossed his ankles and gripped the edge of his desk. "She's a catch."

"I was oblivious." He blew out a long breath. Christ, explaining everything would be a hassle, but she was worth the trouble. "Back then, she was my best friend — still is, but it was different. She was one of the guys and not girlfriend material. But I changed my mind. I'm not oblivious any longer."

"I'm sure Iris is happy to let you go."

"She's got me busy for the next two weeks, but I thought if I didn't go through with it not only would she have a shit fit, but she'd probably take me to court for breach of contract and she'd pull it. I knew we were being used but I thought it was the lesser of all evils." He still believed he was doing the right thing, but Christ, it hurt.

Roscoe didn't say anything for a long while. He drummed his fingers on his thigh.

"What's so important about Molly? You barely noticed us before. We did our jobs and you profited. We never even earned bonuses, despite bringing in and maintaining all of our projects." Austin stood. He wasn't sure why but anger rose within him. Someone wasn't telling him something and he wanted to know what.

"You've been my biggest headache. I never know how careless you'll be," Roscoe said. "I never know how I'm going to have to bail you out."

"I'm not careless." And he'd never brought his love life to work — except with Molly and now Iris. *Fuck.*

Roscoe rolled his eyes. "Your personal life is a mess."

"Has it impacted my job?" Austin challenged.

"Not yet."

"And it won't." He'd already made changes in his life and had a plan for his future. He patted his pocket. He wouldn't let Molly down.

"Look, I don't care how you conduct your personal life as long as it doesn't impact your work or Molly. She was my first hire and I'm partial to her—even if some of her choices are questionable. She's the daughter I never had, and a good scout." Roscoe paused. "If you really want things to work out then get your life sorted out."

"I plan to." Austin offered his hand to his boss. "I'm coming back. This was a screwed-up idea and I can't wait for it to be over. I'm ready to be in my office with Molly and cranking out advertisements for pickles and blue jeans."

"We'll see." Roscoe shook hands with him. "Like I said, sort out your life, then we'll talk."

"Deal." Austin nodded then headed out of Mr. Lee's office. He hadn't been asked back but he wasn't totally out of the loop. Not great, but not awful. He strolled down the corridor to the office he shared with Molly.

One good thing about her, she wouldn't chuck his stuff. He stopped when he noticed the door was already open. Mr. Lee hadn't allowed Tyson to move in already, had he? Austin peeked around the doorframe and into the office. For a split second, he hoped Molly had made it to CDL and was behind her desk. Unfortunately, she wasn't.

Iris folded her hands on Molly's workspace. "Close the door. We've got lots to talk about."

Fuck. He'd been her puppet for only a day and already hated it. He remained at the door.

"Fine." Iris smiled and narrowed her eyes. "I came in because I didn't see you at the airfield. Seems you took a detour. I know because I tracked the location of your phone."

"Why would you do that?"

She shrugged. "I like to keep my assets accounted for."

'Assets'? He'd been relegated to the role of a material item. Jesus.

"Now, you're mine for the next two weeks. Am I detecting an undercurrent of upset?" If it were possible to narrow her eyes even more, she did. "You're not happy. You won't come to bed or let me kiss you anymore. Either you're overwhelmed by me—and many are—or you're having second thoughts. Should I make the call and pull the plug on any future Aura ads? I could make you a star."

"Pull it." He didn't have any second thoughts or regrets. He wasn't meant for stardom with her. He was supposed to be in this office working on advertising for other people.

"I thought you might say that." She stood and rounded the desk. She pinned him between her body and the doorframe. Anyone in the hallway could've seen her groping him. "I'm not the type to beg or to chase. Once I make a decision, that's it. Are you sure you want to give this—me—up? I told you. I can make you famous and rich beyond your wildest dreams. I've already had modeling agencies call. They want the man with the boy-next-door look in all of their work."

"I'm sure I'm willing to give it all up." He nudged her away and ducked into the office. "I'm here to create promotional materials and marketing campaigns, not to be some face on a billboard or your body of the month to play with. I have a job to do and I can't if you're expecting special treatment." His hands shook and he stuffed them into his pockets to hide the trembling.

"You can't do this, remember? You signed a contract." She shut the door. Her smile widened as she crossed the room. "You're *mine*."

Austin swallowed hard. He'd made the fucked-up decision to go along with her whims and was about to pay for it. He tamped down his anger and nodded once. "You're right. Let's go to the airport. I don't renege on contracts." Even if every fiber of his being screamed to run the hell away from her, he'd fulfill his end of the deal.

He left CDL and climbed behind the wheel of his car. He drove the short distance to the airfield and parked. The closer he got to the plane, the more he wanted to run. He forced himself to board the jet and to take a seat beside Iris. He'd made this mess.

Iris clamped her hand on his thigh and sipped champagne. She didn't offer him any or give him any other special treatment. He was her property, nothing more.

Once the plane was airborne and the seatbelt light darkened, the flight attendants left her alone with Austin.

"Did I tell you you're already big? We've used you on the billboards in New York, Los Angeles, Vegas and Chicago. You're huge. The posters of you at the bus stops keep getting stolen." She clapped her hands. "Isn't it fantastic?"

"Sure." Great. Other women were happy to see him, but he wasn't happy. He wanted to be with Molly. Not ogled.

"You don't seem thrilled. Well, maybe this will perk you up. I've helped you in the relationship department. I sent your partner a photo text and I'm sure she loves it. Check your phone."

"What?" Austin fumbled with it. "What are you talking about? Where?" Sent…Molly a photo? Iris hadn't taken any pictures that he knew of—unless she referred to one of the ones Molly had photographed, but wouldn't Molly have copies of those?

"In your messages. While you were in the bathroom, I took the liberty of sending it from your phone." She dug her nails into his thigh. "You won't have to worry about her any longer."

"What the fuck did you do?" He flipped through the screens to his messages. In the thread with Molly's name, he noticed the photograph—one of him and Molly together. Someone had added red writing over the image and blacked out Molly's head. "Beauty and money always win," he muttered. He turned to Iris. "You sent this to her? From me? Why? That's awful, even for you. What was the point of it?"

"To eliminate the competition." She clasped his chin in her fingers. "She's not worthy of you and you're wasting your time. You're going to be huge and you need a woman at your side who is your equal."

"Like you?"

"Exactly. I told you. She doesn't deserve you."

"No, she doesn't. She should be with someone much

better than me, but I'm not sure I can live without her."

"Well, for the next fourteen days, you'll have to. No calls, no texts, no chats. You're mine." She grabbed his phone. "I'll take this."

"No." He wrestled it from her. "You might be in charge of what I'm doing for the next few days but you're not getting my phone."

"Really? She's worth that much to you? I could buy ten of her."

"No, you couldn't. She's…" He stopped himself before he got too sappy and gave Iris more ammunition. She'd already screwed up his life. He wasn't sure how in the hell he'd explain the photo to Molly.

"You'll change your mind. A few premieres, some dinner parties, and all that posing will show you where you belong. By the end of the two weeks, you won't want to go back to your crappy job or your mousy girlfriend." Iris yanked the sleep mask over her eyes and settled in her chair.

Austin glanced through the window. She could say what she thought would happen, but he knew. He checked the messages after the photo. Molly had replied, but she seemed more confused than upset.

Not sure why you're sending me that. Rubbing it in that you're famous? I'm rooting for you. Guess now I can say I knew you when…☺

He peered at Iris' still form then switched his phone to silent. If he had any chance of getting back with Molly then he needed to do some serious damage control.

I'm sorry about that picture. Iris sent it, but I have no idea how she got the photo or my phone long enough to do it. You probably don't believe me and you're smart not to. I screwed up.

He hit send then composed the next text.

I can't ask you enough to forgive me for being myself. I'm trying

171

to be a better man for you. Two weeks and I'm all yours. Promise.
I miss you.

Austin sent the message and slumped in his seat. Life could be so great then turn shitty in an instant. He only had himself to blame. If he'd have been happy with what he had then the whole episode with Iris never would've happened.

He turned the phone over and swiped his index finger over the screen. At least he could play games while Iris slept. The message icon blinked at the top left of the phone. He tapped the icon and held his breath. Could be something innocuous or something important. He hoped for important.

His hope died when he read the words. Dylan wanted to know if he was available for drinks. *Shit.* He typed out a reply and promised his brother he'd call later. So much for a quick resolution with Molly.

He stared out of the window again and sighed. He had fourteen days to decide if he truly loved Molly. He doubted he needed that long, but the contract was binding. He braced himself for what he saw as the roughest two weeks of his life — time without the woman of his heart.

Chapter Eleven

Molly closed the lid on her laptop and rested her head on her hands. The photo of her and Austin never quite left her mind. She saw the red words and the scribble even in her dreams. She'd read the explanation from Austin a hundred times. He was sorry. Unless he'd given his phone to Iris and approved of her defacing the photo, he had nothing to apologize for, but she appreciated the sentiment.

But he was in California or New York—wherever the last text claimed he was—with Iris. Molly had seen a quick story on the tabloid news involving Iris but she hadn't seen him. *Oh well.*

She sat up and raked her fingers through her hair. She'd never get her work done if she kept worrying about Austin. He'd been away exactly fourteen days and had only called once—long enough to make sure she was still alive but not enough to actually have a conversation. She'd heard Iris in the background and figured she wouldn't let him talk for long.

Rain streaked down the window and a clap of thunder rumbled. Lightning flashed, illuminating her townhouse. She'd never been one for thunderstorms, but the cruddy weather suited her mood.

"Molly."

She could've sworn Austin was at her door, but he was out of state.

The person out in the hallway pounded on the wooden door. "Molls? You in there? Please God, tell me you're home."

"Austin?" She raced to the door and twisted the lock. She

gasped when she saw him. "You're soaked." Molly stepped aside and waved him in. "Get in here and dry off. Good Lord."

"No." He stood still in the hallway.

"Do you want your clothes plastered to your body? I'm not arguing the look—it's a good look—but you'll catch a cold or something." She bit back her confusion and the rising hunger within her to snuggle in his soggy arms. "Did Iris dump you or are you avoiding her? You can hide here for a few hours, but just tell me the truth."

"Neither." Austin stepped into the room and scooped her into his arms. He nudged the door shut then carried her to her bedroom. He feathered kisses all over her face then down her neck. Her skin burned and delicious heat raced through her body. She rubbed her crotch against his belly. He'd been working out. His rock-hard muscle felt even stronger. She moaned. The man was perfection on legs.

She pulled her mouth away first. What in the hell was he doing? He'd barely spoken to her for two weeks and now wanted to fuck her right away? Yeah, no. As much as she liked having him back in Ohio, she wasn't ready to strip so he could do as he pleased with her. He owed her more than an explanation. Some begging would be nice. "I'm confused." She brushed her hair from her eyes as he sat with her on his lap on the edge of the bed. "Not that I don't like it, but why are you doing this?"

"Because I fucked up. I can't see my life with anyone by you. Mistake goof-up or my favorite soft, warm place to land—that's you. I love you, Molly."

"Austin." He didn't use that word—not for pizza or beer or even his football team. Love wasn't in his vocabulary.

He crushed his mouth over hers and claimed her. The need within him flowed to her and she groaned. He palmed her breast, pinching her nipple. She writhed on his lap. Being with him felt right.

Austin stood long enough to turn around and place her on the bed on her back. His hungry gaze slid over her as he yanked her jeans and panties down her legs. He dropped to his knees between her thighs and arranged her calves on his shoulders. He buried his face in her pussy. His warm breath tickled her sensitive skin and she grabbed handfuls of the comforter. His scruff scraped along her inner thigh in a wonderful burn. She threaded her fingers into his hair and grabbed two handfuls.

"Don't." Molly bucked against him and opened her legs. Every synapse in her body stood at attention. There wasn't much point arguing with him. He'd do what he wanted and she liked.

Chilly air kissed her labia.

"So pretty." He parted her pussy lips and dragged his tongue over her sensitive skin.

Molly collapsed on the bed and stared at the ceiling. If he wanted to please her then she'd let him. She wanted to experience him on a sensory level. His warmth radiated through her as he flattened his tongue on her clit. He alternated between nips and licks.

She moved on instinct and reached between her thighs. She trailed her fingers over the crease alongside her pussy. The slight tickle added to her pleasure. She wondered if seeing her touching herself turned him on.

"Beautiful," Austin whispered.

She wasn't sure about the 'beautiful' part but she was comfortable with her body during solo play. Why not be okay with touching herself in front of him? She arched her back and spread her labia. "Right there."

Austin sucked on her clit and allowed her to direct the action. His touches sent a tremor through her body. She planted her feet and held on. The man knew how to break her apart inside.

She squeezed her eyes shut and basked in the sweet pressure on the tiny bundle of nerves. A moan bubbled in her throat.

"Tell me you like this." Austin kissed her inner thigh up to the inside of her knee. "It's sexy when you moan."

Did she enjoy what he was doing? Hell yes. "Don't stop." She spread her legs even more, shoving her pussy into his face. "Fuck."

"We're not going to fuck yet." He dragged his tongue down her leg to the apex of her thighs. "Want to make you happy." He resumed caressing her cunt with flicks and nips. He added the occasional jab into her vagina, making her moan again.

"Then don't stop." She opened her eyes. Oh, God, he was so good, but he'd have to go eventually.

"If I could spend forever right here, I would." He scraped his teeth across her clit. "I love you."

Realization swept over her. Maybe she and Austin weren't meant to be together forever, but the passion they shared was real. He loved her in the best way he knew how.

"Mine," Austin murmured. He smoothed his palm over her hip and up her belly to her chest. He moved her shirt away from her breasts then eased her bra down to expose her boob. He tweaked her nipple.

"More," Molly whimpered. Each time he manipulated her body, she loved it. She dug her nails into her skin. She closed her eyes and gasped for breath.

"Anything you want." He continued to massage her breast. At the same time, he slid his middle finger of his other hand into her channel. He pumped his digit and twisted his wrist, touching her all over from within. Within seconds, he worked up a perfect rhythm of sucking, pinching and finger-fucking her.

Molly gasped and opened her eyes. She moved her hands from her pussy to his hair. She didn't tug. Instead, she held him in place. Holy fuck, she needed more from him.

If she'd thought she'd been overwhelmed by him before, the combination of all the sensations on her body blew her mind. He sent her over the edge. The orgasm that started low in her belly spread through her limbs. Her legs trembled and she tensed. Heat engulfed her and everything tingled. Her thoughts blurred.

"Austin," she panted. "Oh, my God." She whimpered and tightened her grasp on his hair. "Austin." She couldn't think or breathe. Everything centered on the way he made her feel. She drew her knees together on either side of his head and shivered as the orgasm washed over her.

"Let go of me, babe." Austin uncurled her fingers, releasing her grip on him.

She closed her eyes and hoped he didn't disappear when she opened them again. Austin knew how to touch her in all of the right, delicious ways. He owned her heart and made her soul sing but he wasn't going to stick around. That's how things went between them. He built her up then walked away.

Austin arranged her legs on the bed then crawled onto the mattress beside her. He dragged a blanket over her partially nude body and rested his head against her shoulder. "Like that?"

She wanted to say yes and to curl around him. Hell, she wanted him to resume licking her pussy, but he hadn't answered her question—not really. She adjusted her bra and smoothed her shirt back into place. "You did that so you didn't have to tell me the truth." She balled her hands at her sides. "Didn't you?"

"No. I'm being as honest as I can. I did everything because I wanted to. Because I needed you." He propped himself up on his elbow and draped his arm across her belly. "Molly, I've jacked up so much, but not this time."

"So you're leaving again." She should've known. She tried to sit up in order to get away from him. The idea of him seeing her crying again wasn't her plan for a good time. Instead of letting her get away, he flopped on the bed and pulled her across his lap. The blanket tangled around her legs, making escape nearly impossible. "Austin, don't do this." She wriggled in his grasp. "Don't do this to me. I can't handle it again."

He managed to sit up and cupped her jaw in both hands. "I know what you're scared of. I'm an ass. I leave you and expect you to not only pick up the pieces but to stick with me. You truly are the most loyal friend I've ever had." He placed his fingers on her mouth when she parted her lips to argue with him. "I know what you're thinking and I'm not pandering to you. Molls, I'm trying to tell you things have changed. I'm not the same asshole Austin I used to be. I'm in love."

She stared at him and processed what he'd said. She wobbled on his lap. *Oh fuck.* He might not be the same person — she'd give him the benefit of the doubt on that — but he was in love like he claimed? "With Iris," she blurted. She moved his hand from her mouth. "This is our last huzzah." The tips of her ears burned and embarrassment flowed through her veins. Tears threatened behind her eyes. No, she wasn't going to cry over him again. *Fuck it.*

"I never said that." He curled his fingers around her wrists. "Babe."

"You're so blind. You used me and knew I'd be loyal, then abused my trust. You have no idea how deep you cut me." She kept her gaze on him but didn't cry. Her voice cracked, despite her effort to stay calm. She scooted off his lap and tumbled to the floor before she righted herself. She kept the blanket around her lower body. "You're getting my bed wet and I think you should leave." She turned her back on him. "Don't come back. Don't call or text me. Just go."

She couldn't handle looking at him. Her heart ached. She'd been used for the last time. She covered her face with her hands and gritted her teeth to keep from letting her emotions get the best of her.

"No."

"No?" She snorted. "Are you serious?"

"This isn't the end for us." He eased up behind her. "I'm trying to tell you I love you." He tucked her against his soggy chest. "I love your vulnerability and your grace. Your smile, laughter and the way you fit against me."

She wanted to believe him, but damn it… He knew the right things to say and how to get to her. "Don't say what you don't mean." Her voice cracked a second time. "My heart can't take the beating. No more."

"I'll have to live with being known as that kind of dick for the rest of my life but I don't care." He turned her around in his embrace and rested his forehead on hers. "Babe, I love you. I screwed up by not saying it when we were in college. I knew my heart and it belonged to you. Still does and always has. You married Linc and I had Carole, but I wasn't happy. *You* weren't happy. We're best together. I don't see any reason we have to be apart."

His words made sense. She even believed some of what he'd said. But to trust him? She wasn't sure the trust was possible.

"I've waited too long to be honest with you and I can't stand it. I'm yours, babe. I love you so much." He brushed his nose against hers. "If you push me away, I'm going to keep trying."

"Austin." Her resistance to him frayed. She wanted to believe him. As much as she'd been hurt in the past and knew he could hurt her all over again, she still wanted that happy ending with him. She'd had little else but she'd had hope.

"I've never let myself be stripped bare like I do with you." He kissed the tip of her nose. "You have my heart in your hands."

"I don't understand. All this time, you loved me? Why didn't you say anything or make a move?"

"I wish I could say it was simple but it's not." He eased back to the bed and sat on the mattress. He tugged her onto his lap. "The first time I saw you, I had this feeling deep in my gut that we'd end up together. I might have been blind a few times and missed my chances but I'm not letting go. I said I love you and I do. One of these days I'm getting my grandmother's ring."

Her lips parted and she gasped. Oh shit. "Austin?" He couldn't mean what he'd said. No way.

"I'm going to marry you." He patted her ass. "That's a

promise."

"What about Iris?" she blurted. He'd been so hot and heavy with the other woman and the last she knew he was still *with* Iris.

"What about her?" He slid his palm beneath her shirt and caressed her back. "She's not the woman I love. Not the one I'm going to make love to." He eased Molly onto the bed again and brushed her hair from her face. "I'm going to show you how I feel and pray to God you're not going to push me away."

If she'd expected something sweet and sensual from him, she was mistaken. The animalistic side of Austin took over. He whipped his shirt up over his head and tossed the garment onto the floor. His hair stuck up at odd angles and passion lit in his eyes.

Molly didn't think. She acted and threw her arms around his neck. She peppered his face with kisses. The bit of scruff on his cheeks burned her face, but she wouldn't push him away. Not now. She bumped noses with him and their teeth clashed a couple of times. Austin continued to kiss her while he fumbled to open his pants.

Molly slid her hands down his chest to his jeans. She popped the button for him and shoved the denim and his boxers down his thighs. The clothing bunched around his ankles. Power filled her—she could make him feel good. She wound her arms around his waist. She nipped her way down his chest. She tasted the salt of his perspiration and the bit of hair on his pecs tickled her nose. The scent of him—something unlike his usual woodsy scent—wrapped around her. She met his gaze.

"Love that." Austin cupped the back of her head and dragged her flush to his body. He kissed her again, sucking on her tongue. He swallowed her moan and swatted her bare ass.

Molly yelped—not from the pain, but because she hadn't expected him to spank her. She writhed against him. Damn, she liked the twinge of pain with her pleasure. She scraped her nails down his chest and tweaked his nipple.

Austin wrestled his mouth free of hers and gasped. "Fuck. I need to be inside you." He kissed her again. "Right now."

"I want you there, too." She bit his bottom lip before letting him go. Her nerve endings sizzled. She felt alive and free in his arms.

As he fumbled in her dresser for another condom, an idea occurred to her. She turned around and settled on her hands and knees. She waggled her ass at him. After the earlier orgasm and the spanking, he had her on the edge. She glanced over her shoulder at him.

"Oh, fuck yeah." Austin still had his pants and boxers around his ankles as he scrambled back to the bed. "So damn hot." He rolled the condom over his erection and filled her to the hilt. "Fuck," he said, drawing the word out. "Love the way you feel around me."

She groaned. From head to toe, her body buzzed. The heat in her lower belly surged to her pussy. She rocked backward onto his dick and the small action seemed to kick-start him.

"Mine." Austin dug his fingers into her hips. He built a steady rhythm but increased his speed with each thrust. The sound of skin slapping skin, along with her whimpers and his groans, filled the air.

Molly grasped handfuls of the bedding and arched her back. Her temperature spiked as her need for him built to a fever pitch.

"Jesus." Austin held onto her with one hand and brought his other hand down hard on her ass. The sound of the spank echoed in the room and was quickly drowned out by her moan.

"Oh, my God." Molly pushed against him, shoving him deeper into her body. "More. Harder. I want to feel you in my soul." She bowed her head. Nothing would compare to this. She'd denied herself and had ignored how much he meant to her, but she knew better. Her heart belonged to him. He knew how to make her body sing.

"Babe," Austin murmured. "My sweet babe."

"Austin." She closed her eyes. Her legs trembled. She wouldn't need much more to come apart. "Shit."

"I know, babe. I'm close." Austin swatted her again. "Oh, Jesus." He added more force to his thrusts and spanked her with each surge into her body.

Molly gritted her teeth and succumbed to the climax. Euphoria flowed through her veins as the orgasm washed over her. Everything trembled.

"Yes. Fuck, that's so sexy." Austin's thrusts turned frantic and his rhythm faltered. He filled her to the hilt and groaned. His dick pulsed within her pussy and she felt the throb all over her body. He moaned then rocked his hips. He added a few more thrusts but with more tenderness than before.

She opened her eyes and parted her lips. He'd wrung her out—again.

"Molly." He encircled her waist and tugged her upright. He held her to his chest. "Damn," he said against her neck. "Just damn."

"Yeah." She had no other words. Her knees weakened and she leaned into his embrace. She sighed and peered down at her clothing. She still wore her bra and shirt. He probably still had his pants around his ankles. Good Lord, she and Austin were a hot mess.

"I've never done that before." Austin nibbled on her neck. "Never needed someone so much that I kept my clothes kind of on." He chuckled. "But you do that to me. I'm not me without you. I'm best when you're beside me." His cock softened and slipped free of her pussy. He kissed her then lowered her to the bed. "Give me a second. I'll be right back."

Once he let go, Molly snuggled into the pillows and breathed in his scent. He was right—she and Austin were better together. She closed her eyes and didn't bother to cover the lower half of her body. The bed dipped as he climbed onto the mattress beside her. He parted her thighs and she opened her eyes.

"Gotta take care of my babe." Austin dragged the warm washcloth over her cunt, cleansing her.

"Thanks." She'd never realized how sweet he could be until he surprised her. He had an odd way of showing he cared about her and loved her. He disappeared into the bathroom for a few moments then strolled back into the bedroom. He'd manage to untangle himself from his clothes.

She drank in the image of him nude. Dear God, he'd become even more handsome. Austin climbed into bed beside her. He dragged the blankets over his body and hers then held her to his chest once again.

Molly nestled in the blankets with her back against Austin's chest. She mulled over the events of the last couple of hours. The switch in him was not like Austin. She twined her fingers with his and sighed. So many thoughts filled her brain. Why'd he finally admit he loved her? Was he being honest? Had he had a falling out with Iris? Learned he might not be cut out for the modeling world? Could they really have a chance at a future together?

"What are you thinking about?" Austin kissed the back of her neck. "Something good?"

"I'm overwhelmed," she confessed. She rolled onto her back and met his gaze. "This isn't like you. Not only will we get fired, Mr. Lee will have a fit. He likes us working together, but he'll never go for us being together. It's against the rules. We're screwed."

"I'm not screwing you. I love you."

"You're not thinking straight." She splayed her hand on his chest. "It's a sweet sentiment, but it can't work." Someone had to be the practical one. "Besides, you were fired."

"Okay. We need to talk—about work and us." He sat up and crossed his legs then faced her. "I lost the Aura campaign because I refused to sleep with Iris. I didn't bite, so the dream is over. I'm not upset one bit. I hated the way she'd paw me and expect me to play nice."

"Really?" He hadn't slept with Iris? She could've sworn she'd seen the spark between them. Iris seemed to like him and he knew how to work with Iris' attention. Everyone wanted to be around him. "I want to trust you and believe you but I'm not sure. I've been a consolation prize for so long. I guess I'm doubting myself. You don't confess love or settle down. How can I be sure this is what you really want?"

"Fuck." He bowed his head.

Had he been figured out? She should've known. Austin and honesty weren't buddies. He took what he wanted and left the moment the situation got too difficult. She'd become the sticking point. He wanted to stay friends with her and have sex, but long-term...yeah, probably not in the cards.

"Hey, I get it. I do. You want something else out of this and used the word love without thinking." She wanted to say she wasn't upset, but damn it, she couldn't lie.

Austin leaned forward and curled his fingers under her chin. "You're not second best. You're the woman I've needed but was too blind or scared to see. I'm shit at speaking my mind when it comes to my feelings but I can't not be truthful with you." He brushed his thumb across her bottom lip. "Will you give me a chance? I'll figure something out at the office. For now, we'll keep this quiet and continue on with our jobs."

"I'm a secret? Or is that part of what we need to talk about? You've been fired. There's nothing to hide."

"Yes—no—kind of." He frowned. "That's not what I meant."

"Then explain it to me. As I see it, we're never going to make this work. I'm terrible at keeping secrets." She shook her head. "I'm still having a hard time wrapping my head around all of this."

"I'm not exactly known for my poker face." He kissed her hand and kept his mouth on her knuckles. "With CDL, I got my job back. Mr. Lee rescinded my resignation. The problem is my partner. He won't pair me and you up.

According to him, you've been reassigned and I'm up shit creek."

"Oh." She had so much to think about. The office situation wasn't great. She didn't mind her partner but she'd rather work with Austin. But then if she got back with Austin, she'd have to fake the relationship—if that even worked out. The more she thought, the more she wanted to move around. She sat up and raked her fingers through her hair. His wet clothes were still on the floor. They'd probably dried a bit, but not much, and they'd end up smelly if she left them in a heap.

Austin kissed her shoulder. "Give me tonight. I swear, I'll come up with something. I created this mess and I'll fix it. Besides, I'm not done being with you. I meant what I said. If it takes forever to prove I love you, I'm willing to go the distance."

Willing to go the distance... He sure knew how to come up with the smooth lines. Not like he hadn't had practice. She scooted out of bed and gathered up his clothes.

"I need to hang these up," she said and made her way to the bathroom.

Truth be told, she needed space to think and took the reason to get some air. Part of her wanted to go along with his grand idea. He'd never said any of those sweet things before and never to the girls she knew he'd dated. She doubted he'd mentioned love in order to get her into his bed—he'd already fucked her a couple of times. Part of her refused to believe love was possible with Austin. She draped his clothes over the railing and breathed in the scent of him. She could lose herself in that smell—woodsy and spicy.

He'd used the word 'love'. She'd only ever heard him use that word when he spoke to his mother. Never to a date or lover—at least that she knew. His ex-wife Carole had claimed he'd never told her outright that he loved her. So what made Molly so special?

She sighed and faced the mirror. She appraised her

reflection and groaned. The liner around her eyes had smudged, reminding her of a raccoon. Still, the blush on her cheeks hadn't gone away and the smile returned to her lips. She looked mussed but happy and she hadn't been the poster girl for happy in a long time. For the first time in forever, she didn't see the cellulite or wrinkles. She saw herself and felt pretty.

"I'd ask you if you got lost, but this apartment isn't big enough for that to happen." Austin strolled nude into the bathroom. "There's that smile I love." He wrapped his arms around her waist.

"You've used that word a lot lately." She leaned against him and snuggled in his embrace. She drank in the image of their reflection in the glass and bit back a gasp. They did make a striking couple — well, he was handsome and the blush of love helped her appearance. She wasn't bad on her own, but having him beside her gave her strength.

"Because that's how I feel." He kissed the top of her head and grinned. "Do you think I'm worthy of a…what…fourth try?"

She paused. He'd won her over, but she wanted to keep him guessing. Maybe she'd lost her mind but she'd fallen head over heels for him all over again. "I suppose."

"You *just* suppose?"

"I'm willing." She turned around in his arms and smoothed her palms over his chest. If he wanted to make this work then she'd go along with his choice. But if they were going to do this, she wasn't letting him get off easy. He'd have to work for her affection. "I'm willing to give you that chance, but there are rules. We're honest with each other — if this turns into something you can't handle then say so. We don't hide it at work, either. We act normal. We're pretty close as it is and people already think we've been fucking for years."

"We should've been." He wriggled his eyebrows. "If I'd have gotten my head out of my ass then this conversation wouldn't be necessary."

God, he knew the right words and how to smile at the right times. Her nerve endings tingled. With every touch and kiss, her resolve melted. No, she had to keep talking. If she didn't finish, she'd never get the words out. "Promise me that when you decide to move on, you'll let me down gently, okay?"

"And If I don't plan on moving on?"

"We'll take things one day at a time." The hope blossomed in her soul and grew. For a split second, she allowed herself to imagine a future with him. A little wedding—maybe on a beach and barefoot—their own place and children. She could see them growing old together. Things could be so bright, but he had to prove himself first.

"One day at a time?" Austin kissed her again. "Deal, but tomorrow we go to my place. I've got more room and a bigger tub...oh, and more rubbers. We'll have to buy stock in a condom company. I don't want to not be with you."

"You're awfully sure of yourself." She'd fallen for him but she wasn't above challenging him. "What if I decide this is enough?"

"I know you." He eased her shirt over her head then unhooked her bra. "You want to be taken care of but you don't say that because you don't want to appear soft. I love you strong and soft." He reached into the shower and turned on the spray. "Let me take care of you."

Like she could resist him? She allowed him to tug her into the stall. The hot water stung her body. She leaned into him and groaned. Bone-deep weariness settled within her as he pressed his soft dick into the cleft of her ass.

Austin nuzzled her neck and grabbed the washcloth. He lathered it. "You've been so strong for me." He caressed the suds over her breasts and down her belly. "Strong when you should've given up on me."

"You're worth fighting for." She moaned as he smoothed his fingers between her legs and over her clit. She'd come twice already, but when he touched her he set her nerve endings ablaze.

"So are you." He nudged her under the spray to rinse her and squirted shampoo onto his hand. Without speaking, he worked the lather into her hair and massaged her scalp. He rubbed his burgeoning erection against her butt.

"Feels good," she whimpered. "I can't remember the last time someone washed my hair for me."

He turned her around to rinse the shampoo out of her hair and feathered a kiss on her lips. "Did I ever tell you every time I smell whatever scent your shampoo is, I think of you? It must be in a perfume or something, too. My brain goes right to you."

With each word, he broke her down a little more. She believed him, even if she still wanted to guard her heart. She cuddled with him as he conditioned her hair then rinsed. The hot water on her back woke her up from her relaxed state. She grabbed the washcloth, but he took it from her hands.

"You've taken care of me plenty. I can do this myself." He scrubbed his body clean, leaving suds on strategic parts of his anatomy.

Molly couldn't help but watch. The soap accentuated the already strong parts of him. He stepped under the spray to rinse then turned the water off. He grabbed one of the towels. Instead of drying himself, he wrapped her up.

"You'll spoil me." She wobbled in his arms as he dried her. Each kiss he pressed to her skin, to her neck, shoulders, breasts, belly and inner thigh, pushed her closer to breaking.

"I like spoiling you." He nuzzled her breasts again. "Love it."

Her synapses misfired and she sizzled from within. When he scooped her into his arms and carried her into the bedroom, she clung to him. She never wanted the night to end.

Austin placed her on the bed. Still damp and skin glistening from the shower, he picked her brush up off the dresser then joined her on the bed. He ran the brush through her hair. "I read once that brushing your woman's hair was right up there with oral sex. It's the same kind of relaxing pleasure."

She swayed into him. "I don't know about being equal to oral sex but I like having the knots brushed out and the bristles on my scalp are relaxing."

Austin kissed her shoulder. "If you're happy, then I've done my job."

Molly turned around as best she could to face him. "You have."

He tossed the brush onto the nightstand and removed the towel from around her body. He rummaged through the drawer for a condom.

Molly rolled onto her belly to warm the front of her body. Her nipples ached from the temperature change. She pressed her face into the pillows and breathed in his scent on her sheets.

"Hiding from me?" He kissed along her spine and Molly softened beneath his touch.

She turned her head. "No. Just cold."

He patted her ass. "You've got one sexy butt." He eased his fingers between her ass cheeks. "So wet for me, too."

"I want you." She whimpered. "I'm still reeling from the first two orgasms."

"Good. Then the third will be the charm." The bed jiggled as he left her side.

She didn't have to look at him to know what he was doing. The snap of the condom wrapper told her plenty. He eased up behind her and lifted her hips. Austin straddled her legs. He slid into her with slow thrusts. He kissed her back and nipped her shoulder blades.

Molly moaned and arched her back to send him deeper into her pussy. She felt him not only in her cunt, but in her soul. He surrounded her. She'd never felt anything so exotic in her life. She balled her hands in the sheets. Whimpers and groans bubbled from her throat.

"Yes, babe. Let me know you like it." He increased the speed of his thrusts but not much. If he wanted to draw things out and bring her the most pleasure, he was doing the right things.

"Austin." She arched her back even more. His balls slapped against her pussy lips, sending shivers through her body. "Austin. I'm close." She tensed around his dick. He knew how to play her in order to get her to climax—or he'd figured out how to amplify the last orgasm. She wasn't sure and didn't care. She loved the gooey, weightless feeling in her limbs.

Austin bit her shoulder once more then pulled out. "Roll onto your side, babe. I want to look into your eyes."

She allowed him to move her. He pinned one of her legs between his and hooked her other leg around his waist. Hunger shimmered in his eyes. He parted his lips and sank back into her. Once again, he fucked her with slow thrusts and overwhelmed her. He palmed her breast.

"Fuck yeah." He smiled and met her gaze from under heavy-lidded eyes. "You're blowing my mind."

He'd blown hers, too. She wasn't sure how she managed any coherent thoughts when all she wanted to do was experience him.

Austin smacked her ass and surged into her. The combination of pain and pleasure pushed her closer to orgasm. She tensed again. Austin punctuated each thrust into her pussy with a spanking. Her ass burned. She grabbed his wrist. She didn't want to stop him, but rather she needed to hold on to him. She teetered right on the edge of climax. She opened her mouth to tell him she was coming, but the sound lodged in her throat.

"So beautiful." He pistoned into her. Harder and faster. He stopped spanking her and focused on making love to her. He grunted as he slammed into her channel.

Molly couldn't think. The world evaporated around her and only Austin existed.

"Jesus." Austin's thrusts turned feral and he groaned. "Goddamn it." He shoved himself deep into her and curled over her. His hot breath feathered over her shoulders and the back of her neck. "You know how to blow my mind."

"Uh-huh," she managed.

Austin eased out of her pussy and collapsed on his back beside her on the bed. "I need to get rid of the condom but I don't want to move."

She rolled onto her side to face him as he sat up. He scrubbed both hands over his face and stood. He removed the rubber and tossed it into the waste basket then settled beside her again. "I'm never going to stop loving you, Molly." He kissed her temple and held her tight to his chest. "Like I said, I'm a better man when I'm with you."

She sighed. For their sexual relationship starting out as a mistake, he'd become her closest friend and lover. Now she had to hope he wouldn't end up smashing her heart to bits.

She wouldn't worry about the future—even the one he kept promising. The present was good and what she wanted from her life. Austin wasn't perfect, but for the moment, he was hers.

Chapter Twelve

Austin scratched his forehead and stared at the laptop screen. In the last two weeks, his life had changed in so many ways and he didn't regret a minute. He liked the way Molly had made his gigantic apartment feel cozy. She seemed right in his space and at home with him—just like their college days but with more maturity and sex. She smiled more and seemed happier, too. He liked her scent on his sheets and his clothes. Molly tended to wear his T-shirts to bed and around the apartment. He bit back a groan. She made his clothes look so much better than he ever could. Sure, she'd agreed to keep their relationship on the down-low, but he wasn't sure how long he could keep his mouth shut. Maybe he'd have to take a trip down to Mr. Lee's office and see if he could get the rules changed.

He snorted. He'd never thought he'd be able to live with someone—not after the Carole debacle—but from the moment Molly had walked into his place, she'd settled him.

He looked at the other desk in his new office. She should be with him. He worked better with her to bounce ideas off of and to shut him down when his ideas went too far out into left field. But no. She was down the hallway with a new partner—Tyson.

A twinge of jealousy hit. He and Molly were a good combination. He had no idea how well she got on with Tyson. She never talked about him. Hell, the only person he knew she'd collaborated with besides him was Ben Reynolds. The jealousy subsided. He trusted her. If she wanted a change, she'd let him know.

He could go down and check on her but decided against

it. He stood and stretched then headed down to the break room. He poured a fresh cup of coffee and dumped two packets of creamer into the tart brew. He glanced over his shoulder and his irritation increased. Speaking of the devil, Ben...

"There's the man." Ben stood beside him and rinsed his navy-blue coffee mug. "So the great team of Dean and Neff has split up. I thought her office looked a little less full of you." He laughed. "She's not your other half any longer."

"I don't know about that. We still bounce ideas off each other." And spent most of their time together outside of work. Making love to her was better than the best.

"Yeah, but since she's not working with you, she's happier. Looks to me like you've held her back." Ben sipped his coffee. "Am I right?"

"Nah." Realizing he loved her had been the best tonic for what had ailed them both.

"I see why you kept her to yourself, though. She's awesome. Ask Ty. They get along great and their work has been off the charts. Did you hear the jingle for the Crescent Bikes campaign? It's awesome." Ben leaned against the counter. He crossed his ankles and sipped his coffee. "I'd like to have her on my team."

I bet. Austin blew out a long breath. He refused to let Ben see him upset. Molly could do what she wanted, but he doubted she liked Tyson nearly as much as Ben claimed. Austin stirred his coffee once more.

As if on cue, Tyson ambled down the hallway. He passed the break room then doubled back. "What? I'm getting a death glare."

"Molly." Ben chuckled. "Old Austin, here, is jealous."

"Hey," Tyson said. "She's sweet and cute. I'm debating asking her out. She's not a knockout but she's loyal—and Austin would know."

Austin tamped down his anger. He didn't like listening to his co-workers talk about his girlfriend like she was a piece of meat.

"Sometimes you've got to lower your standards to find a great one." Tyson clinked coffee cups with Ben then shrugged. "I'd rather get with Iris but I know my limits."

"If you don't ask her out, I will." Ben held up his coffee mug. "I'd tag her." He slid his gaze over to Austin. "What about you? Or is that why she left you? You had her and moved on?" He laughed. "Probably, and good for us. We'll take your leftovers."

Austin gritted his teeth. He could've sworn smoke billowed from his ears or at least clouded his vision. Of all the times to keep his relationship with Molly quiet, he had to choose now. But he had to keep a lid on his anger. If he blew his lid, he'd never hear the end of it and would probably get fired again. Fuck it. He knew of at least two other advertising firms that would take him in a heartbeat. He crossed the room and closed the door.

"Whoa. Gonna get all private," Tyson said. He plopped onto the plastic chair. "What crawled up your ass?"

"Okay, here's the deal." Austin gripped his coffee cup. "Molly is your—*our*—*co*-worker. She's our equal. Don't talk about her like she's anything less than that."

Ben snorted. "Territorial much?"

Ty stared at Austin. "He can't design shit without her. Boy Wonder here is a blunder." He laughed again. "Is that your problem? No Molly makes Austin a dull little boy?"

"Sounds about right," Ben snapped. "Molly makes us all look better on paper and we make her look better in person."

"For fuck's sake, shut up." He hadn't planned on blowing his secret with Molly, but the two assholes deserved to be put in their collective place. "You said she was second best, right? Not a knockout, but loyal, correct? You've got a lot to learn. She's a wonderful woman. She's smart, dignified and if I ever hear you or anyone talking shit about her, you'll answer to me. You mess with her then you're messing with me."

Ben and Tyson shared a glance. The color drained from

Tyson's face. Ben appeared less ruffled. "Messing with you? Are you two together? You're not working together." Ben drummed his fingers on his cup. "That's got to be it. She moved on and you're not ready to let go."

"Moron," Austin murmured. Some people would never learn. "Enough."

Tyson's lips parted and after a moment, he finally spoke. "You could have Iris Sommerville and you took Molly instead? Are you crazy? I'd totally fuck Iris over Molly. But then we all thought you were already with Iris. Crazy bastard."

"Crazy?" Austin growled. "Molly's my best friend and my creative partner. No, I'm not crazy. I took what I wanted and not Iris."

"Because you've got Iris on the side. It's on the quiet." Ben winked. "Smart. Have every woman, not just one or two. I like it."

"Asshole." Austin dumped his cooling coffee down the sink. "Hands off Molly."

"'Cause she's yours?" Tyson asked. He snorted and shook his head. "You're so fucked-up."

"Yes, I'm dating Molly. That's why you need to leave her alone. That and because she deserves better than you." She deserved more than Austin, too, but he wasn't giving up.

"Dude, at least it's legal for you to be with her." Tyson shrugged. "She's old news."

"What?" Austin paused at the door. "What the fuck are you talking about?"

"She got a promotion or something. We finished up our projects and I got a new office," Ben said. "Sweet office, too."

"Good." Austin opened the door and left the break room. He pieced through the conversation. Iris on the side? Not hardly. Having Molly as a second-rate date? What the hell? The guys were blind and full of shit. He stormed down the hallway. A new fucking office. Ben deserved to be stuck in one of the cubicles. Whatever. Austin stepped into Molly's office, and she grinned then frowned as he closed the door.

"Don't you look happy?" She smiled but it faded fast. "What happened? Got the news about me?"

"Yeah. I'm not sorry, though." He leaned against the door and clicked the lock into place. He didn't want any interruptions. His shoulders sagged and his fury melted away, only to be replaced by embarrassment. He'd blown everything sky high and needed to do some damage control. He also needed to clear a few things up — his future depended on it. "Remember how you felt when I married Carole? How pissed you were because I made the wrong decision and you knew it but I wouldn't listen?"

"Yeah. I also remember what Carole said that day. She told me to go make some hot friends and to move on because you'd never be mine." She gripped her stylus in both hands. "At the time, she was right."

"No, she wasn't — well, no. Yes. Fuck." He pinched the bridge of his nose. "That's the thing. We'd find a way — you and me. We always do. There's something between us that can't be denied. Hot friends or not, we're supposed to be together. What she should've said was for you to get loyal friends." He focused on her. Instead of the normal clutter on her desk, the space was clean. Only her tablet, phone and a file folder remained. Her cheeks were rosier than normal. She'd put makeup on that morning, but he could swear most of it was gone. *What the hell?*

She scooted her chair back and frowned. She sighed. "Loyal. That's Remy to a T. Why? Aren't you?" She stood and rounded her desk then met his gaze. "Austin? Is there something you should be telling me?"

"I'm very loyal." He'd just demonstrated his overzealous and slightly neurotic devotion to her back in the break room.

"Then the rumor about you and Iris is crap. Okay. We're cool." She shrugged. "Or is there something else?"

"You were worried? Honey, I never slept with her." His heart sank. He'd worked so hard to prove Molly was the only one he loved, but apparently he hadn't done enough.

"No, but I'll admit to being a tad jealous. I mean, she's so much better suited for you, even if you haven't slept with her. I'm what Ben and a few others have deemed second-rate." She tucked the stylus into the top of the tablet.

"Ben and Tyson are full of shit." He'd given them a piece of his mind and still didn't believe they'd gotten the hint.

"They are, but they don't matter." She hooked her fingers in the front pockets of his slacks. "What are you getting at? You're not jealous of Ben or Tyson, are you? I'm not attracted to them. Remember? I'm loyal. They've told me that a hundred times, too. You're leftover and loyal. I don't agree with them, but my opinion doesn't matter to them."

"They're assholes." He appreciated knowing he had nothing to worry about, but things were still touchy.

"Why would they spread a rumor about you and Iris or say that shit?" she asked.

"Jealousy. You and I have a good thing—in and out of work." He held her close. "You're important to me."

She pressed her chest to his and rested her head on his shoulder. "I like hearing that."

He'd been so strong for her but not nearly as much as she propped him up. He draped his arms around her shoulders and toyed with the downy soft hairs at the base of her neck. She hadn't exactly told him she loved him in return. Call him sentimental, a romantic or whatever, but he'd fallen deep for her and needed to know she returned his love.

"Austin. Talk to me. What else is bothering you?" She met his gaze. "Huh?"

The blue in her eyes sparkled. He could get lost in those eyes. He couldn't see his life without her. "Do—do you love me?" There. He'd asked the question. Part of him wanted to hear her answer. The rest of him wanted to run and hide, especially if she said no. "You've said it a couple of times, but I—I don't trust myself. I've screwed up so much. I need to know what you said was the truth."

"I've *always* loved you."

No hesitation from her, just an honest answer. "Like you want to get married and grow old together? Maybe have a couple of kids with me? Or is this pity?" He sounded like a dick, but she unnerved him. "Be honest."

"Where is this all coming from? You've got the biggest ego I've ever seen and you usually don't scare easily. What happened to your confidence?"

"God. I've never been this unsure about anything in my life. I've always known where I was going and what I wanted to do. Now, I'm all fucked in the head." He slid his hands into her back pockets and squeezed her ass.

"So Ben and Tyson ran their mouth. So what?" She didn't pull away. Instead, she smoothed her palms over his chest. "I've told you I loved you so many times and you heard the words, but you weren't ready to believe me."

"Molls?" Fuck. Was that right? He'd been listening. He'd longed to know she returned his feelings. But he knew and she was right—she'd told him over and over how she felt, but he'd expected her to change her mind. She'd been the only one to trust and stick with him and he'd still refused to believe her.

"I've loved you since I first locked eyes on you. Crushing on you, pining for you...yeah. That's was me. Then I saw the real man the night you walked me to my room because Reyland dumped me. You were kind, patient and smelled so good. You hugged me as I cried—I wanted to stay there in your arms forever. You moved on and so did I, but you were right—whatever that link was, it was always there. I married Linc but I wanted you. His jealousy was justified."

His heart ached. He cupped her jaw in both hands and kissed her. This was why he loved her—she knew how to get him to crack. He didn't understand how he'd passed her up for so long but he wasn't going to any longer. She owned his soul.

"I guess what I'm saying is it doesn't matter where we work or who we work with. I trust you and I love knowing that when go home, I know I'm coming home to *you*." She balled her hands and rested her head on her fists. "And right now, I should gather my stuff so I can head home."

"Babe."

"I love you, Austin Dean," she whispered. "All the way."

"I love you, too, Molls." Calm, relief and desire swept over him. A thought occurred to him. "You know. We've never properly initiated our office. Your office. Whatever." He tilted her chin and kissed her lips, nose and cheeks.

"No, but we can after we leave. Then it won't be our office, or mine."

He paused. "Wait. What? It won't? I'm confused. Ben said he was getting a new office, but are you, too? Tell me you're getting to come back to me."

"Not exactly. I got my pink slip today." Tears slipped down her cheeks. Her makeup ran, leaving pale black streaks on her skin. "Mr. Lee said he'd thought it over. We'd violated the no-staff dating rule and he wasn't convinced we'd stay here anyway, despite our track record for CDL and work ethic here. You might be back for now, but he wasn't playing games any longer — especially after we both took time off for the Aura debacle. I can't say that I blame him. The past month and a half has been crazy."

"For that, you got fired. You're the brains of our operation. Fire me, but keep you. Jesus. Ben or whoever was right, I'm a blunder without you." He groaned. "Besides, plenty of people have second jobs. Who cares? You do what's asked of you here, most of the time more than what's asked. I'm the one who should've lost their job."

"Well, it doesn't matter since you're not getting fired and I did." She wiped her cheeks with the back of her hand. "It's a good thing. Doesn't seem like it, but it is."

"I don't like it. *We* broke the rules, not just you." He'd march down to Mr. Lee's office and resign. Fuck it. Then he'd beg for her to get her job back. He'd been the issue, not her.

She shrugged and straightened in his arms. "It kind of works out for the both of us."

"How?" As far as he was concerned, she'd been given the raw end of the deal. "I want you to move in with me, so that's fewer living expenses for you, but you've still got the lease on your apartment."

"That's not what I meant. I don't want you to feel like you've got to pay my way."

"You're mine and I take care of what's mine. Might take me a while to get there but I do."

"I know." She toyed with his collar then unbuttoned the top button of his shirt. "Remember last year when I entered the design competition for the museum group downtown?"

"Yeah. The logo thing. I remember. I encouraged you to try it. The ideas you showed me were awesome." He wished he'd have been able to help her if only to have his name on the project, too. But he'd wanted her to shine and besides, he hadn't come up with anything worthy of entrance into the competition. Her ideas rocked.

"I almost forgot about it because it took them nearly a year to decide. According to the board, they were trying to get the okay from Mr. Lee to let me do it and until recently, he wasn't going to. If it was free or earned us promotion then he was all for it. Otherwise, no way."

"Well? What happened?" Excitement ran through his veins, combined with the irritation from knowing she'd been fired.

She smiled again and sighed. "Mr. Lee refused until today and I've got the feeling that our relationship was what changed his mind. He probably told them I was fired before he mentioned it to me."

"That's nuts. If they said no then you're screwed." His skin prickled. Damn it. He wanted to fix this for her but didn't know how.

"Yes and no. Getting fired wasn't the end of the world. I can find something elsewhere. I've had offers but I liked being here — because it kept me close to you." She shrugged. "I wanted to talk to you about it, but you were with Iris when they initially offered me the job. Then Mr. Lee said no, so I kept my mouth shut. No point in telling you about something that wasn't going to happen."

"I wish you had, but it's done now." She'd been so strong and kept her wits about her when others might have lost faith. She wasn't perfect, but he didn't want perfect. He wanted her. He needed the open line of communication with her, too, but he'd helped to make that difficult.

"I really want to work for the museum group. I like their flexibility, allowing me to do more than half of the work from home and I get to do some photography for them. Sure, there'll be some traveling, but not tons, but the health benefits are better, they match half of my contributions to my 401k and we get free admission to all of the museums." She paused. "Austin, it's a great opportunity."

He rested his forehead against hers and closed his eyes. "You really wanted to leave CDL, didn't you?"

"I've got no choice now. He's already hired my replacement."

"Who?" *Holy shit.* He'd missed so much. Now he wouldn't be able to see Molly every day at work, but really, did that matter? If he'd won her over then he'd have her in his life and bed forever.

"Her name is Angela. She just graduated in the fall from Kent with a bachelor's in design. Ben and Tyson won't know what to do with her. She's pretty." She shrugged again. "Right up your alley. Young, blonde, pretty." She averted her gaze. "She's sweet."

"She must be with Ben or Tyson, because Mr. Lee informed me I'd be flying solo from here on out."

She still wouldn't look him in the eye. "We're not going to be at the same office. Think this will still work?"

He curled his fingers under her chin and redirected her gaze. "I'm sure of it. You're going to rock that job." He tugged her across the room to her chair and sat on the leather seat. He pulled her across his lap. "I'm proud of you. The museum stuff is the kind of job you love. You went for it and got it. Plus, you stuck with me. I don't need anyone else." He threaded his fingers into her hair and removed the elastic from her ponytail. "I want you."

"Austin." Her hair tumbled down her shoulders. When she kissed him, her tresses tickled his face.

Hell yeah. He breathed in her scent and brushed his lips over hers. The need to make love to her overwhelmed him. The idea that they could get caught spurred him on. He slid his hands beneath her blouse and caressed her back. He loved the feel of her smooth skin under his fingers.

Molly sat up long enough to yank the blouse over her head. She tossed the shirt onto the desk and faced him again. "This is so unprofessional—us right now. I kind of don't care."

"Me either." He eased the cups of her bra down and exposed her breasts. The straps slipped off her shoulders. She threaded her fingers into his hair as he latched on to her nipple. He rolled the sensitive skin between his teeth then sucked. Her moan turned his insides out. Fuck. He needed to take her. Right *now*. He switched his attention to her other nipple and palmed her chest.

Molly muffled her second moan against his hair. She shivered. "Austin," she murmured.

He let go of her boob and flicked his tongue across her nipple. "Right here."

"Make love to me." She slid off his lap and turned her back to him. She shoved the stuff on her desk to the side and leaned over. "Please?"

"Don't have to beg." He reached around to the button on her jeans. He unzipped the denim and eased the jeans and her panties down her thighs. He dragged his nose and mouth along her ass cheek then bit. He could've sworn the temperature in the room spiked.

Molly smothered the yelp into the crook of her arm.

Hell, he wouldn't need much time before he came apart. He stood and leaned over her, pressing kisses to her back as he popped the button on his fly. He shoved his pants and boxers down around his knees then stroked his dick a couple of times. His hand on his cock felt great but being inside her would be the best. He paused.

"Fuck. I don't have rubbers," he whispered.

"In my bag. Front flap." She tucked her arms under her body as he rummaged through her purse. He located the condom and blew out a long breath. Thank God, she was prepared. He tore the foil wrapper then sheathed himself.

"Prop yourself up on your elbows." He slid his arm under her as she complied and tweaked her breast through the fabric of her lacy bra. Desire welled within him. Fuck. He lined his erection up with her cunt and pushed. Her heat enveloped him.

She grinned and a whimper bubbled from her throat.

"Good girl." He pinched her nipple again. "Mine," he said against her ear. "All mine." He let go of her chest then grasped her hips. Fucking hell. He wouldn't last.

Molly eased into his arms. She met his gaze and spurred him on.

Austin pumped his hips, thrusting into her. Each slide into her body nudged him closer to climax. His nerve endings tingled and his thoughts blurred. Nothing mattered. Not the possibility of being caught, not her firing, nothing except being in that moment with her. He gritted his teeth and pistoned into her body. The sweet scent of her wrapped around him.

She shivered beneath him and bucked. Each muffled whimper and moan turned him on and increased his desire for her. He loved her and couldn't see his life without her. He leaned over her and buried his face in her shoulder blade to keep from making much noise. From head to toe, he shuddered and the orgasm washed over him. He closed his eyes and filled her with his seed.

Austin kissed her skin and stilled within her. For a moment, the rest of the world melted away.

Molly collapsed on the desk with him on top of her. She laughed into her arm. "Someone will catch us."

"Oh well. If I get fired, I won't argue." Austin kissed her

again then eased out of her. He tossed the used rubber into the waste can. He hiked his pants back up and stuffed his cock inside. He plopped onto the chair and sighed. He wasn't going to be able to get any work done now. Sure, she relaxed him, but he wasn't in the mood to write advertising copy for pineapples.

"You're so bad." She grinned and eased her jeans over her hips. She settled on his lap and rested her head on his shoulder.

"Feel better?" He snugged his arms around her and kissed the top of her head.

"I'm sad I was fired, but not that I'm leaving, although this did help." She glanced up at him and smiled. "I forgot to mention something. Since I've been let go, Mr. Lee did offer me a nice severance package—which I accepted—but since I'm out as of this afternoon and I don't start at the museum for another two weeks, I've got some time off. I'm supposed to meet with the museum group when I leave tonight."

"At least you got some cash out of it." He held her tight. "Why don't we go out tonight and celebrate? Wherever you want to go. I'm spoiling you."

"I'd like that. I've got another idea—for afterwards." She paused. "What if we used our vacation time together?"

"I doubt Mr. Lee would appreciate me using my last few vacation days, but I'm game. What were you thinking?" He liked where she was going with this.

"What if we went to Vegas and bet on ourselves?"

What she said sank in, but it took him a moment to understand. "And get married? Who would be the witnesses?" He loved where she was going with the idea. He'd go to Vegas in a heartbeat, especially if it meant a lifetime with her.

"Remy and his new beau, Dylan. I haven't said anything to him but I know he'd agree if I say the word Vegas." Her grin widened. She grabbed her shirt from the desk and threaded her arms through the sleeves.

"Wait." He smoothed the hem of her shirt down. "Remy and my brother?"

She nodded. "I wondered how long it would take you to figure that out. They started seeing each other last week. You know Remy. He can't do anything half-assed. Once they got together, they're *together*."

"I'm happy for them. They're good for each other." He grasped her left hand. "Then will you marry me?"

"Did I just half-assed ask you that same thing when I mentioned Vegas?"

"You did but you deserved the real thing." He cupped her jaw in both hands. "I will marry you if you will marry me. I love you, Molly Louise Neff." He needed to get his grandmother's ring out of the safe deposit box. He'd do that after they'd hit the museum. Until then... He slid the ring he wore on his middle finger past his knuckles. She'd made him the piece of jewelry back in college and he hadn't been able to part with the ring. "It's too big but it's my most prized possession." He kissed her left hand. "I'll get you a little better one as soon as possible, but Molly, will you be my bride?"

"You're being all formal." Her blush stretched from her hairline to below the neckline of her shirt. "Of course I will."

"Hot damn." He kissed her hard on the lips and bit back the whoop. No more mistakes. He had the woman of his dreams in his arms and she was about to become his wife.

"We should unlock the door and go." Molly winked. "The faster we clock out, the faster we can hit the museum then have dinner. Whatever happens afterward...I'm game."

"That's the best idea I've ever heard." He patted her ass as she left his lap. He zipped and helped her gather up her electronics. Austin followed her out of the office then stopped in his own to grab his computer and tablet.

Molly waved then headed out to the reception room.

Austin locked his office and when he turned, Mr. Lee stood in the hallway.

"Can I have a word with you?" Mr. Lee bowed his head.

"Austin?"

"Sure." He stopped and gripped the strap of his messenger bag. "What's up? I heard about Molly."

"It's best for all of us. She wanted to move on and wasn't happy here." The boss looked him in the eye. "How long will it be before you go, too?"

"I don't plan on quitting, unless you're going to fire me as well." He gripped the leather a little tighter. *Fuck.* Was he about to get his pink slip, too? He didn't care but he really didn't want to look for another job.

"Oh no. I'd like to keep you on." Mr. Lee nodded and stood taller. "This will settle you down, I believe. Working with her was good, but you needed to get out of her shadow. This will help you do that."

"I agree. I do have a request, though. I'd like to use the remainder of my vacation time." Austin held his breath. This would be the moment he got the axe. He just knew it.

"Oh? I trust I'm not losing you to another Aura campaign." Mr. Lee rocked on his heels.

"Since Molly's got time off, I'm taking her to Vegas to get married."

"That's wonderful. I knew it would happen and hoped you'd both realize you were meant for each other." Mr. Lee clapped his hands and laughed. "What do you need? Two weeks?"

"If you're serious, then yeah." That should give him plenty of time for a decent honeymoon after the wedding. His heart hammered. He was about to get everything he'd ever wanted. *Holy shit.*

"Deal and congratulations." Mr. Lee shook hands with him then waved. "See you when you return."

Austin watched his boss stroll the rest of the way down the hallway before he moved. Holy hell. He'd never heard of being given that much time off, besides the fact that Mr. Lee wanted him to stay on with the company. Was Mr. Lee thinking straight? Not that he'd argue with his boss. He pumped his fist. Fuck yeah. He couldn't wait to tell Molly.

He bounded out of the building and down the stairs to the parking garage. Molly waited beside his sedan.

"What took you so long?" She grinned. "Seriously, what happened?"

"I got two weeks off. Mr. Lee told me about your leaving and informed me he wanted to keep me on. I mentioned getting married to you and he basically said, 'Duh. We all knew you'd get married.' He gave me extra vacation time so we could go to Vegas."

"Then it's settled. We check flights tonight and break the news to your mom and brother." She clapped her hands then settled on the passenger seat of his car.

Austin rounded the hood. He couldn't wipe the smile from his face if he'd tried. A man couldn't get that lucky, but he'd managed to score Molly as his wife, keep his job and would have the life he wanted to lead. Hells yes.

Chapter Thirteen

Austin sighed and his stomach finally settled. He hadn't expected his nerves to go out of control on his wedding day. Coming to the tiny club had been a stroke of genius. They could have a party but without the hassle of a gigantic mess. He liked simple and easy and so did Molly. Right now, he didn't care about anything but Molly. He'd made her his bride that evening and once they returned to the hotel suite, he'd make love to her all night long.

He sipped his whisky and cola and gazed at his bride. Molly danced with Remy and laughed in his arms. Austin's brother, Dylan, stood beside him and leaned against the bar.

"She's really happy," Dylan said. "Mom came up with the perfect dress, too. Looks like you scored twice."

Austin drank in the image of Molly once again. The simple ivory-colored dress hugged her curves in all the right places. The thin halter straps and deep 'V' accentuated her cleavage, and the way the silk gown fell around her hips blew his mind. He loved how the corset emphasized her hourglass figure, too.

"I hit the jackpot." He soft-punched his brother in the arm. "You and Remy. Looks like you scored, too."

"It wasn't planned. Hell, we couldn't seem to make connections. He'd be out or didn't have his phone when I called and I was always working. Can't really have a relationship when neither one of you is available." Dylan held up his glass of vodka and lime to his boyfriend and Molly on the dance floor. "I get you married her and I'm honored to have her as my sister-in-law, but you're sure you won't fuck her over?"

"Ouch." Austin sipped his drink again and the whisky burned down his throat. He'd had the question coming. Until he'd sorted out his life, he would've been the one to dump the relationship. Not now. "I'm not the same man I used to be. If you'd have asked me six months ago, I wasn't ready for a relationship with her. Back then, I wasn't in the right mindset. I am now and have been since she turned my thinking around."

"Good."

"What about you?" He focused on his brother. "Until I showed up at the store, you and I weren't exactly on speaking terms. What made you change your mind about me and coming along? The trip to Vegas?"

"Remy was a pretty good reason, and so was Molly. She and I bonded when she was at the store. She's a sweet woman with a big heart. Her confidence is in the toilet, but I bet you can help her fix that. She's devoted to you." Dylan turned his back to the dance floor and placed his empty glass on the bar. "Just appreciate her the way she should be. She's not fragile but she's been kicked around too much. Let her know every day that she's the center of your world."

"You bet your ass I will." Austin leaned on the bar beside his brother. He'd missed so much with Molly before. He'd missed a lot with his brother, too. The rift between them had been huge, and all because of attitudes. He bowed his head and looked at Dylan. One of them had to bend a little more. He'd be that man. "I'm sorry we haven't talked."

"We could've." Dylan clasped his hands together. "I'm just as much to blame as you are. I didn't try, either. Life got in the way, then different boyfriends. My life was a mess for a while."

"Yours was a mess? You should've seen mine. I couldn't keep a relationship to save my life. Besides that, I was jealous of you." He glanced sideways at his brother. The weight of his confession threatened to kill his good mood, but damn it, he'd get this off his chest. "Everyone liked you better.

You were the sweet one. You got along with the girls. Your grades were better than mine by a mile. I had this neurotic belief I had to compete with you. Mom certainly seemed to like you better."

"Austin, you're my brother. We're equals — especially to Mom. Why would you think that?"

"Mom always talked about you like you were God. Whenever I was within earshot, that's all I heard about was you and I let it get to me." He rubbed his forehead. Maybe it was childish to feel second best to his brother but that's how he'd grown up. Dylan was the better brother. Shutting his family out of his life had made things easier for Austin. Less complications meant he could screw his life up in other ways. "I didn't talk to you for the last three years because I didn't think I could. I'd pick up the phone and lose my confidence." Admitting that truth cut him deeply. "Sucked."

"Really? I'm that scary?" Dylan frowned. "Austin."

"I know. You're not — it...it was just before I left for college, then three times when I came home, I kept trying to convince Mom what I wanted to do with my life wasn't a mistake." He turned long enough to glance over at Molly. She didn't see him, but damn, she made him happy.

"I'm sorry that happened and even more sorry I didn't know. Mom's very proud of you. I'm sure she never thought one of us would go into advertising, but I bet you she never expected me to get into fashion, either." Dylan clinked the ice against the side of his glass. "When you called her asking for help with Molly and the ball...she was in her element. She liked being needed by you. She gave Molly that special necklace. I don't think she'd have ever given Carole one like that. She might not say it all of the time, but whatever we do, she's proud. We're equal and that's that."

"Really? She didn't like Carole?" Austin had an idea his choice for his first wife hadn't been the best, but he hadn't known his mother disliked her that much. "Why didn't she tell me?"

"You weren't ready to hear it." Dylan shrugged. "They clashed about as much as you and Carole did. She called Mom a lot, asking for help and how to get through to you. That's part of why Mom took a step back. She had no idea how to help Carole—but then no one did. You two were so far apart in personality, temperament and I'm surprised it lasted two years."

"I am, too." The Carole years had been pretty hard on him. He should've seen how he'd used Molly during that time. He might not have waited so long to get to her.

"I'm glad Carole left and you finally tried to get Mom back into your life. If you want me there, I'm here for you. I'm not your rival or your problem. You've got your strengths in life and I've got mine. I forgive you for whatever you've done and whatever you think you've done. It's over."

"Thanks. I'm not your rival, either. I forgive you, too, even if I'm not sure what all happened." He waited as the bartender filled his and Dylan's drinks, then Austin turned his back to the bar. "So she likes Molly?"

"Let's just say she's got grandchildren on her mind." Dylan bumped shoulders with Austin. "Take your time. You've got tons."

"I do." Just not tonight. He needed her more than the air he breathed.

Molly and Remy strolled up to them, Molly flushed and glowing. Remy stuffed his hands into his pockets and averted his gaze.

"To what do we owe what appears to be a greeting card moment?" Molly asked. She took Austin's drink and sipped. "Whew, this is strong."

"He's been making them with a lot of kick." Austin rested his arm around her waist and held her to his side. "What happened with Dylan was just brother stuff."

"And me begging him to let you shop at the store for all of your fancy galas at the museum." Dylan wriggled his eyebrows.

"You never said that, but it's a good idea," Austin replied.

211

"It *is* a good idea and I will. Absolutely." Molly kissed Austin on the cheek. "Thanks."

"Remy. You're quiet." Dylan tugged Remy's neck tie. "Already bored? Or just wanting to be upstairs instead?"

Remy met Austin's gaze. His blush ran from his hairline to below his collar.

"That's a yes." Dylan downed the rest of his drink and whistled. "It's a good thing we're staying here tonight or I'd be in trouble." He turned to Remy. "You're taking me home, right?" He wriggled his brows again and whispered something into Remy's ear.

Remy blushed but didn't say a word.

Dylan grinned. "Goodnight. See you whenever we surface for air or when we've got to be at the airport to head home — whichever comes first." With Remy beside him, Dylan left the club.

"That's our cue to leave, too." Molly squeezed Austin's ass. "It *is* our wedding night and I don't want to dance or drink any longer."

"Our wedding night." He couldn't get over those words. Hearing them sounded so good. As he left the club, a voice grabbed his attention and it wasn't Molly's. He looked over at the television by the bar. Iris Sommerville's face flooded the screen. He shuddered and Molly wrapped her arms around him.

In the next clip, Iris stood on the red carpet with a twenty-something man at her side. Austin snorted. The guy was handsome in a classic way — probably all created at Iris' request.

Iris mugged for the camera. "To me, loyalty is everything. Each of my models and boyfriends understands that. I'll make you a star if you're a team player."

The red carpet reporter interrupted Iris. "Is that what happened to Austin Dean? He seems to have vanished at the cusp of stardom."

Nah. He simply figured out what he wanted from life and who he wanted in that life.

"You can teach a man to look hot, but I couldn't teach him to model." Iris waved her hand. "Besides, I don't take no for an answer or accept anything less than complete devotion. Look for the next Aura campaign. Douglas will be front and center. He's a natural in front of the camera and understands the price of loyalty."

"Loyalty, my ass," Austin murmured. The poor bastard probably wanted to be famous and saw her as his ticket to the top. *Good for him.* Austin turned his attention back to Molly.

"She has no idea what genuine loyalty is." Molly rubbed his forearm. "Did you really want to model for the rest of your life?"

"No. I wanted to try it, to do it with you and maybe make some money. I did that and now it's time to move forward—with you." He escorted her out of the club to the elevator. "Mrs. Dean."

"Mr. Dean," she said as the doors opened. "I like the way that sounds. Mrs. Dean."

"I love it." He gathered her into his embrace and stepped into the car. "This is oddly how I saw our wedding going— you, me and a zillion lights. By the way, you look fantastic." He removed his tuxedo jacket and draped the garment around her shoulders, then pinned her to the wall of the car. He cupped her breast and nipped her neck. "Want to fuck you right here in the elevator."

"We can't—God only knows where the cameras are and I don't want to get arrested." She smiled and kissed him. "You look good, too."

As the car ascended, she wobbled into him. Her eyes widened and her lips parted. Within seconds, the bell dinged for their floor.

"That went fast," she whispered.

"Not fast enough. The card is in my front pocket. Inside." He scooped her into his arms and carried her down the hallway. He stopped outside their door long enough for her to swipe the card then carried her into the suite and set her

213

on her feet. Molly scrambled over to the bank of windows overlooking the strip. She clasped her hands together.

Austin locked the door. He had one more surprise up his sleeve. "Molls? I forgot my wedding present for you."

"You can do it when we get back to Ohio," she said. She smiled at her reflection in the dark windows. "I didn't have the chance to get you anything."

"It's here, not in Ohio." He dug through his bag for the flocked box then eased up behind her. "Once I give this to you, I'm kissing every inch of you and staking my permanent claim."

"Didn't you do that already?" She faced him and rested her arms around his neck. "The whole Mr. and Mrs. thing?"

"Oh, so you don't want to make love to me now that we're married?" he joked.

"I can't wait." She toyed with the hairs at the base of his skull. "I figured we'd be naked already."

"You deserved a reception of sorts." He owed her a better one, but that would have to happen later. He opened the box and eased the delicate chain from the velvet. "I had Remy make this. It's braided silver and one of a kind. May I have your wrist?"

She yanked the sleeve up for him. "What does it say?" Once he affixed the jewelry on her arm, she turned the oval plate over. *Molly & Austin 8/29.* She met his gaze. "Austin, it's beautiful. I feel guilty for not getting you anything."

"You gave me a hundred chances and never gave up on me. That's the best gift I could ever get. Like the clasp?" he asked.

She turned the bracelet around. "It's a lock."

"Now that we're together, nothing can tear us apart— no mistakes or bullshit. You belong to me and I'm yours forever." He eased the jacket down her shoulders until the piece of clothing landed on the floor. "Now, about making love to you…" He grasped her hand and led her to the bed. He couldn't get her naked fast enough.

Austin mashed his mouth down on hers while he opened

the fastener holding the straps of her dress in place. When she broke the kiss, the front of her dress drooped, revealing her lack of a brassiere.

"No bra?" he blurted and met her gaze. How'd he missed that?

"I couldn't under this dress." She tugged the zipper at the side of the bodice. The gown slipped down around her ankles, baring her body to him.

"No panties. Hells yes." He gasped and slipped his hand over her thigh. He stroked the hairless patch above her pussy and slid his middle finger between her cunt lips.

"I didn't want lines under the silk." She wobbled forward and collapsed on top of him. The teardrop pendant glittered against her skin.

The passion he felt for her bubbled over and love filled his brain. She was everything he'd ever wanted and a few things he hadn't realized he needed. He eased his finger from her pussy then rolled her onto her back. He scrambled to his feet and paused a moment. Fuck. Molly looked so appealing and beautiful. She might not see her attractiveness, but he sure did.

Austin couldn't get into her fast enough. He loosened his necktie and eased the silk from around his collar. He opened the buttons on his shirt as fast as he could without popping the little plastic discs from it. He owned the tux but he didn't want to ruin it. He shrugged out of the shirt and yanked his undershirt up over his head.

"I can help." Molly sat up and eased the pins from her hair. Her dark tresses spilled over her shoulders as she moved forward on the bed. She grasped the front of his pants. "I've always wanted to strip a man in a tux."

Austin groaned. "You're doing a good job." He stood still as she freed the hook holding the front of his pants closed. The soft article of clothing dropped to his ankles. "I see you did wear underwear."

"I wanted to give you more to unwrap." He eased his fingers beneath the waistband of the boxers and shoved them down his legs. He kicked out of the balled-up clothing then scooped her into his arms. He sat on the bed with her on his lap. "Ride me."

"Anytime." She draped her arms around his neck and scooted forward. She closed her eyes as she sank onto his erection. Her nipples grazed his chest and her warm breath fanned over his skin.

He grasped her hips. *Holy shit.* He'd dreamed of this moment and fantasized about how the day would go but he'd never expected to be in Las Vegas and married to Molly.

"More." She kissed him then bit his bottom lip. "Austin."

"I'll give you whatever you want." He rolled her onto her back again and pinned her to the bed. Being inside her, skin on skin, pleased him. He surged in and out of her pussy, filling her to the brim before pulling out. Each thrust pushed him closer to orgasm and reinforced his love for her.

Molly dug her nails into his shoulders and arched her back. She met him thrust for thrust. "Damn." She writhed, twisting her hips and adding a new dimension to the act. "Austin. Oh, my God."

"Yeah." He spread his knees for better leverage. "My baby." He folded her legs up, sending his cock deeper into her heat. When she whimpered, she spurred him on. He tilted his head back and pistoned his hips. The climax came on strong and fast. *Fucking balls.* He gritted his teeth then forced himself to look her in the eye. He focused on her gaze and rocked his hips.

"Austin." She wrapped her arms around her legs and her lips parted. She tensed beneath him. "Austin." She whimpered his name and shattered his restraint.

Austin bore down on her and thrust his hips with abandon. Heat filled his body and he couldn't pull her tightly enough to him. His balls ached as he curled forward and came. Everything within him trembled.

Molly closed her eyes and sighed. She relaxed. She rested her head on the sheets and her legs went slack. A giggle erupted from her.

Austin pumped his torso, working through the orgasm and the trembling. His cock throbbed and his back ached a little from tensing, but he didn't care. He braced himself on his hands and knees and rested his forehead on hers.

"Mr. Dean." She opened her eyes and brushed her mouth against his lips. "Congratulations."

"Mrs. Dean." He loved the way that sounded. He'd belonged to her the whole time and now everything was official. He smoothed the loose locks of her hair away from her face. "My wife."

"It still feels like a dream," she said. "You're supposed to be a mistake or a fling. I never thought…we'd be here."

"I hoped we would, but I knew me." He grinned and toyed with a few strands of her hair. "No regrets?"

"None."

"Good." He eased out of her pussy and collapsed beside her then rolled her onto her side to face him. "Love you."

"I love you, too." She flopped over and spooned against him then dragged the comforter over their bodies. Molly sighed and her breathing evened out.

Sleeping? Already? Part of him wanted to keep her awake but only for selfish reasons. He wanted to gaze into her eyes and kiss her. The rest of him allowed her to rest. They'd both had a long day and they had the rest of their lives to be together.

He sighed and draped his arm across her side and belly. He should've known his heart belonged to her. Should've realized long ago that she was meant to be his wife. But that was all in the past. What mattered was she'd married him and loved him. She might have thought being with him was a mistake. But if the relationship initially had been a mistake then she was his favorite of them all and now he never had to let her go.

WENDI ZWADUK

HER MAN

The love of her life isn't the man she expects but he just
might be the man she never saw coming

Her Man

Excerpt

Chapter One

Trouble. That's what most women were—too much trouble! When Logan Malone's last movie had ended, so had his love life. He'd decided women weren't worth the effort—not right now.

Well, no, that wasn't the case—not entirely. Red-hot American blood still charged through his veins and he needed a woman, someone soft in all the right places, tough as nails and unafraid to fight to warm his bed. Why not go for totally impossible?

Logan shifted in his seat. The olive-colored plastic creaked and scratched against the ceramic tile floor. The other three men in the drafty room glared as though he'd ruined their concentration.

"Quiet," the blond man to his right growled.

"Sorry," Logan muttered. He caressed the worn cover of

the book jacket as he convinced himself he could play the romantic lead better than the rest of the competition sitting in the drab hallway. Who else could embody the sexy, romantic boy-next-door role better than Romeo Malone, the hunk of the silver screen? He smiled, but quickly lost faith. He faced the biggest roadblock of his career—convincing the directors, producer and author that he was the man for the job. Yeah, another impossible task.

He sighed. Was he the man? Logan took a deep breath to relax before another glance at his competition. Mark Lanigan stood hunched in the corner with his index finger in his ear as he spoke on his cell phone. *Shit.*

Logan flexed his jaw and turned away. His heart dropped to his stomach with a sickening thud. Mark Lanigan wasn't a slouch in the looks department. His baby blues melted even the iciest of hearts with ease. Romance publishers begged for his services as a cover model and Mark had the honor of being selected the 'Sexiest Man of the Decade' according to *Delish* magazine. Last year the man had won an award for his performance of a baseball phenom in love with a farmer's daughter in *Flowers in the Outfield.*

Logan ground his teeth. He should've had that role, but no! He'd spent the two-week casting call screwing around with Katrina Butterfield, romping in the Virgin Islands, answering her darned booty call and living up to his womanizing Romeo image. When he realized he'd forfeited his chance at the part of the year, he'd just about wrung her pretty little neck. He sighed. At least he'd learned from his misstep.

Logan gripped the unforgiving black rubberized armrests. He had to get his career in order. Andrew Speedle exited the conference room through the thick wooden auditorium door. Logan's heart plummeted to the floor. *Great.* More competition he didn't need. Andrew's crooked smile could be both sinister and sweet at the same time. His rumpled, straight-out-of-bed look graced the covers of countless magazines. And he was only twenty-seven! Not only that—

he had three supporting roles under his belt, with a lead coming up at the end of the year. Audiences had flocked to see his last film, making it the third highest grossing movie of the year. Andrew could play the sexy hunk-next-door role in his sleep and Logan hated him for it.

Logan pinched the bridge of his nose. Shit. Another part down the drain and he hadn't even tried out yet.

Please let them turn him down. I can do this.

"Malone? Are you giving in already?"

Logan's gaze met Andrew's glare. "They laughed at your sappy credits, didn't they?"

Andrew gave him the finger. "Piss off, Malone. Once she finds out you've screwed the producer and the director, that writer will have your balls in her pocket. Go home and try for a fitting job, something you can handle without dialogue. This ain't the role for you."

Logan's eyes narrowed. "Thanks, asshole."

Andrew sauntered away. Jealousy crashed in Logan's body like a tidal wave. What did that man have that he didn't? He mentally tallied his own assets—broad shoulders, six-pack abs, toned legs and tight buns. Women drooled over his hazel eyes and perfect grin, and he looked hot with any hairstyle. So what was the issue? He was the man for the job without a doubt—case closed.

He sighed. That line of reasoning worked, but Andrew had roles and money, lots of money. A tight ass meant nothing without dollars in the bank.

He thumbed through the book. There were no answers in the battered pages, but simply holding the paperback gave him comfort. He could identify with the hero who wanted true love and honesty with no pretensions. He shook his head. That wasn't possible in Hollywood. Maybe not even in California. Possibly not the world.

Logan flipped to the black and white picture of the author on the inside back cover of the book. Her dowdy professional clothing covered her figure and she smiled sweetly over her shoulder. He'd stared at her so many times and dragged the book around so much over the past three months that the edges of the paper had ruffled. He wondered if she was the actual writer or a model meant to trick the reader. Women that beautiful didn't write romance. Or did they?

Desire curled in his stomach. If she weren't a model, he'd love to tangle his fingers in her dark hair, kiss her lips raw and make her scream with pleasure. Did her skin feel as soft as it looked? Logan guessed it would and she'd do just fine as his arm candy for the premiere. Hell, he'd love to love her for quite a long time.

Love? Too bad it was all a load of crap and nothing more than an act of foreplay involving fictitious emotions. Who actually believed in love? Logan drew a deep breath and let it slide between his lips. He'd never meet a woman who could change his mind and his heart. Women like that didn't exist. Not that lasting relationships mattered much. Paying the bills—that was important. Keeping up the movie star lifestyle had drained his already dwindling bank account. Another flop would mean the end of his career. Career over before the age of thirty-three, hard to envision...but it looked like a very real possibility.

Maybe it was time to go home. No, he'd begged too long and hard to get the chance for the audition. He couldn't back down now. *I will earn this role.*

"Malone?"

Jostled back to reality, Logan looked up. His throat constricted at the sight of another ex. Perfect. "Well, hello, Nikita. It's a pleasure to see you again. Is it my turn, or did you fill the role? I saw Speed walk out earlier."

Nikita Cline pushed her black-rimmed cat's eye glasses back up the bridge of her nose. "It's your turn. We haven't made a decision, yet, but you might do."

Logan felt her heated gaze travel the length of his body. He shivered. He should switch to a different production—one without Nikita. He pasted a wolfish grin on his face and stood to meet her in the doorway. "Well, I'd better dazzle your socks off, then, shouldn't I?"

She grabbed his arm before he entered the room. "You could dazzle other things off instead." Her lips grazed his ear. "I miss you."

Logan shivered again as her perfume wafted to his nose, demanding his undivided attention. He didn't miss the arguments, the accusations, the experimentations she loved so much. She liked to play the field with multiple partners, toys, role-play and whatever she could find for kink. He liked a little kink, but she wasn't his style. "How about I just pass the audition, huh?"

He spotted the women at the table and pasted on his most wicked smile. His voice caught in his throat and a ripple of excitement ran the length of his spine at the sight of his audience. The writer? Was she really there? Or did she moonlight as a screenwriter? Maybe a friend of the producers? *Oh, my, my, my.*

Nikita gestured to the table. "I'd like to introduce the heads of this production. This is Maggie Bowles, our associate producer." She shrugged a shoulder to the woman on the right. "And this is the writer, Cass Jensen."

Logan forced a nod. Maggie had worked on *Break* and co-directed *Maia*, both mega box office hits. She had a reputation for fairness and impartiality with her actors and crew. But the other woman—oh man. He blinked. Cass Jensen penned *Wrong Turn*, *Slingshot* and toyed with his fantasies from the safety of a black and white photo. Crossbeam Studios had translated three of her earlier novels into box office hits. Now she sat across the room, in living color and completely unaware of his innermost desires.

Had the heat just kicked on? He licked his lips. Something had happened and not just between his legs.

It seemed as if everyone else in the cavernous conference room had evaporated except him and Cass. She wasn't his normal blonde model-type, quite the opposite. She had curves and porcelain skin. Her dark chocolate-colored hair glittered slightly under the harsh glare of the fluorescent lighting, and she brushed the silky strands off her face, revealing her lack of a wedding ring.

Score!

Her mouth curled into a faint smile, accompanying the sparkle in her startling blue-gray eyes. Color rushed into her pale cheeks.

Oh man.

Logan's eyes slipped greedily over her body. Would she flush during sex? The light scent of her perfume muddled his brain. Lilac? Rose? Whatever it was, it was enticing. Logan swallowed hard. Tightness invaded his chest. Such a rapid reaction to a woman knocked him for a complete loop. Cass was the kind of woman who ended up being a cherished lover, not a plaything. He glanced at her once more. His throat went dry. Damn, if she blushed too much longer, he'd be in trouble. If he got time alone with her, he'd be a goner. How would her hands feel gliding along his body? Heaven, probably.

More books from
Totally Bound Publishing

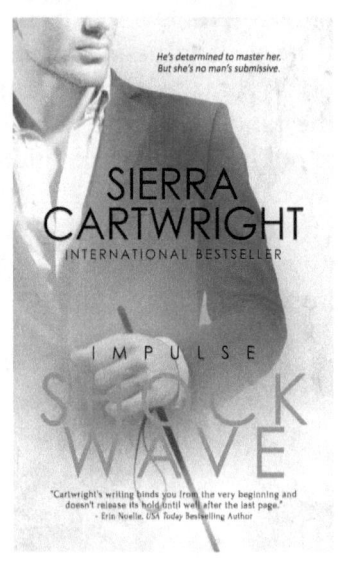

Book one in the Impulse series

When Master Nathaniel Stratton catches Alani Dane, a professional submissive, yawning during a scene with one of his club's most prestigious members, he vows to personally deal with her.

Book one in The Dark Side serial

Who knows where pain ends and pleasure begins?

Part of the Totally 5 Star collection

Can Tanvi alter kismet's path?

Book one in the Bound for Justice series

Targeted by a drug cartel, Teague is out for vengeance until Chantel lands in his lap. Is this fiery, redheaded submissive his lifeline or his downfall?

About the Author

Wendi Zwaduk

I always dreamed of writing the stories in my head. Tall, dark, and handsome heroes are my favourites, as long as he has an independent woman keeping him in line.

I earned a BA in education at Kent State University and currently hold a Masters in Education with Nova Southeastern University.

I love NASCAR, romance, books in general, Ohio farmland, dirt racing, and my menagerie of animals.

Wendi Zwaduk loves to hear from readers. You can find contact information, website details and an author profile page at https://www.totallybound.com/

Home of Erotic Romance